Echo Mountain

Praise for *Wolf Hollow*

'Harper Lee has a worthy successor. Wolk is a big new talent'
The Times

'Extraordinary . . . A timeless story, beautifully placed in an evocative
and brilliantly realized historical setting' *Guardian*

'Suspenseful, wise, beautifully written and emotionally engaging'
Sunday Times

'Haunting . . . Full of grace and stark, brutal beauty'
New York Times

'Atmospheric, haunting and beautifully written,
this is a wonderful and very moving story'
Robin Stevens

'This book is extraordinary. It is a gripping, moving, living, breathing
tale written by a highly skilled hand. I cannot recommend it enough'
Philip Ardagh

Praise for *Beyond the Bright Sea*

'Lauren Wolk has the ability to stun with a very simple sentence'
TES

'Beautiful'
Kirkus

'A tense and moving adventure story, this book's real strength
is in the characters and the understated but overwhelming love
that binds solitary people, no matter what their blood links may be'
Daily Mail

'Lyrical and heartrending . . .
A stellar story full of heart, action and emotion'
School Library Journal

Echo Mountain

LAUREN WOLK

PUFFIN

PUFFIN BOOKS

UK | USA | Canada | Ireland | Australia
India | New Zealand | South Africa

Puffin Books is part of the Penguin Random House group of companies
whose addresses can be found at global.penguinrandomhouse.com.

www.penguin.co.uk
www.puffin.co.uk
www.ladybird.co.uk

First published in the USA by Dutton Children's Books
and in Great Britain by Puffin Books 2020
001

Text copyright © Lauren Wolk, 2020
Illustrations copyright © George Ermos 2020

The moral right of the author and illustrator has been asserted

Edited by Julie Strauss-Gabel

Set in Adobe Garamond Pro
Printed and bound in Great Britain by Clays Ltd, Elcograf S.p.A.

A CIP catalogue record for this book is available from the British Library

HARDBACK ISBN: 978-0-241-42415-5
PAPERBACK ISBN: 978-0-241-43755-1

All correspondence to:
Puffin Books
Penguin Random House Children's
One Embassy Gardens, New Union Square
5 Nine Elms Lane, London SW8 5DA

For my husband, Richard,
and our remarkable sons,
Ryland and Cameron

Maine

1934

Chapter One

The first person I saved was a dog.

My mother thought he was dead, but he was too young to die, just born, still wet and glossy, beautiful really, but not breathing.

"Take him away," she said, sliding him into my cupped hands.

Her voice was cold. Perhaps that was why it shook a little.

But I knew her better than that.

Maisie, curved around her three living pups as they poked blindly toward her milk, watched me with aching eyes.

I could feel how much she hurt, too.

"What should I do with him?" I asked.

"Bury him far beyond the well." My mother turned to tidy the bedding straw. It was as red as Christmas. We'd all had a hard night. But it had been hardest for the last of the pups. The one in my hands.

I cradled him close against my chest as if I had two hearts but only one of them beating, then carried him away from the wood-shed, into the pale spill of morning light. Past the cabin, toward the well and a grave waiting beyond it.

But then I stopped.

Looked back.

And there, on the cabin's broad granite step: a wooden pail brimming with cold water, waiting to be useful.

I didn't know what was about to happen, but a little flicker in my chest flamed at the sight of that water full of green and blue from the tree, the sky overhead. Calm. Simple. It spoke to me with a voice louder than my mother's as she stood at the door of the woodshed, bloody straw bundled in her arms, and said, "Go on then, Ellie."

But I didn't go on then.

The flicker, the flame, the voice all tugged me toward the bucket, where I plunged the baby dog deep into the cold, cold water and held him there until I felt him suddenly lurch and struggle.

"Ellie! What are you doing?" my mother said, dropping the straw and rushing toward me.

But she stopped and stared when I lifted the dripping, squirming pup and pulled him back against my chest.

"He's not dead," I said, smiling. "Not dead at all."

Which made my mother smile, too, for just a moment.

"Then he's yours," she said, turning back for the straw. "See that you keep him that way."

I didn't know if she meant that I should keep him alive or keep him mine, but I intended to do both.

I sat on the step and dried the pup on my shirttail, roughing up his slick pelt, which made him breathe harder—which made me breathe harder, too, a series of sighs, as if we'd both been starved for air.

Then I took him back to Maisie, who lifted her head and watched as I wedged him between the other pups and showed him the teat meant for him.

When Maisie laid her head back down again, she sighed, too.

The pups all looked mostly the same. Dark. Perfect. One of them had a white forepaw. Another was bigger than the rest. Another, some color in his coat. And my boy had some brindle, too, and a white tip to his tail, as if it were a brush he'd dipped in paint. So that set him apart.

But I didn't need a marker.

I was sure that I would know him again in an instant. And I was sure that he would know me.

"I'll have to think of a name for you," I told him as he began to gulp down his new life.

And I did just that all through my morning chores.

While I pulled winter grass from the potato patch, I decided against *Shadow* (though he was dark and it suited him).

I thought of *Possum* (because he hadn't really been dead, not really) as I bundled the grass and set it aside for the cows.

I considered *Boy* (which he was) and *Beauty* (which he also was) as I weeded early spinach come up from autumn seed.

I thought about *Tipper* (for that white tip) as I bundled kindling.

And finally—while I stowed the wood in the bin by the big kitchen stove—chose *Quiet*.

My little brother, Samuel, said, "I like that," as we ate a breakfast of dried blueberries, fire-black potatoes, and milk still udder-warm. "It's a heartbeat name."

My mother said, "A what?"

"A heartbeat name. You know: two parts. *Ba-bum. Ba-bum.*"

And *I* liked *that.*

Esther said, "Quiet's a dumb name." But she was my big sister and thought everything I did was dumb. "He'll wander off somewhere and you'll go yelling 'Quiet!' at the top of your lungs." She shook her head. "Dumb."

But I disagreed, though I did think that Quiet was an odd name. Which was all right with me.

I myself was odd in many ways, and I liked other things that were odd. Questions worth answering. Like the ones that would soon lead me to Star Peak, to a boy who could make a knife sing, to a hag named Cate, and the other *else*s I came to know during that strange time. Some of them good. Some of them bad. All of them tied to the flame that burned more brightly than ever on the day when Quiet was born.

Chapter Two

Quiet's grandmother, a sweet dog named Capricorn, had started her life as I had started mine—in a town where my father was a tailor and my mother a music teacher, before the stock market crash that made almost everyone poor and sent us to live on Echo Mountain.

"But who crashed?" I had asked my father when our own lives began to spin toward disaster.

My father told me that too many people had gambled with their money and then panicked when it looked like they might lose it . . . which, in fact, made them lose even more, and made them poor, and us along with them.

"I don't understand." I remember looking up at him, expecting a better explanation than that. "Did we gamble with our money?"

He shook his head.

"Then why did we lose ours, too?"

"Not ours, right off. But people who have no money don't pay a tailor to make their clothes, and they don't buy new clothes when the ones they have will do."

My father was more than a fine tailor. His clothes fit us like second skins. And the vines and flowers he stitched into his hems and cuffs were more than beautiful. They were like signatures. Like signatures on paintings.

"But Mother is a teacher," I said. "Do you mean that people are too poor now for school?"

He shook his head again. "No, I don't mean that. Quite the contrary. More music right now would do everyone a world of good. But I'm afraid music is one of the first things to go when a school is in trouble. And we're not the only ones leaving. Half the town has gone away, moved in with kin, or just . . . moved. To live on the road, in the rough, looking for work. Which means not so many children in the school anymore. And no need for all the teachers they once had."

No need for my mother.

And so we lost his shop first. And then our house. And then the life we'd always known.

Which was when I understood the other name that people used when they talked about the crash. The Depression, they called it. The Great Depression. Which meant something dreadful and dark.

I didn't need my father to tell me that. It was in my mother's face. My sister's face. Somewhere more distant than that, in my father's eyes, but there all the same.

We took Capricorn with us when we left town, though we didn't know how we'd feed ourselves, let alone a dog.

When we arrived at our little portion of mountain, we tied up our new cows, piled our belongings under a canvas to save them from the weather, and lived in a crooked tent while we built our cabin.

Poor Capricorn was baffled by our new life in the woods. She had always been happiest under the kitchen table while we ate or at the foot of a bed or in the garden we'd had before the crash. But we had no kitchen anymore, no kitchen table, no garden to give her comfort, so we took her into the tent each night, where she managed to give *us* some comfort instead.

It was Capricorn who growled warnings in the night when a bear came close, sending my father out with a torch to scare it away.

It was Capricorn who trembled and cried so hard when thunder came that we all felt brave in comparison.

And it was Capricorn who brought me the strangest gift I'd ever received: a tiny lamb, carved out of wood, tied with a bit of twine to her collar.

"What's that?" I said when she came through the trees one morning, already skinny, learning to hunt for the first time in her life, much as my father was. But she had a choice between field mice or bean soup, so hunt she did.

I untied the little lamb and held it up to the light.

"Where did you get this?" I looked her in the eye, but she had nothing to say.

I peered into the trees all around me but saw only my father, cutting popple. Esther, gathering firewood. My mother, lugging a pail of water up from the brook, Samuel clinging to her skirt.

No one else.

We had come to know the other four families that settled nearby. They were all good, solid, hard-boiled Mainers who saved bits of string and sucked the marrow from their soup bones. None of them would have dulled their knives with such whimsy.

But Capricorn would not have let just anyone get close enough to tie something to her collar, so I judged that one of those people must have carved this little gift and sent it home with her. Who else?

Perhaps they had hoped that Samuel would find it.

But I knew he would lose it in the mud.

And it felt like it was meant to be mine.

So I stashed it in the toe of a church shoe I was unlikely ever to wear again. And told no one.

If anyone was going to unravel its mystery, I wanted it to be me.

Chapter Three

We spent our first spring on Echo Mountain damp and dirty and tired, as hungry as the animals that crept from their burrows after months of winter fasting.

Building a cabin was our work, our play, our church and school. The other families helped us with the heaviest parts, just as we helped them, but most of it we did ourselves, and so slowly that at times I thought we would never again have a roof over our heads.

Samuel was too small to help much, except by making us laugh and love him, which was plenty. Sometimes that's all a person needs to do: be who they are.

Esther and my mother worked as hard as they could, their soft town hands ruined, their hair a mess, and they cried at night when we lay down to sleep. They seemed to blame the mountain itself for what people had done.

Every shrieking storm reminded them of the day my mother had lost her job: the last goodbyes to the students she'd come to think of as her own children.

Every coyote that howled us awake reminded them of the day my father had closed his shop, his face like a wet stone, everyone too poor now for his beautiful clothes, for the ivy he embroidered through every hem and cuff.

And every long, gray rain that found its way into our sad tent reminded them of how we had lost our house. Sold nearly everything we owned. Took what little was left. And went looking for a way to survive until the world tipped back to well.

But I didn't blame the mountain. It was, after all, what saved us.

For the first few weeks, we lived on a watery soup of beans and salt.

We ate rabbit when my father could kill one, but he was a slow and clumsy hunter in those early days, and the rabbits of Echo Mountain were fast and clever, so we were far more likely to eat turtle when we could.

But neither my mother nor Esther ever took to possum, which was easy to catch but greasy and gamey and tasted like whatever the possum itself had eaten. A hungry possum will eat almost anything. But a hungry person will, too, so possum we ate when possum we had.

It was hard. All of it. Especially for my mother and my sister, who lived in a brew of fear and exhaustion, lonely for the life they'd left behind.

My first spring on the mountain was a kinder season.

Like my father, I loved the woods. From the start, the two of us were happy with our unmapped life. The constant brightness of the birds. The moon, beautiful in its bruises. The breeze that set the trees shimmering in the sun, fresh and joyful. And the work we did together to build ourselves a home.

For every difficulty, there had been some kind of good work we could do. So we'd done it.

But this bond with my father and the wilderness itself made a rift between me and my mother—and my sister especially—who both seemed to think I had somehow betrayed them by being happy when they were not.

Nothing about life on Echo Mountain was harder for me than that rift: the idea that I should be sorry for being different. And I made up my mind early on that I might miss my mother, miss my sister, and be lonely, but I would not be sorry for what set me apart.

I loved the mountain. And I loved what it kindled in me. And that was that.

But it wasn't easy.

If I needed another reason to love where I was, I got one on a morning in May when the whole world hummed and the air was sweet with the first of the lilac.

I found it in the pocket of my jacket, which I'd hung from a tree branch and forgotten.

My father had made that jacket in his shop before the crash, stitched it with spring flowers, carved the buttons from hardwood, made it with plenty of room for me to grow. And I wore it whenever

I could, through work and weather and mess, while Esther and my mother kept theirs packed in brown paper, safe from harm, and scolded me for every new rip and stain.

When I plucked my jacket from the branch and slipped it back on, I found in the pocket a perfectly carved snowdrop sprouted from a bulb, so fine and delicate that I lifted it to my nose, expecting a whiff of meadow.

This time, I didn't turn to search the woods around me.

This time, I let my eyes look past the carving and into the trees.

And there, just in that thicket there: a face.

Framed by leaves, as if it were part plant itself.

And then gone.

I blinked. Looked harder.

"Hello!" I called, but no one answered.

So I slipped the snowdrop back in my pocket and spent the rest of the day wondering about that face. Those eyes. Watching me.

After that, I looked more closely at the faces of the others on that mountainside, peering at them thoughtfully until more than one said, "Is there something in my teeth?" Or, "My wife has an old pair of glasses that might suit you."

But none of the faces looked like the one I had seen. They were all too old. And none of them had enough . . . loneliness in them. So I went on as before, working hard, learning so much every day that I thought I might pop like corn in a kettle, and watching the woods to see who might be watching me.

When the first room was done, we moved out of the tent and into the cabin.

I remember: It was June and we were no longer cold except at the very darkest part of night.

For me, that was enough.

But my mother and Esther made my father put a bolt on the cabin door, so they could lock us in each night and sleep, finally, in peace. Dry. Safe. A thick wall between them and the wilderness.

By the time our first mountain winter came, we had a snug, safe home with four good rooms—one for us children, one for our parents, one for our kitchen, and one for everything else. A root cellar for what we'd grown the whole summer long. A place where we could start again. The know-how to make our way in this new world. And, for some of us, the blessing of knowing that we were blessed.

But that was before my father's accident changed everything.

Chapter Four

"Mr. Peterson shot a doe," my mother said as we lingered over our tea on the morning when Quiet was born. "Ellie, after breakfast you and Samuel go on up and get our share."

Once the winter ice had melted, none of the five families who lived on the western slope of Echo Mountain had a way to keep meat fresh, so we'd come to share our kills, eating the best parts in short order and drying the rest for jerky.

Everyone knew that our next kill probably wouldn't come anytime soon. My mother was a terrible shot, and she didn't have time to lie in wait for a doe. Esther was gun-shy. Samuel at six was still too young and quite small for his age, besides.

I myself was two opposite things at the same time. One: I was now an excellent woods-girl who could hunt and trap and fish and harvest as if I'd been born to it. Two: I was an echo-girl. When I clubbed a fish to death, my own head ached and shuddered. When I snared a rabbit, I knew what it meant to be trapped. And when I pulled a carrot from the sheath of its earth, I, too, missed the darkness.

There were times when this two-ness made me feel as if I were being stretched east and west, my bones creaking and crying as they strained back toward one.

But hunger has a way of getting what it wants. And the hunger of a brother or a sister or a mother or a father is a very strong hunger indeed.

Before his accident, my father had provided plenty of meat, firewood, river fish, furs, and sometimes honey. But I was now the one who caught fish. And I snared rabbits. And if we grew hungry enough, I knew I would be the one to shoot a deer.

If I had to.

I hoped I wouldn't have to.

One more reason for my father to wake up.

While he slept, we paid for our venison with cream and butter and things the other families didn't grow: potatoes mostly, but carrots, too, and beets. Onions and turnips. Parsnips and rutabagas.

And my mother gave the best haircuts to be had. And she made soft shoes from deer hide lined with rabbit fur and traded them for things we needed from town: stove and pump parts, sewing needles, other things we couldn't make for ourselves.

Since Esther and Samuel and I were the only children among the five families, my mother could not offer schooling in trade for meat or metal. And although she could sing like an April breeze and stun angels with her mandolin, she refused to think of those things as currency. "Music is not something you keep in a wallet," she said. "I can't just open my purse and pull it out."

"People would trade anything to hear you," I said soon after my father's accident, when we were still learning how to pay our way without him.

But she had sung very seldom since coming to live in the woods. Not at all since my father had been hurt.

I was amazed that such a wild, beautiful thing could be silenced, especially in a place as wild as a mountain.

I missed that voice. That mother.

And other things, besides. When she stopped singing, she stopped teaching the three of us how to play her mandolin as well. In town, our lessons had been as much a part of our lives as church and school. But though she continued to teach us our letters and numbers, she left both prayer and music to us now, though we knew better than to touch the mandolin that my mother had set aside.

I missed Capricorn, too, who had died a year after we'd moved to the woods, soon after giving birth to a litter of four scrawny pups.

She had seemed to let go too easily, as if she were less afraid of dying than of living in the wild, and I had cried long and hard when she'd gone to her grave. And I had been the one to feed cow's milk to her puppies until they were old enough to be traded away (which also broke my heart). And I had been the one to choose the pup we kept, though my father had decided she should be Esther's dog, not mine.

"Maybe having a puppy will help her be happier," my father had whispered when he took the little dog from my arms. *"You and I are all right here. But Esther needs something more."*

So I had handed over the puppy I'd bottle-fed for weeks, watching sadly as my sister changed her name from Willow to Maisie and made her into a new doll of sorts, tying a strip of rag around her little neck like a ribbon, brushing her soft fur until it gleamed, and training her to sit. To stay.

Just as Esther and my mother tied their hair back, and polished their shoes, and did everything they could to keep Samuel, too, from growing up wild.

Chapter Five

By the time Quiet was born, I had found many more of the strange and marvelous gifts left by the stranger I'd glimpsed in the trees, each of them tiny, each of them enormous, like shooting stars.

One of them I found next to Maisie's water bowl, in the yard near the cabin door.

It was a little dog, the spitting image of Maisie, right down to the perk in her tail, the tip of her head. So wonderfully done that I held it gently, as if it were made of sugar.

And then I looked up carefully. Turned slowly in all directions, as if I were a lazy clock, looking for a glimpse of who had left the tiny dog for me to find.

This time, I saw something move in a grove of birches. And I burst toward it like an arrow from a bow, straight and fast, intent on only one thing: to see more than a face this time.

But when I reached the birch grove, there was only a place where some twigs were freshly broken and, on the ground there, a few pale curls of wood, fresh from someone's blade.

I was disappointed. But I was also worried that running into the woods like that might have ruined everything.

Sure enough, the next few days were empty ones: no new carvings, no glimpse of anyone among the trees, and I was sorry all over again that I'd been so impatient.

I told myself that I wouldn't make the same mistake again. That I would wait, and be careful, and do what I could to prove that I was worth another chance.

But at the end of a long week of waiting and wondering, I decided that the next move would have to be mine.

So I left my jacket hanging from a branch as I had before and went into the cabin for the night.

I thought doing that might seem like an invitation. A sign of friendship. A bridge. But in the morning, when I went out to fetch my jacket, I found nothing in its pockets.

And I wondered whether perhaps the jacket had felt too much like a trap.

Or whether I had indeed ruined everything by running into the woods, like a hunter chasing her prey.

Finding another gift a month later was like a yellow sunrise after days of rain.

It was a full-moon face, left by the brook where I always went first thing to wash the night from my eyes.

This time, I didn't even look around. I simply kissed the face of that moon, smiling, and hoped that someone was watching.

That someone would see how much I loved such a beautiful gift.

And then I called out, "Thank you!" and "Whoever you are, thank you!" before I turned and went back toward the cabin again.

My church shoes weren't big enough to hide more than the lamb and the snowdrop, so I had long since dusted off a high shelf in the woodshed and lined the carvings up at the back of it, where no one could see them without standing on a stool.

I couldn't see them either as I traveled through my days, but I knew they were there, the way I knew the sun was in the sky. And I knew that the friend I had not yet met was close by, too.

If Maisie suddenly stood at attention and barked at the woods, I figured I was being watched, but all I ever saw was a shadow of a shadow. If she barked in the night, I lay in bed and thought about what I might find the next day when I searched the cowshed, the woodshed, the root cellar, the trail through the woods. All the places that anchored my days like the points of a compass.

I thought of those little gifts as clues because they told me things about the carver and myself, too. Whoever had made them was sweet and clever. And I was someone who noticed things that others missed. There was a reason I was the one who found the little creatures before anyone else did. Most eyes would have passed right over a little wooden treasure tucked among the leaves at the edge of the brook. But not mine.

And there was another clue, too. The most important one. Those gifts had been meant for *me*. I was sure of it. Which meant that whoever was making them *knew* me and understood that I was the kind of girl who would love finding them tucked in the corners of my world, all of them carved from good hardwood, all just short of alive: a milk cow with one ear up and one ear down; a hunch-backed inchworm; an acorn with a tiny feather in its cap; a chicka-dee as round and fat as a plum.

And then, soon after my father's accident, I found another one.

This time, it was a carving of me.

I found it perched on the stump of the tree that had nearly killed him.

And I wondered whether there had been a witness to what had happened on that terrible day.

Whether I was not the only one who knew the truth of it.

Chapter Six

The months after my father's accident were every kind of dark and cold, but on the morning of Quiet's birth I felt three kinds of light, three kinds of warmth: from spring itself, from Quiet, and from the flame growing inside me.

But my mother still seemed as cold and dark as the January day when he'd been hurt.

"Go on now and finish your chores," she said after we'd had our breakfast. "And don't forget the venison. Mr. Peterson will be done with the butchering by now. He'll have our share ready."

"How come Esther never fetches the meat?" Samuel groused, though he loved venison and visits to the Petersons, too.

"How come you never darn your own socks?" Esther said.

"Or make your own cakes?" my mother said, and by that she meant corn cakes or fish cakes or potato cakes. It had been a long time since we had had the kind of cake that wore candles in a crown.

"And how come Ellie gets a puppy?" Samuel said.

My mother cast him a baleful eye. "Where were you when Ellie was helping me with Maisie last night?"

Samuel sighed. "Sleeping."

"And where were you when Ellie saved that puppy from being buried too soon?"

"I would have saved him if I'd been there," Samuel said.

"If," said Esther. "Such a word."

"You know the rule." My mother wrapped her hands around her mug, warming it as it warmed her. "One puppy at a time. When Maisie has another litter, it'll be your turn, Samuel."

"But Ellie already has Maisie," Samuel said.

And he wasn't really wrong. Esther had lost interest in Maisie as soon as the cute had worn off, so I was the one who fed her and made sure she was locked in the woodshed at night, safe from coyotes and bears. And I was the one who sometimes snuck her into my bed on cold nights, where she warmed my feet and soothed my sleep no matter how high the wind.

And now I had a pup of my own, too.

Quiet.

"Nonetheless," my mother said to Samuel. "You'll get your turn when it's your turn, and not a minute sooner."

After I'd washed up under the kitchen pump and filled a pail for Maisie, I said, "I'm going out to the woodshed to check on the puppies."

My mother nodded, the tea still cradled in her hands, while Esther tidied the table and Samuel said, "I'm coming, too," close at my heels.

Since my father's accident, Samuel had taken to following me around, watching me work, asking me questions, and I tried to teach him some of the things my father had taught me, though he often didn't want to do the work or listen the way he needed to listen.

Even so, I stopped him on the way to the woodshed and reminded him about what happens to a dog when she has a fresh litter. "Maisie growled at me a lot last night," I said. "She even showed her teeth when I got too close."

"At you? Maisie?"

I nodded. "Something takes over when babies are new."

At which Samuel made a face. "You're twelve, Ellie. What do you know about it?"

So I let him go ahead of me into the woodshed.

Let him see her fangs when the door opened.

Let him step back so fast he tripped and went down hard on his butt while I waited for Maisie to get used to the idea of us. And then I went forward slowly, murmuring soft words, careful to reach out the back of my hand until she calmed and licked my knuckles, crooning a little.

"There, there," I murmured, stroking her ears. "That's my good girl. That's my good Maisie."

When I poured water into her bowl, she raised her head enough to lap some up and then lay back down again.

The puppies were sleeping, their tummies fat with milk, and I didn't want to upset Maisie, so I didn't touch them, though the sight of Quiet made me long to hold him against my neck.

Samuel eased up behind me, murmuring as I had, reaching

down slowly to run his hand along Maisie's neck again and again. *"How was I supposed to know she would get so mad?"* he whispered to me. *"First time you've ever been right about anything."*

Which I ignored.

Being a middle child had made me good at turning the other cheek. But being good at something didn't make it easy.

While Samuel was looking at the puppies, I stepped silently onto the stool in the corner and reached up to touch each of the carvings I'd hidden on the highest shelf.

There was no reason for them to feel warm, though they did.

The carving of me looked calmly back into my eyes, and for a moment I wanted to be that little girl with her solemn face and her steady gaze.

"They're pretty ugly," Samuel whispered.

I turned to look down at him kneeling by the birthing nest. "So were you when you were born." I stepped off the stool and pushed it back against the wall. "Much uglier."

"Was not." He peered at the puppies more closely but leaned away again when Maisie raised her head. "What made you dunk the dead one?"

To that, I replied by leading him out of the woodshed, leaving the door open so Maisie could come and go.

"I just did."

Samuel huffed. "No, you just didn't, Ellie. Nobody just dunks a dead puppy for no reason."

Which was true, but I wasn't sure how to explain what had happened without getting it wrong.

So I said, "I remembered how it feels when you stuff snow down my neck." Something he did too often but which maybe had led to some secondhand good. "I guess I wanted him to gasp."

Samuel nodded grudgingly. "The second time you've been right. Probably the last time."

Which deserved no answer.

Instead, I listened to that voice, that flame in my chest as it suddenly rose again, bright and wordless as the sun, as it had that morning when I helped Quiet find his way back to life.

This time, it spoke to me about my father.

Chapter Seven

"How's our Maisie?" my mother asked as we went back into the cabin and found her still in the kitchen, grinding dried corn into meal. We'd have johnnycakes for lunch and maybe the last of the eggs.

"She's tired," I said. "But the puppies are all fine."

Samuel took off his boots. "They're ugly as bugs."

"Not for long." My mother had to raise her voice over the grumble of the mill. "In a week or so they'll open their eyes and fluff up."

My back to them both, I worked the pump until I had a pitcher brimming with cold well water.

My mother didn't pay me any mind as I carried the pitcher past her, out of the kitchen toward the little room where we kept our basins and soap and the big metal tub we used for weekly baths. The floor had a drain to wash it all down the hill when we were done, though sometimes it let a snake come up . . . until Esther's screaming would chase it back down again.

But I went on past that washroom and carried the pitcher to a door beyond it, closed as always.

Inside, I found my father not asleep but something deeper. More constant. As he had been for months now.

There was a terrible pink scar on the top of his head where the tree had felled him as he had felled it.

After the accident, Mr. Peterson had gone straightaway to fetch a doctor, though it had taken a whole day before he arrived on horseback, Mr. Peterson leading the way.

The doctor was as clean as any man I'd ever seen. Tidy, even after the rough trip from town. In a black suit and hat. His face as round and shiny as a dinner plate. He went straight to the bed where my father lay and examined him carefully, pricking his feet with a needle, listening to his chest. Holding smelling salts beneath his nose.

Then, "Coma," he said. Which wasn't a word we knew. "He might wake up tomorrow or never again. Can't tell if he'll be all right. Can't tell much of anything except he's hurt and his body has decided that rest is what he needs most. So rest he'll have, until he either gets better or doesn't."

My mother and we children had stood in a huddle listening.

I remember trying to think of a question that wouldn't have a frightening answer.

I remember failing.

I remember watching as my mother picked up the mandolin my father had bought for her as a wedding gift. I remember how she cradled it in her arms as if it were a fourth child. And then she put it aside, took her mother's silver locket from around her neck, and handed it to the doctor as payment for what he had not done.

After he went away, I remember trying to find a way to explain what it had been like when that tree fell, what my father and I had tried to do.

I remember failing.

And so I had held my tongue.

We had learned, since then, how to care for my father. How to prop him up and pour soup slowly, carefully, into his mouth, just drops at a time so he wouldn't choke. How to tuck his chin down close to his chest and stroke his cheek and massage his throat to help him swallow.

How to turn him, again and again, in an endless battle with the horrible, leaking bedsores that came from lying still for so long. Esther always took Samuel outside to play when I helped my mother clean those sores with vinegar. We couldn't know if my father felt the terrible pain of that acid on his raw flesh, but I worried that he did, though he was not the one who cried.

Most of all, we learned how to make his little room into a world apart.

As soon as there were spring flowers in the world beyond the cabin, there were flowers in my father's room, too. Jonquils and crocuses and snowdrops in little vases everywhere.

My mother had dragged in the gramophone, the one impossible thing she had insisted on keeping from our town house, the horse struggling to haul it up the mountain on a sled, and she played it for my sleeping father as she once had, though there'd been no dancing since we'd come to the woods to live.

When I asked why she no longer played her mandolin, not once since nearly giving it to the doctor in trade, she answered by sighing and shaking her head. Laying her hand flat on her chest. And I didn't ask again.

Before the accident, Esther had read to me and Samuel at bedtime each night. Now, she read to our father instead, though Samuel and I lay at the foot of the bed and listened. She read nothing sad. Only happy stories.

Samuel's part was to lie next to our father and tell him about the day. Funny episodes filled with dog-play and mountain business: a moose stranding Mrs. Anderson in the privy; Mr. Peterson, with only a weak lantern for light, mistaking a skunk for Dinky, his mouser. Things like that. Harmless. Gentle.

I had always done likewise, taking nothing into that room but light and loveliness, all of us sworn to tempt my father back into the life he'd had before. The life *we'd* had before he'd been hurt.

But I brought him something different on the day when Quiet was born.

Sun slanted through the window by the bed to light his thin, still face.

I watched him breathing.

And then I dumped the pitcher of cold water on his head and chest and waited for him to revive, as Quiet had.

"Mother!" Esther shrieked from the doorway, dropping her book and rushing to the bed.

My mother flew in behind her.

Saw me with the empty pitcher hanging from my hand.

Saw my father drenched, the wet bedclothes glued to his bones.

"Ellie!" she cried. "What's the matter with you?"

She rushed to the bed and pulled my father into her arms, warming him against her chest, while Esther tugged away the wet bedding behind him . . .

. . . and I stood frozen in place, riveted by the sight of my father's right hand.

It was twitching, just slightly.

Chapter Eight

"They aren't the same," my mother said when my father was once again dry and the room once again a place apart. "The puppy . . . what happened just now . . . they're not the same."

"But why not? I saw his hand twitch. The water woke him up a little!"

I knew how tired my mother was. I knew how much she wanted my father back. And I knew that it vexed her if anyone shook what she tried so hard to make calm. But I was sick and tired of calm. "He moved, Mother. For the first time since he got hurt."

I wanted her to be hopeful. To say, at least, "Maybe. It's possible." But instead she took me by the shoulders and said, "A body does things with or without our say-so, Ellie. Your father's hand twitched because you made it cold. That's all."

But I wasn't convinced.

"What if he's trapped in there and we could give him a way out?"

She looked half sad, half impatient. "We do that every day," she said. "Every day."

She meant by speaking softly and reading to him. The feel of his small son tucked up against him. My hand in his.

"All we give him are lullabies," I said, though I didn't want to make things worse. "Why would he wake up for those?"

She took her hands from my shoulders and stepped back. "Go apologize to him," she said.

Which made no sense. If he was too deeply asleep for cold water to slap him awake, how could he hear me say I was sorry?

And that, right there, was the first time I understood how complicated hope could be.

But all I said was "Sorry." Because I was. Sorry that she had lost so much. That she might lose even more.

"Say it to *him*," she said, turning away.

I bumped into Esther as she bustled out of his bedroom, her arms full of wet bedclothes.

"That was a terrible thing to do," she said. "Do you want him to get sick?"

Which I ignored. None of us wanted him sick.

But sick he was.

And after months of watching him lie there, I was suddenly convinced I could do something about it.

My mother would have called that pride.

My sister: stupidity.

My brother: silliness.

But it was my father whose opinion mattered most.

"Daddy," I whispered into his ear, up close, though a sourness had replaced the good, clean sweat, woodsmoke, dusty dog smell

he'd had before. *"Mother says I have to apologize to you, so here: This is my apology."* I paused and took a long breath. *"I'm sorry if that water was cold."*

But, like Esther had said before, *if* was quite a word.

"I'm sorry," I amended, *"that* the water was so cold. But I wanted you to feel it."

I told him about the puppy. About Quiet waking in the cold water.

"You felt it, too, didn't you?" I asked, but he didn't move again. Not even a little.

I leaned away from him, looked toward the empty door, leaned back. "We're in a bad way without you, Daddy. Mother is tired all the time and never laughs. Never. Hasn't sung or played her mandolin since you got hurt. Samuel acts like a kid, but he's as sad as a stump. I can tell. And Esther thinks she's got to be grown up all at once." I paused and gathered myself.

"And I want to burn down every tree on the mountain." And I did. Though I didn't. I loved trees. Even the dead ones. Even the one that had hurt my father as it fell. "It's terrible without you, Daddy. We need you back."

It wasn't a lullaby.

No more lullabies from me.

"And you're the only one who knows it wasn't my fault," I said, my voice breaking.

Although that wasn't really true.

I knew it, too.

And maybe someone else, watching from the woods.

But none of that would matter, if he woke up.

When he woke up.

Before I left the room, I kissed my father on his head. On the scar there.

It felt like a map against my lips.

So I followed it.

For lunch, my mother and Esther and Samuel ate johnnycakes and eggs fried in butter.

I ate gruel.

"You need to learn a thing or two," my mother said, though there wasn't much bite in her bark. "Next time you have a wild idea, maybe you'll think twice."

"Or thrice," Esther said. Every hair on her head was in place. Her shirt was buttoned at the cuffs. She was only three years older than me, but she acted like she lived in an older world. A smarter world. One where everything followed the rules, though I knew there was no such place.

So I ate my gruel in silence, and I washed the dishes without complaint. If that was the price for heeding the flame in my chest, it was a small one.

Then I took the table scraps—which we'd all left deliberately on our plates, hungry as we were—out to Maisie and fed them to her bit by bit while she lay in the straw, the puppies again at her milk. She was as thirsty and hungry as they were, and she licked my hand over and over until every trace of the food was gone. And then she drank the milk I'd brought her, as they drank hers.

Slowly, slowly, I reached out toward the puppies, and she did not object as I touched their tiny heads, lingering over Quiet, who pressed back briefly against my hand as if to say, *I'm busy now but just wait. I'll be along soon enough.*

Then I left the shed and walked up the path and, after a bit, into the woods, through a hemlock grove so full of shadows that almost nothing grew between the trunks of the old trees, the deep layer of dead needles underfoot like the soft coat of a great, sprawling animal that didn't mind the weight of me. The feel of my boots on its brown back.

And before long I came to the spot where I did my best thinking.

It was an old place, left behind by people who'd come long before us, built a cabin, and abandoned it, so now nothing remained but a big hole lined with granite blocks and boulders, a caved-in well, and wood rotten and pocked by bugs and birds, weather and wear.

When I put my hand on those boulders, I could feel how much they missed the steady weight of a cabin above them. The idea that they had been of use.

And when I touched the soft timbers that had once stood firm against blizzards and hail, I could feel them dreaming of the time when they were stronger than storms.

That place made me sad and lonely, but when I climbed down to sit in the bowl of that ruined home, cupped in that granite hand, sheltered by the trees growing up in it, I felt strong and able, too. A mountain girl. Smart. Quick. On my way to wise.

I sometimes found old bottles there. Shards of rusted metal.

Once, the head of a doll, its eyes forever open, still blue. Signs of life long gone. All of them wistful for what had been.

And I had found one of the gifts waiting for me there, too—the fat chickadee—perched on the stone where I myself often perched.

On the day Quiet was born, I sat among the tumbled boulders and slowly, carefully followed the map of my father's scar, through every kind of cure I knew, and considered how they might help him wake.

I thought about what the balsam fir gave us for head colds, sores and cuts, and plenty more.

Jewelweed for ivy poison.

Barberry, in winter, so we never had scurvy.

Mustard plaster for clear lungs.

Mud for bee stings and spider bites.

The twin nurses—onion and garlic—for what's coiled in a gut, and vinegar, as well, for the gut and cuts, too, when they festered.

I would try all of these, and more besides.

When I thought of the jonquils by my father's bed and how they had failed to rouse him, I considered their opposite, and I came up with a plan that would surely earn me a week of nothing but gruel. Maybe worse.

When I thought of the songs that my mother played on the gramophone and how they had failed to rouse him, I considered sounds of my own, and I came up with a plan that would surely mean a mouthful of fresh horseradish . . . which gave me yet another idea to try.

Beyond that, I couldn't think another thought. My stomach was sore with such ideas. I didn't relish the thought of upsetting my mother. And the prospect of giving my father pain made me hurt, too. But the flame that lit my way felt true to me. And brave.

That's what my father needed me to be.

That's what I needed me to be, too.

So that's what I would be.

Chapter Nine

"The *venison*," my mother said when I came back to the cabin and found her in the yard, hanging wash.

I'd forgotten.

"Samuel!" I called.

We waited for his answering yell, which came from below the cabin where the brook crossed the slope and paused long enough to make a shallow pool where crayfish sometimes paddled foolishly into my brother's waiting hands.

"See that you come straight back after the Petersons', Ellie."

There were two places my father had told us to fear. One was the river, which sometimes raged after a heavy rain and was, at all times, apt to drown things. The other was the part of the mountain above where the families lived. "Bears," he often said. "And coyotes. And steep rock faces. And ledges that drop off into nothing. So don't wander up too far, you hear me?"

And we did hear him, and we did obey, especially since there was a warning in his voice of something else besides bears and broken bones, though I didn't know what that might be.

I knew that beyond the river was the road into town and beyond that more people than I could count, and buildings and bridges and trains and much, much else.

Beyond the mountaintop? Other mountains, old forests, caves and caverns, and more of what I didn't know than what I did.

But here, on this mountainside above the river, there was some of each. Some tame. Some wild. Some of what I knew. Some of what I did not.

And here, on this mountainside, among the families, in broad daylight, with two of us together—Samuel making enough noise for ten boys—there was little chance of a bear or coyote meddling with us.

But we'd be carrying a sack of fresh meat, which would be like hoisting a big come-and-get-it sign in the language of carnivores.

So, "Straight back," I said, looking her in the eye, nothing soft about either of us.

I was the first to look away. I knew I was right about those lullabies. But that didn't make her wrong.

I picked up a tangle of wet laundry and shook it out: my father's bed shirt. It was marbled with brown from where his sores had bled.

I pinned it on the line.

"What?" Samuel called as he came out of the trees into the yard, faceless in the shadow of his hat but all Samuel, still, in the set of his shoulders, the way he pumped his arms as he climbed the tilted yard. He was, in many ways, my father, cast small.

"We're going to the Petersons' now," I called.

"Says you," Samuel muttered, but we heard him.

"Says me," my mother said, swinging her head around to look at him.

"Well," Samuel said, "I'm going up first." And he charged past us, past the cabin, toward the path to the Petersons'.

He did that a lot. Charged through life without paying much attention to where he was going.

"Like a little bull." My mother shook her head.

Finally, she'd said something beyond the barest of bones.

And I wanted to do the same. To tell her about the treasures I was hiding on the shelf in the woodshed. How lonely I was. What had really happened on the day my father got hurt.

Instead, I nodded. "Like a bull. Or a puppy." Which led to "When can I hold Quiet again?"

She shrugged, Samuel's long johns like a headless puppet in her hands. "As soon as Maisie says so."

Which meant I would visit the litter again after I'd brought the venison home.

Perhaps if I smelled enough like both a harmless deer and a juicy dinner, Maisie would let me hold my pup.

"Tell the Petersons I'll bring up a peck of potatoes later on," she said. "You take the pail of milk I left by the well."

That was another way we paid our way on Echo Mountain.

Our two milk cows, Venus and Jupiter, had a little fenced-in yard of their own below the cabin, but we loved those big, mooey girls too much to keep them locked in a world of mud and flies. So my father had threaded barbed wire through the trees in a big hoop around their pen, and every morning we let them out to roam in the woods, feasting on wild grass and moss, scratching their shoulders on the trees, napping in the shade. At dusk, we herded them into their tiny stable, just big enough for the two of them, a net of hay, a trough of water, and nothing else.

One time, a mountain cat had climbed onto the roof and screeched at them through the tin and wood, and they had lowed and hollered in fear until my father had come out, a torch in his hand, to scare the cat away.

I would remind my father of that. How the cows needed him, too.

I thought about such things as I lugged their milk up the trail to the Petersons' that morning, Samuel far ahead of me.

The trail was steep, the milk heavy, and I knew what would happen if I tripped on a root and spilled it, so I kept my eyes on the ground until I reached that tree, there—that big old balsam fir that curtsied a little in the wind as if it had been waiting for me.

I set the pail carefully aside and, taking my knife and a scrap of leather from my pocket, ducked under the tree's prickly skirts and ran my hands along the rough bark until I felt the blister where I'd recently cut a branch to chip into tea for my mother.

The tree hadn't seemed to mind sharing what it had to share.

The blister was the size of my thumb, its skin tough, a hard bubble. When I pierced it with the tip of my knife, the sap inside oozed out onto the blade, and I wiped it onto the scrap of leather over and over until I had a sticky dollop that I folded up carefully and slid into my pocket.

Then I cleaned my knife by plunging it into the dirt and scraping it against a rock again and again before slipping it, too, into my pocket.

Until now, the sap from this tree had healed our small wounds, glued the tip of my mother's finger back on after she sliced it nearly off with a carving knife, made us new skin when we needed time to knit ourselves back to whole.

I didn't know if it could fix anything already scarred over, but I saw no harm in trying, though I knew it would make an unholy mess.

I also knew a mess was not the worst thing that could happen.

There was no jewelweed yet—the spring too fresh for that—so I contented myself with balsam for the time being, happy in the knowledge that there was mustard, powdered and waiting in a tin in our kitchen. And cinnamon, too, though not much of it. Vinegar and onions. And mud, of course, whenever I wanted to make it. Honey, soon, if I could manage to steal it from a thousand bees. Maybe the next time the Lockharts went to market for coffee and salt they could ask for ginger, too, though I would have to find a way to pay for it.

I was filled with such thoughts as I ducked back out from under the drooping branches of the balsam tree, picked up the pail of milk, and turned toward the Petersons'.

And realized that I was not alone.

On the path ahead of me was a creature I'd never seen before, his paws braced, head low, ears pricked.

At first I thought *coyote*, but it wasn't. Too big.

And then I thought *wolf*, though I'd seen only one of those. But he wasn't a wolf, either. Too . . . blunt. Not enough snout.

And then: *dog*, though not the kind I knew.

Wild dog, maybe.

He had a big head, a lean body, and was well brindled—some of him brown, some red, some gray—with an ample tail and a coat still winter-thick.

Even from five paces away, I could see an enormous tick hanging from above one eye, so full of blood it waggled as the dog tipped his head to one side, his face fiercely curious.

I didn't move.

"Who are you?" I said carefully.

As if in answer, he took a slow step toward me, his eyes dropping from my face to the bucket of milk in my hand, then lifting to my face again.

I carefully set the bucket down and took off the lid.

But when I looked up again, the path was empty.

If he'd been my dog, I would have called him *Ghost*.

Chapter Ten

I waited for the dog to reappear, but there was no sign of him.

I waited some more, hoping he would come back. Hoping he wouldn't.

Nothing.

So I put the lid back on the bucket and started again toward the Petersons'. I wasn't afraid. Not exactly. But I was careful, watching for the dog as I climbed.

"Samuel!" I called, though he usually ignored me and was, besides, bound to be with Mr. Peterson by now, following him around like a shadow, yammering about nothing of importance. He seemed to crave the company of men lately, and I couldn't blame him. I knew he loved me and Esther and our mother, but I also knew how much he missed our father.

"You must be careful around a horse, even a friendly one," Mr. Peterson was explaining to Samuel as I reached the edge of the yard and found the pair of them examining the hoof of a big tawny workhorse named Scotch. "If you hurt him, even by mistake, he might very well boot you over the hill."

I watched as Mr. Peterson showed Samuel how to cradle Scotch's hoof in his left hand so he could clean it with his right. "There, that's it," he said, as Samuel carefully dug out a wad of accumulated muck. "You're born to it."

Samuel looked up at Mr. Peterson, smiling, and caught sight of me standing at the trailhead, the milk in my hand.

"Took you long enough." Samuel put down the hoof and straightened up.

"Did a big dog come through here just now?" I asked, but they both shook their heads.

"No," Mr. Peterson said, glancing over his shoulder and around the yard. "No dog at all."

"What big dog?" Samuel asked.

"That's what I want to know," I said.

"What did it look like?" Mr. Peterson asked, a little worry on his face.

I thought back. "He was . . . rough looking. Brindled. Nervous."

Mr. Peterson glanced up-mountain, thoughtful, then back at me. "I do believe I've seen that dog before. Once or twice. But there's nothing for him around here." He turned back to the horse.

"Something wrong with him?" I said.

Mr. Peterson shook his head, not looking at me. "He's a wild mutt," he said. "Not a dog you want."

"No, I meant Scotch." Though now that I'd been told I wouldn't want the dog, I found that I did. "I meant is something wrong with Scotch."

"He'd been favoring his hoof," Samuel said, in a voice much like Mr. Peterson's. "But I've cleaned it out now."

As we watched, though, Scotch lifted his sore hoof and rested his weight on just the front edge of it.

"Still lame." Mr. Peterson pulled the hoof into the light again so he could look more closely.

Samuel peered at it, too, near as he dared. "Is that a thorn?" he said, gently probing with a fingertip until Scotch threw his head back and shifted his weight enough that Mr. Peterson let go the hoof and stepped back.

"A thorn or the tip of a stick, straight in." Mr. Peterson made a face. "Scotch isn't going to like me pulling it out." He ducked into the stable. Came out with a pair of pincers.

"I'll hold his head," I said, putting the milk beyond kicking distance.

"Stand well away, Samuel," Mr. Peterson said as he lifted the hoof again.

But Samuel came to stand with me as I took Scotch's bridle in both hands, at the corners of his mouth, and put my face close up to his. *"There, boy,"* I whispered again and again. *"This is only going to hurt for a second."*

And I felt his answer. How he loved Mr. Peterson.

"It's just a lousy thorn," Samuel whispered. *"It's—"*

But then Mr. Peterson pulled the thorn and Scotch lurched

away, dragging me with him, and we all ended up in something like a dance for a moment or two, Mr. Peterson scrambling free, Samuel reaching for the reins, me hanging on to the bridle, and Scotch prancing in place until he calmed . . . calmed . . . came back to still, and we all took a breath.

"Wouldn't want this in my hoof either," Mr. Peterson said, holding up his pincers and the long, bloody thorn in their beak.

"Aren't you worried that it'll fester with all the muck he stands in?" I said.

Mr. Peterson sighed. "It's his own muck. And I can't very well put a boot on him."

I pulled the leather scrap from my pocket and offered it over. "Fresh balsam," I said.

"For a hoof?"

"Works on a hand. Why not a hoof?"

Mr. Peterson pulled back a flap and lifted the balsam to his nose. "That's fine."

"You always carry balsam in your pocket?" Samuel said, squinting at me from under the brim of his hat.

"I do today."

And we both watched as Mr. Peterson took a knife from his pocket, opened it, scraped out a portion of balsam, and spread it where it was needed.

Scotch swung his head around to stare at me. The look in his eye warmed me to my bones.

"I'm in your debt," Mr. Peterson said, though we all knew that any debt was one we owed him, not the other way around. He held out what was left of the balsam.

"Oh, keep it. I can always get more. And I brought you some milk," I said, fetching the pail.

"*We* brought you some milk," Samuel said. But pride quickly stepped into the shadows, and something quite different took its place. "We would have brought meat if we had any. Or fish even."

"But meat I have," Mr. Peterson said gently. "And milk I need. And balsam, too."

He led us to a granite lid atop a narrow hole in the shade of a big hemlock, shoved aside the stone, hauled out a bundle of meat wrapped in cloth, and handed it to us both.

The hole was his cache, deep enough to be cold still, lined with rocks and narrow enough so no bear or coyote or mountain cat could get in, even if they managed to wrestle off its lid.

"That ought to do you for a bit." He pushed the lid back in place. "And hold on," he said, turning toward his cabin. "There's tallow as well."

He took a step and called, "Molly!" and then, "Molly!" again, even as she came out on the porch in an apron, her hands white with flour.

"Good morning," she said to us, smiling. "And how is your mother?"

"She's well."

"And your father?"

I paused, remembering that hand as it twitched. "The same."

She nodded briskly. "I'll get the tallow." She stepped just through the door to fetch a lump of deer tallow tied up in an old kerchief. "Rendered and ready," she said, bringing it to where we stood in the yard, the pouch of meat slung between us, dripping a little blood onto the ground.

That was a trail we did not dare leave along the path, so I blotted the belly of the sling against the ground, Samuel getting my gist and lowering his end, too, while Mrs. Peterson tucked the tallow into a fold at the top.

"That ought to make you a fair bit of soap," she said. "Or candle, if you like."

We nodded our thanks, said it, too, and then our goodbyes.

"Tell your mother to come along next time," she said. "I could do with a visit."

"She'll be up in a bit with some potatoes."

"And I'll be back soon to visit Scotch," Samuel said.

And off we went back down the mountain, the meat swinging between us in its hammock, Samuel's end mostly dragging on the ground, leaving a trail of blood despite our best efforts.

Chapter Eleven

It's not easy to gather stink, but I decided I would go out before dark and do just that.

Supper almost changed my mind, it was so good and made me so sleepy, the venison a lovely change from soup.

I wanted to say to my mother, as she seared it in a black pan, "If that smell doesn't wake Daddy up, nothing good ever will."

But I knew I would soon be raising her dander again, so in the meantime I was the girl she wanted me to be. I helped with the meal, thanked her for it, and cleaned up afterward, my voice quiet, my smile steady, until I thought perhaps she and even Esther had forgiven me for dousing my father that morning, though I knew they still blamed me for much more.

"I'll take supper to Maisie," I said when the kitchen was clean and the lanterns lit.

"And then we'll make soap," she said.

My mother didn't notice when I took a jar with a tight lid and snatched the last egg, the one that had been meant for my lunch.

Since it was, in some ways, mine, I reckoned that I had the right to spend it as I wished. But I wasn't sure my mother would see it that way, so I took it when she wasn't looking and carried it out with the scraps for Maisie.

"Oh, how spry you are!" I said to Maisie when I crept into the woodshed and found her on her feet, her tail wagging a little.

I knelt down and let her come to me, the puppies squirming and squealing in their nest of straw.

She put her nice, wet nose into the hollow of my neck and snuffed at me, licked my cheek, put one forepaw flat against my arm until I knuckled her ears and kissed her in return. She gobbled the venison as I fed it to her on the flat of my hand, piece by piece, not just the gristle but soft meaty bits, too.

I knew that twilight would soon come creeping across Echo Mountain, and the night critters with it. Deer, wherever fire had left a clearing. Coyotes, wherever there were deer. Raccoons, masked for plunder. And skunks, hunting for grubs and worms and frogs too young to be quiet on a spring night.

But skunks loved eggs most of all.

And I had one.

A nice big one from Mrs. Anderson's Rhode Island Reds, who feasted on marigolds and wheat berries and laid hearty eggs for all of us who lived nearby.

I had planned to crack the egg into a notch of a big rotten stump below the cabin, where I'd often seen skunks digging for termites, and then wait for its thick, gamey smell to draw a skunk close while I waited in the trees.

But I looked into Maisie's eyes, ran my hand down her wash-board ribs, thought about the milk she made for her puppies, and fed the egg to her instead.

I cracked it with one hand into my other and held it out while she lapped and lapped until it was gone.

"So you can sleep well," I whispered into her silky ear. *"So you can come out of here soon and see the springtime."*

And I was startled by the swell of happiness and fullness that swept over me as she laid her head against mine.

When I crept into the nest with her puppies, she trembled a little but didn't protest. Not even when I lay among them and they belly-crawled up to my warmth and butted me with their hard little heads, Quiet the one to find my neck and claim it for his own, curling against my pulse and sighing as if he'd found what he was looking for.

"That's my little one," I said, the rumble in my throat a new music to his tiny ears. "That's my Quiet."

After a while Maisie crooned at me until I gave back her bed and her babies, and then I hid the jar I'd brought to collect skunk stink and went out into the twilight to start again from scratch to gather the makings of a cure.

There was still light enough in the sky to coax me across the yard again toward the path that led to the balsam tree.

But the woods were darker, and I'd forgotten about the trail of blood that Samuel and I had left on the path not long before.

Chapter Twelve

It wasn't a coyote that found me. Or a bear. Or even a fox.

I didn't hear anything as I stood under the tree, collecting balsam on a paddle of wood I found in the litter around its trunk. Nothing but the whisper of its long roots reaching deep into earth still cold from the long winter.

And I didn't see anything, either, as I tapped the patient old tree again and took what I needed.

I didn't know I was being watched until I turned back to the path and found myself face-to-face with that big dog again.

This time, in the poor light, he looked even more like a wolf. Even more like something wild.

I hoped that he hadn't followed the blood trail, expecting something wounded. Something he could eat.

When he lowered his head and took a step toward me, I knew a moment of fear, but the sound he made was not quite a growl—it was more question than threat—as if he needed something but couldn't quite make up his mind about me.

Then "Ellie!" came the thread of my mother's call from down the path.

And I turned instinctively toward her voice.

Turned back to find the path empty, the dog gone.

Just as before.

This time, I didn't look for him in the trees or follow up the path.

This time, as darkness came, home felt like a better choice.

My mother was waiting for me in the yard.

"What were you doing up there?" she said, her hands on her hips.

I might have told her then about the dog, but she seemed a little too much like him in that moment. The way she looked at me. As if she wanted an explanation. An answer to a question she could not quite put into words.

So I said, "Just walking." Something I did often. Something I had once done with my father, who also liked an after-supper ramble and the softness of dark air.

"Well, walk back out and get some kindling for the soap fire." She turned toward the stone pit where we cooked things better made outside.

I almost echoed Samuel then. I almost said, "How come Esther isn't helping with the tallow?" But I didn't.

Esther did her fair share. It didn't matter that she *liked* house-work. What mattered was that she *did* that work, leaving me free to do some of what my father had once done. Yard chores. Gardening. Fishing. And anything involving fire.

My mother didn't notice the paddle of balsam I carried behind my back. She didn't notice when I tucked it behind the woodshed. But I knew she would notice when I spread it on my father's scar. The place where the tree had struck him. Which was as close as I could get to what ailed him.

I knew his wound was on the inside. And I knew that balsam was mostly good for wounds on the outside. But what about the things I didn't know? What about the possibility that all we had to do to make him well was try harder? Try anything. Try everything. And admit that there were things we didn't understand.

Working with my mother to build the soap-fire, stirring the tallow into the kettle of lye water that hung over the flames, made me sorry for the silence between us, so I broke it.

"I saw a dog on the trail earlier today."

In the golden firelight, my mother seemed softer, but there was nothing soft about the look she gave me.

"What dog?"

"That's what I want to know. It was a big one, brindled, with ears that stood up. And it didn't seem quite tame."

My mother added a stick to the fire. "You sure it wasn't a coyote?"

"Dog," I said. "Come down the trail from above."

"Maybe someone on the hill has a new one."

I shook my head. "There wasn't anything new about this dog. And Mr. Peterson didn't know him."

"I wonder if that could be the hag's mutt. Except it's never come down from her camp before."

The hag. I hadn't heard that name for a long time.

Not since a foggy morning long before, when I had been tempted by how the mountaintop disappeared into the mist, ignored my father's warnings, and climbed beyond the last of the five families, where there were no trails except what the deer and moose made . . . and smelled a fire up above. I had run back down to warn my father. Wildfire, I had thought. And I hadn't been entirely mistaken.

When I found him splitting wood and told him there was a fire above, he set his ax aside and said, "It's all right, Ellie." He wiped the sweat off his face with his hands. "That's just the hag up there."

"'Just the hag'?" The only hags I knew were in storybooks. Gnarled old creatures who cast spells and ate children for supper. "What hag?"

"The only hag I know of. And I met her only once myself, when we first came here. Didn't know she was up there when I went looking for the mountaintop. She was in her little yard, skinning a deer, and I tell you, Ellie, I had a hard time standing still when I saw her. She was that odd. And she had a dog with her. A big one. With a dark eye."

"What, you mean one eye black and one eye not?"

"No." He laughed. "A dark stare. No welcome in it. Not in hers either."

I pictured that. "Did she say anything?"

He nodded. "She said, 'You need a leech on that ear. Then honey if it's hot.'"

I remember him smiling at the look on my face. "I had a hurt ear. From a fall. It was swollen. She told me I should go down to the marsh and get a leech or two to drain the blood off or I'd have a ruined ear."

"And did you?"

He shook his head. "I had your mother lance it instead. It bled so bad I thought we'd made a mistake doing that, but the pus came with it. And then I recall we did put some honey on the open cut, and it healed right and quickly. So."

I remember how he picked up his ax again. Went on with his work. But I stopped him with a fresh question. "And what about the hag? Did you go back up after that?"

At which my father shook his head.

"You don't ever even talk about her," I said. "Why doesn't anyone ever talk about her?"

My father set a fresh log on the stump and hefted his ax. "Nothing to say. And no sense pointing you children toward something better left alone. Which is what you'll do, Ellie. Leave her alone." And there was something so hard in his voice that I'd obeyed him.

Now, much later, as I stood with my mother by the fire and stirred the tallow, I wondered if the hag might have carved the little lamb and the dog and all the other small gifts I'd been given.

"How old is the hag?" I asked my mother, remembering the face

I'd seen in the woods, which had seemed too young for someone called a hag.

"I have no idea," she said. "But from what your father said, I'd imagine 'old' would do."

So: not the wood-carver. But perhaps something better.

"Did you ever ask her to come see Daddy?" I asked. "After he got hurt?"

My mother looked at me like I had two heads. "The hag? When the doctor said there was nothing to be done? Don't be foolish." She fed another stick to the flames. "I don't know if that dog was hers or a stray, but if you see it again, you keep away and let me know." She kicked an ember back into the fire. "Tame or wild, a hungry dog will eat. And your brother's still little enough to be dragged away."

I imagined Samuel in a set of jaws, and my shoulders went up around my ears.

For a tiny boy who never looked where he was going, the woods could be especially unkind.

"I'll tell you if I see it again," I said. And I meant it. I truly did. But I didn't know where that dog would lead me. Or what it would lead me to become.

Chapter Thirteen

That night, when we gathered around my father to wish him good night, I laid my hand on his forehead and closed my eyes and told him, without a word, that I was going to bring him back.

I concentrated so hard on that thought that I could feel it pulsing in my ears, and my hand grew hot on his cool skin, as if the flame in my chest had spread.

I was startled when Esther pulled my arm away and said, "What are you doing, Ellie? Daddy doesn't need your sweaty hand on his face."

"Do you have a fever?" my mother said, pressing her lips against my forehead, and I closed my eyes and let myself feel that almost-kiss until she pulled back and said, "You'd better get on to bed. Your father is already sick enough."

Later, as I tried to sleep, I touched that spot on my forehead again and again, but it was no softer than the rest of me.

I hoped it would send me quickly to sleep—perhaps even to dream of my father waking and rising and growing brawny and brown again—but instead I lay in the darkness as I always did now, jangled and jarred by a memory that kept me wakeful and sad long into the night.

While my mother, my sister, my brother, my father all slept, I lay, wakeful, and remembered that January day, Esther gathering kindling under the trees at the edge of the yard where the snow was thinnest, watching Samuel while my mother was inside making stew.

I remembered helping my father clear trees at the edge of the garden so in the spring we could plant more beans and peas and squash.

I remembered him showing me where to stand as he swung his ax. How to keep a safe distance in case the tree kicked back like an angry horse as it fell. How to make the cut so that the tree fell mostly where he wanted it to fall. In this case, downhill. In this case, away from him. Away from me. Where it could do no harm.

But my mother was busy with the stew. And Esther was busy with her chores. And my father was busy with his ax. And I was the one who suddenly saw Samuel running across the open ground where the snow had drifted away and the bare dirt was burned pale with cold. I was the one who saw that he was running after a rabbit, his eyes fixed on the white smudge of its tail.

The tree broke just then. Began its fall. Began its great arc toward Samuel, its branches thrashing, slowing as it snagged on the branches of other trees, spinning heavily, and I charged beneath it, grabbing Samuel as I ran, both of us shoved from behind to land hard, just out of harm's way.

I remembered lying on the cold ground with Samuel in my arms. How he struggled to get free, yelling, "Why did you do that, Ellie?"

I remembered holding him tight as I turned to see my father lying still under the tree's branches.

His blood on the snow.

I remembered not knowing what to think about that.

I remembered pulling Samuel away before he could see my father, dragging him toward the cabin as he tried to break loose from my hand clenched tight around his wrist, hauling him farther from the garden and the tree and my father, casting him into the snow where Esther was gathering wood, where Esther was supposed to be watching him, where Esther was unaware of any trouble until I raced into the cabin yelling for my mother, until I ran back to where my father lay, my mother with me, Esther chasing us, calling, "What's happened?" and Samuel chasing her, all of us climbing through the chaos of branches and dirt and snow to try to lug the tree off my father, all of us pulling at it together as he lay so still beneath it that I was sure he was dead.

We couldn't reach him through the tree's sharp, tangled limbs, no matter how Esther yelled his name, no matter how hard my mother worked to break the smaller branches, her hands torn up from trying. But we all, together, finally managed to pull some of it off him, and then I bent away the thinnest branches until they bowed, taut and difficult, in my arms while my mother and Esther tugged him away inches at a time, Samuel crying "Daddy!" again and again but too small for anything else, my mother reaching through the branches, feeling my father's neck, feeling for his pulse, finding it, and then with a mighty surge pulling him from the last of the tangle and onto open ground, to turn him over and call his name, holding his face in her hands, the blood matting his hair, his skin a shocking white, all of us calling him, my sister holding one of his hands in both of hers, Samuel tugging on the hem of his pant leg, my mother kneeling alongside him, then scrambling to her feet, looking wildly around, her hands dripping with blood, and then running for an old blanket that we made into a hammock to drag him, his poor body bumping along the frozen ground, and then slowly, horribly, up onto the cabin's step and through its door and across the floor, into the washroom, laying him near the drain and pouring warm water over his wound to clean it, waiting for him to wake up.

I will never forget the moment when we all stopped and sat back, exhausted, and looked at each other, at him, at the pink water trailing from his head, all of us breathing hard, Samuel still crying, crawling into my mother's lap, his face red and snotty and swollen.

"Run to the Petersons', Ellie," my mother said, her voice shaking. "Tell them to fetch the doctor. Tell them to hurry."

Chapter Fourteen

It was only days later, after the doctor had come and gone, after we had had time to consider the idea of my strong, laughing father never waking again, that my mother asked how he had come to be in the path of the tree as it fell.

She looked at me, who had been with him. Esther looked at me, who had been with him.

Samuel said, "Did you see what happened, Ellie?" He turned to my mother. "Ellie knocked me down."

And I simply could not say, *I knocked you down to save your life.*

I simply could not say, *And the tree knocked Daddy down because of you.*

I loved him too much to do that to him. And I knew my father would wake up—I *knew* he would—and tell everyone the truth of it. By then it wouldn't matter that Samuel had chased a rabbit into harm's way. My father would be well again. My mother would smile again. And everything would be all right again. I knew it would.

So I said, "No, Samuel, I didn't see what happened. One minute, Daddy was cutting the tree, and I was . . . dragging some branches into a pile. And then the tree fell. I didn't mean to knock you down, Samuel. I was running to get help and I didn't mean to knock you down."

He frowned at me for a long moment, and I hoped that he wouldn't work too hard to unravel that thread. To sort out the jumble of what had happened.

"You were in the way, weren't you?" my sister said.

At first, I thought she was talking to Samuel, but then I realized she was looking at me. Talking to me.

Esther wasn't a mean girl. But she never tried to be more gentle than she was. And it was clear that she needed a reason. An explanation. Someone to blame.

My mother looked at me, too, waiting for an answer. She wasn't angry like Esther was, but it was clear that she had no extra space in her heart just then for anything except my father.

Part of me wanted to tell them that it was Samuel's fault, if a little boy could be blamed for such a thing. But when I thought of saying the words, I felt sick and sad. When I thought of Samuel someday learning that he had drawn his father into this disaster—perhaps even into death—I felt even more terrible.

And I knew how Esther would feel—she who should have been watching Samuel.

Which was when I decided that it would be worse to pass the blame than to shoulder it.

If I'd learned anything from the mountain—and from my father—it was that I felt stronger and happier if I was able to do a hard thing and do it well.

So I kept silent. And they took my silence as a confession.

It was difficult to tell, as I lay in the darkness remembering, my face wet with cold tears, whether I had slept and woken or never slept at all.

Esther was quiet but for the slow tempo of her breath. Samuel sighed and murmured in his dreams.

I slipped from my bed and out of the cabin, closing the door behind me without a sound.

The trees wore gowns of starlight.

The dew was cold and luscious on my bare feet.

From somewhere up-mountain, an owl sounded lonely. Forlorn. Beautiful.

It seemed a terrible shame to sleep through such a night, and I was glad to be up before the sun.

I whispered Maisie's name as I opened the door to the woodshed.

She lifted her head and slapped her tail against the ground as I crept inside and found the jar I'd borrowed for gathering stink.

I unscrewed the top and scraped the lip of the jar against my cheeks until I'd captured what tears remained on my face. Almost nothing.

I carried the jar back outside and dragged its mouth through the grass, gathering dew.

Then I retrieved the balsam I'd hidden behind the woodshed and scraped it into the jar, too.

Perhaps tomorrow I would climb down to the river that had carved a valley through the mountains. Its cold, clear water had never failed to make my father smile.

And after that maybe I'd harvest honey from the hive down beyond the brook, ready with a pouch of mud for the stings I was sure to get along the way.

But for now, I contented myself with the stars pulsing overhead, the trees reaching eagerly up, the feel of April on my skin.

When I stirred them, the embers from the tallow fire glowed hungrily, so I fed them bits of dry wood, and leaves, and pine cones, until I had a good fire going.

"Ellie," my mother hiss-whispered from the cabin door, a blanket around her shoulders. *"Have you lost your mind?"*

"I couldn't sleep," I said softly. "I was visiting Maisie."

"And the fire?"

I shrugged. "It was lonely, too."

Which made her smile. So . . . *unexpected,* to see her standing on the step in the darkness, veiled in starlight, the white of her smile a quick surprise, then gone, as she turned to go back inside.

And I stood there for a while, the fire popping and hissing, and thought about that smile. And then I thought about it some more.

When the fire wore itself out, I took my jar of tears and dew and balsam into the woodshed and put it high on the shelf with my other secrets.

"I'm making some medicine," I whispered to Maisie as I lay down next to her, the puppies a muddle of dark softness against her belly. *"Maybe I should add some of your milk."* But she didn't answer me, and I fell asleep and dreamed about nothing at all until morning woke me again.

Chapter Fifteen

The morning began as any morning might—a matter of yawns, squinting at the weather, wobbling on the tightrope between yesterday and tomorrow—but the day to come would be one of the longest and most interesting of my life.

After a proper breakfast with no punishment in it, I went out to finish my morning chores. To these, I added new ones:

Took Maisie her breakfast and sang her a small song I made up on the spot, full of barn cats and field mice and goldenrod bowed down with yellow.

Coaxed her outside for some air but stayed in the shed with the puppies so she wouldn't fret.

Laid my hand over Quiet like a warm cape and told him things like, "You are beautiful. You are a beautiful, silly little dollop of a dog."

When Maisie returned, I decided to go for honey and river water, but my father had taught me never to pass up the chance to get what food I could. ("You never know when there won't be any to be had.") So I gathered his fishing gear and put it with the medicine jar and some oilcloth for wrapping my catch, a pair of work gloves, and some tinder in my pack, the pack on my shoulder, and set out for the river.

Samuel followed me, and I let him, sure that he would tire before long and head back home.

"Where are you going, Ellie?" he said as I went down the path toward the river.

"To see if I can catch a fish for supper," I said, though that was only one of the things I meant to do.

"With so much venison to eat?"

"Mother will make most of that into jerky. For when there isn't any fresh. Besides, I like fish."

"I don't, much," he said, though Mother always fried it crisp and gave it to us with pickles and cream.

"Well, I don't much like jerky. And I don't like being hungry. But if you'd rather eat pickles and cream without fish, that's fine with me."

At which he said "Huh" and nothing else.

The path was steep and rocky in places, but there were saplings all along it, and the ones nearest the difficult spots were smooth from where we had grabbed them again and again to steady ourselves. I had long since learned to find a handhold before I took a hard step down, but Samuel preferred to hop from rock to rock, and it wasn't long before he fell.

"Oh, good grief," I said as he lay crying on the path, banged up but with no real damage done. "How many times do you have to fall before you realize you're not a mountain goat?"

He looked up at me with a wet face. "I don't think I'm a goat. Why would I think I'm a goat?"

"Never mind," I said, helping him up. "Just slow down. I have a fish to catch, and you're here to help or go home."

He brushed himself off. "Help, then. I'll go home when I want to go home and not because you said so."

Which I ignored completely.

And we set off again, the river still far below us, Samuel scooting ahead as soon as the path leveled out a bit, determined to lead the way.

I let him, since it was easier to keep an eye on him if he was ahead of me, but I wished he would stay near.

That was always one of my wishes: to keep him near.

There were many things that tempted me as we went down the mountain: a fresh-green meadow where fire from lightning strike had cleared a few acres of trees before rain had put it out; a vernal pool where peepers sang so loudly at twilight that we could hear them even far up-mountain; a granite ledge big enough for me to sit on, like a turtle in the sun. But I decided to keep those things for another day. And I left the honey, too, for the trip home, since it would be harder to fish with bee-stung hands, but I heard the hive hidden in an oak as we passed, and the old tree, too, humming with excitement as its buds erupted into leaf.

As we passed by there, I saw a brand-new gift, sitting on a white rock at the edge of the trail where even Samuel might have seen it if he hadn't been in such a hurry.

A honeybee. Made of wood and something I couldn't name.

I held it up in the light. Smiled. Peered into the trees. Said, "Thank you," in case someone was listening. "I wish you'd come out and meet me."

"And I wish you'd hurry up," Samuel said from down the path a bit. "Or the river's gonna dry up before we get there."

I put the bee in my pocket and held it there in my hand.

Looked long into the trees all around me. Saw nothing.

Waited until Samuel disappeared around a bend and then, feeling a little foolish, said, "I don't know why you won't show yourself."

The trees stood quietly, waiting as I waited, but nothing moved. Nothing answered.

And I did not dare let Samuel reach the river before me.

But when I hurried down the trail, I found him standing quiet and still, with his hand up to stop me. He whispered, *"Look there, Ellie."*

I saw, over his head, not on the trail but in the trees to one side, the ghost dog, a rabbit hanging limp from his mouth.

He stared back at us.

Samuel must have seen something in that dark eye, because when I came up alongside him he slowly worked his way behind me, put one hand flat on my back, peered out from around me, and said, "I don't like him."

I felt sorry for the poor rabbit in those jaws, but I'd been known to eat a rabbit, too. *"He won't hurt us,"* I whispered.

"How do you know?"

"Because I've met him twice before and he didn't hurt me.

Remember when I came up to the Petersons' and said I'd seen a dog?" I said nothing about the hag or whether this might be her mutt. I imagined Samuel climbing up to her camp. Ending up in a pie. And I understood why my parents hadn't talked about her. "He's just a hungry stray."

"Then let's catch him and take him home for ours."

But I had no intention of doing that. Maisie and Quiet and, for a while, the other puppies were ours if they were anyone's, but this dog was not. If he was the hag's, something had changed up there at that camp. Something had sent him down among us.

I wondered what. And I decided, just then, to find out.

"Git!" I suddenly yelled, waving an arm, and the dog loped off through the brush and out of sight, the rabbit flopping in his mouth, and I thought it odd that the dog had not eaten it right away, as most hungry dogs would, while it was still warm.

"What did you do that for?" Samuel said, coming out from my shadow to glare at me. "He could have been my dog, Ellie."

"Or you could have been his boy, more likely. He's too much dog for you. And wild, besides. Otherwise, you wouldn't have hidden behind me."

At which Samuel glared harder. "I wasn't hiding. You make me sound like a baby. I'm not a baby, Ellie."

"Of course you're not," I replied. "You haven't been a baby for years and years."

"And years," he said. "Third time you've been right."

Chapter Sixteen

The river was where we'd left it, endlessly traveling down its own winding path, through shadow and sunlight, under fallen trees furred with moss and over boulders polished by the current.

Someone, somewhere had named this the Androscoggin, but we generally called it "The River."

At the end of the path and across some marshy ground, a flat rock above a deep pool at the edge of the current made a perfect place to drop a line. "Find me some bait," I said to Samuel, who would have been happy to hunt crickets in September when they were thick on the ground but was less eager to forage for April slugs.

"I don't like things that are slimy," he said, making a face.

"Help or go home," I said again, so he sighed a huge sigh and crawled into the undergrowth to hunt for a slug, which he found and brought back to me on a leaf veined with its glimmer-trail. "Go get me another," I said.

I wasn't fond of slugs for bait, either. They really were slimy. And they tended to leak their guts when I put them on a hook, leaving not much more than skin and slime behind, but I hadn't brought a spade to dig for worms, and I didn't like to use salamanders with their big, glossy eyes and their little hands. So I said, "Sorry, sorry, sorry," and, gritting my teeth until my jaw ached, threaded the slug onto the hook as quick as I could, and dropped it in the pool, my end of the line wrapped around a good, strong stick, and waited.

Some fish were as unimpressed with slugs as I was, but a trout will take a slug, and soon one did. I yanked the line up and away, hooking the fish by the mouth, sorry as I did it, sorry as I wound the line around the stick and pulled the trout up to the rock, sorry as I beat it senseless with a rock, sorry as I put a fresh slug on my hook, sorry as I sent it down into the pool.

I shivered with their pain. Cringed as they died. But none of that stopped me from doing what I had to do.

"Let me try," Samuel said, reaching for the line.

He was only newly big enough for this, and I myself was newly sad that my father would not be the one to teach him, but I gave Samuel the line and taught him how to hold it in two hands, how to move it slowly so the slug seemed to swim though it was dead, how to wait, wait, wait, and then yank hard to set the hook. No good hesitating if you meant to do a thing like that. Do it and be done with it, good and quick. That's what I told him as the fish took the bait. That's what I told him when the fish thrashed and fought so hard to be free that I had to hold on to Samuel and the line both, regardless of how determined he was to do it on his own. That's what I told him when we hauled the trout up onto the rock, its gorgeous scales flashing in the sun, its eye wild before I beat it to death. That part I spared Samuel. That part . . . I'd never done that part before my father went to sleep. But I had done it ever since then, never without being sorry.

Samuel yammered about how much nicer his fish was than mine, and I hoped that meant he'd eat some of it. Muscle came from meat, and Samuel was so little. I wanted him bigger. Stronger. Tougher.

Some fresh fish would do him good.

So I agreed that his fish was by far the better. And I hunted up another slug so he could try for a third. And I stood close but without touching the line as he cast in again, and caught another trout, and did everything else that needed to be done except that last part with the rock.

I made him watch while I cleaned the fish and threw the guts into the river to wash downstream like big, gory worms, a feast for turtles and bottom-fish and flies, but unlikely to attract bears to the place where we fished.

"Those are the best fish anyone ever caught," Samuel said of his two trout. "And yours is pretty nice, too."

The three fish were identical.

"You're right. And they will be delicious." At which he smiled.

I wrapped the fish in oilcloth and tucked them into my pack, setting aside the glass jar I'd brought with me.

"What's that?" Samuel asked.

The balsam inside had melted a bit with the heat of the sun on the rock, turning the tears and dew a nice shade of copper.

"Nothing." I climbed down to the edge of the river to let a little cold water flow into the jar. Just enough for some wildness. "It's something like tea. Nothing you'd like."

And then I made a mud pie and wrapped it in my kerchief, for the bee sting that was sure to come.

Chapter Seventeen

When we reached it, the hive was wide-awake, which is not a great thing when a person wants honey. But I was there, and the hive was there, and I would try.

"Sit," I said to Samuel, pointing at a log just off the path. "And don't move."

He gave me a look. But he sat where I pointed and watched as I buttoned my shirt to the neck.

"Aren't you afraid of getting stung?" he asked.

"Not afraid, so much, though I hope I don't."

From my pocket, I took my knife and a flint spearhead I'd found when my father and I were planting potatoes. "Keep that with you," my father had said. "It could save your life someday." I'd thought he meant as a weapon until he showed me how to strike the flint on his shovel to make sparks. "Fire," he had said. "Few things more valuable in this world, and you can make all you'll ever need if you know how. That's the secret to everything. Knowing how."

"And you'll teach me." Which was as much statement as question.

"I will. But you'll learn best by doing."

I had thought about that. "How am I supposed to do something that will teach me how to do it if I don't know how to do it in the first place? That's like a circle."

My father had laughed. "It is. But it's true. Though you can read about how to do things, too."

"What about learning things from people who don't know how to write?" Like some of the others on Echo Mountain. Like babies. Like dogs. "And what if someone doesn't know how to read? That takes lessons."

"Everything takes lessons," my father said. "Though some you'll give to yourself." And my father had been right. Sometimes I was my own best teacher. He taught me how to make tinder and how to strike the flint with my knife and how to coax a flame, but in the end, I had to do that work myself before I truly learned how.

"How come we don't use matches anymore?" I had asked him.

I remember him sighing. "Same reason we built our own cabin and grow our own food now. Matches cost money, Ellie. And the nearest mercantile is a world away."

So I had practiced with the flint until I had blisters, but it had still taken me a very long time before I could start a fire. The day I first made one without any help was a very fine day indeed.

"Look here," I said to Samuel as he sat on the log and I cleared some ground near his feet. From my pack I took what looked like a bird's nest: a ball of oak bark I'd shredded into coarse wood-thread and molded into shape. I carried one with me always, usually several in the bottom of my pack.

"This is your tinder," I told him, setting the little nest aside. "Which you can make yourself from threads of dead bark or dry grass as long as it's very fine." Then I gathered small twigs and built a tiny pyramid, just big enough to hold some dried leaves with room left over for the nest of bark thread.

Then I scraped the flint hard and strong with my knife until sparks flew into the tinder and then caught, suddenly, making a small flame that I blew on gently, gently, until it strengthened. I quickly slid the burning tinder among the twigs, which caught, making a stronger flame. Before long, the fire was burning well enough to add more sticks and finally a big one I would use as a torch.

Samuel watched it all in silence, with round eyes, and I felt at least ten feet tall.

"Who taught you to do that?" he said, his face serious.

"Daddy did." I blew on the flames and fed them with dry leaves to make sure the torch was well and truly engulfed.

"Why didn't he teach me?" Samuel looked so small that I nearly scooped him up into my arms.

"He will. Soon."

I did not say *Or I will.* Our father would do it. *He* would.

The biggest stick was flaming well when I lifted it into the air and swept it mildly enough to feed it, feed it, coax it hotter and hotter. Then I held it aloft as I scooped dirt and stomped on the fire I'd built.

"What did you do that for?" Samuel said. "That was a good fire!"

"And I got what I needed. Now stay right here and don't move."

The hive was so close to the trail that I thought maybe I should send Samuel farther away, but I didn't know any words that would make him leave. So again I said, "Don't move," before I turned up my collar and pulled on my gloves and crept through the thicket around the oak hive. As I came closer to it, I held the torch straight up until it began to go out, then blew the last of the flame away so it gave just smoke.

With the smoking branch in front of me, I edged up to the oak tree, the hive in its big, dark mouth humming away, and then gently poked the stick into the hole, not too far, just enough to fill the hive with smoke, which would make the bees drowsy and dumb.

After a bit, a few stumbled out, stunned, and flew lazily to the ground.

Others, coming in from their work, spun crazily, looking for a foe, but I stood as still as a broken clock and waited until the hive grew quiet.

Then I pulled the stick away and plunged it, hot end first, into the ground and slowly reached my gloved hand into the hive, feeling for the comb.

The bees in the hive covered my glove until it trembled with their sleepy buzzing.

I could feel the comb where they stored the honey that fed them all winter, that kept them alive in the year's hardest, leanest months, that was meant for them and their young. And I felt their terror. Felt their panic as they choked and nodded in the smoke, their queen weeping. And I let go of the comb and slowly drew my empty hand from the hive.

It was covered with bees slowly regaining their wits, baffled by the smoke but waking as I watched. I shook my hand gently as I backed away from the hive and some of them fell softly away. Others clung without moving and I knew they had stung my glove and died doing it. Which made my heart hurt.

"Go, go," I said to Samuel as I cleared the thicket. "Quickly now." And off he went, up the path ahead of me.

Oddly, it was only then, as I was leaving, that a lone bee flew up and stung me on the cheek.

One of the hardest lessons I had ever learned concerned honeybees and how they died when they stung. How they couldn't leave just the stinger behind, so they had to leave some of themselves behind, too. And died. As the ones on my glove had. As the one who had stung my cheek had. Which made no sense to me.

I hadn't taken a drop of honey. I was well away. And now a bee had died, regardless.

My cheek was on fire, no less when I pulled the soft, fuzzy bit of bee off my skin, but somewhat better when I pulled open the kerchief full of mud and pressed it against my face.

I told the bees I was sorry as I flicked their sad remains off my glove and dragged it through the dirt until it was clean.

Samuel came back down the path toward me.

"What's wrong?" he said. "Why didn't you come with me? And why do you have mud on your face?"

"Bee sting," I said, wincing with the pain of it.

He came close, peering at my cheek. "You've got a big bump there."

I nodded. "It'll go away."

"Why aren't you crying?"

I shrugged. "Won't help me to cry." Though there were times when tears did me some good.

He looked thoughtful. Reached out to wipe away some mud that was dripping down my jaw. "Where's the honey?"

"I didn't take any."

"What?! Why not? You got stung for nothing?"

I headed up the path. "The bees didn't have enough to spare. Not yet."

But Samuel wasn't impressed. "You could have got a little for our porridge," he said bitterly. Porridge without something sweet was unfortunate.

I didn't tell him that the honey had not been meant for porridge. Instead, I told him what my father had told me. "The bees need it more than we do, especially in the winter and the spring. For their babies. And their queen. And themselves."

I thought again of the egg I'd fed to Maisie instead of using it to gather stink.

"Let's trade one of the fish to Mrs. Anderson for some eggs," I said.

Samuel said, "As long as it's your fish."

But, as it turned out, a snake came first.

Chapter Eighteen

When we reached the yard, we found my mother and Esther taking turns at the butter churn.

"I caught fish for supper!" Samuel cried, rushing toward them while I lugged our catch the last of the way up from the river, tired now, wiping traces of mud from my cheek.

"We didn't know where you'd gone," Esther barked, but not at Samuel. At me. "We were worried, Ellie. You should tell us if you take him with you."

I might have said any number of things to that. Always, at the end of every list, was the one answer I couldn't give her: *You were the one who was supposed to be watching Samuel the day Daddy got hurt.*

"And why did you go fishing when we have venison?" she said.

"I'll dry the fish so it will keep," I said. "Or we can use it to make broth for Daddy."

But she just shook her head. "You know Samuel can't swim. You shouldn't have taken him with you. And you should have told us."

"He followed me. I didn't mean to take him along."

"And Mother didn't mean to trade Maisie's puppies to Mr. Anderson for one of his milk cows."

"Esther!" my mother snapped. "That's enough."

But she was wrong. It was not enough. "You gave the puppies away?" I said in a voice that was far too small for the big thing that rose in my throat.

"Promised them, yes. As soon as they're old enough," my mother said. "We need that cow. She's much younger than Jupiter and Venus. We can't expect them to give milk forever."

"But *all* the puppies?"

"Mr. Anderson is a hunter," she said, churning so hard now that she was in danger of busting the dasher into kindling. "He's the main reason we have meat on our plates. He needs new dogs, coming of age behind his old ones."

"But all of them? You gave him Quiet?"

She didn't look at me. "We have barely enough food to spare for Maisie. We don't need another dog. Another cow, we need."

"But you wouldn't even have Quiet if it weren't for Ellie," Samuel said, close by my side. "She saved him."

"And she'll drink the milk we get from this new cow. And the cream. Eat the butter. The cheese." My mother still wouldn't look at me. And I had no desire to look at her. Or at Esther, who wasn't smiling exactly but didn't look the least bit sorry. "You can visit Quiet anytime you like," my mother said.

But that was cold comfort. I had seen what became of a dog that lived in a pack. A dog that hunted for a living.

"This isn't because one more dog will eat too much. Mr.

Anderson would have left us one puppy if you'd asked. This is to punish me." My voice was even harder than hers. "You can't make me give him up."

"We all give up things we love," my mother said. "Whether we want to or not."

I thought of the things she'd lost when we'd left our town life. I thought about my father, slowly thinning away. The sight of his hideous sores. And I thought about Quiet as he had struggled in that water, waking.

I went into the woodshed. Maisie gave me a curious look. She was on her feet, licking one of her pups. She didn't object when I crawled into the nest and put my head among those little dogs. And cried. And cried. And knew it was Quiet who licked the salt from my cheeks, soothing the last of the bee sting, while this new hurt took up a place in my chest alongside the flame that burned hotter, now that I had even more work to do.

Chapter Nineteen

I left my pack with the jar of balsam and tears and dew and river water in the shed and carried the fish back out to the yard.

"Where's Samuel?" I said to Esther and my mother, still at the churn.

Esther turned. Looked. Turned back to me. She didn't say anything.

My mother said, "He must have gone in to wash the fish off his hands."

I went into the cabin and left the fish in the kitchen, by the pump.

"Samuel?" I called.

He didn't answer.

I went through the kitchen to the washroom. The door stood open.

Samuel wasn't in there.

But something else was.

I'd seen a snake or two in the washroom before, but not like this one.

This one was as long as I was. Black and shiny. Lying in a tangle, like a dropped rope, in a patch of sun near the floor drain. It had pushed away the little lid we put over the drain, slithered up from its shelter under the cabin and onto the plank floor, and gone to sleep.

I knew that as soon as I stepped into the room it would wake.

My first thought: Stomp on the floor and let it escape down that drain.

My next thought: Trap it.

It was a black racer. I knew it wasn't a poisonous snake. My father had always said racers were harmless, though a mouse or a cricket might disagree . . . and so did I, since I also knew that it had a mouth full of needle-teeth. I knew that it would writhe and coil in my hands if I picked it up. Heavy. Smooth. Angry. I knew that it would bite me if it could. I knew that I would have to try very, very hard not to shriek and holler as it twisted and whipped around my arms. But I also knew that it would make Esther scream loud enough to wake the dead.

No more lullabies.

One big leap and I was at the drain, my foot over it, as the snake burst from its nap and thrashed out long and swift, racing around the room like ink from a quill.

I'd left the door open behind me.

I couldn't let it past me, out of the washroom, or it would hide and be still and come in the night to warm itself on one of us sleeping.

So I lunged for it as it swept past me.

It's not easy to grab a snake in full-blown panic, but I did. With both hands, as close to the head as possible so it couldn't curl around and bite me. Its big eyes were wild. Maybe even as wild as my own. And I suddenly saw its black-and-white world. Felt the tight choke of a frog in its throat. Its ribs arcing like slender moons inside the dark galaxy of itself.

And I almost set it free.

But I didn't.

I made myself hold it tight, as far away from my face as I could, as I hurried out of the washroom, back to the bedroom where my father lay sleeping. I hung on with one hand while I opened the door and tossed it inside, pulling the door shut and then leaning against it, breathing so hard my lungs hurt.

My hands trembled as they tried to forget the feel of that snake. The giantness of it.

I saw the snake's shadow from under the door. Felt it butt up against the sill. Heard it scraping along the too-narrow gap.

I pictured it racing around the room, trying to find a way out, hole seeking, peering into the mouth of my mother's dusty mandolin, and then, finally, slithering up the post of my father's bed, coiling on his warm belly, its tongue flicking like a little blade, its eyes wide and anxious.

I knew that snakes only bit what they ate or what tried to eat them. I knew it wouldn't bite someone sleeping.

I knew Esther would come in soon from the churning.

I knew she would go to my father's room to check on him, as she always did when he'd been without us for a time, which was one of the reasons why I loved her.

I knew she would be the one to find the snake.

And I knew that if screaming could wake my father, he would wake.

Chapter Twenty

Before I left the cabin, I unwrapped two of the fish and left them for cooking. Wrapped the third in the oilcloth again. Put it back in my pack and took it out into the yard.

"He's not inside," I said to my mother, who was scooping butter out of the churn and into a bowl in Esther's hands.

"Then go find him," Esther said.

I held up my pack. "I'm taking a fish to Mrs. Anderson to trade for eggs. I'll look for him on the path."

My mother nodded. "And then bring him straight back for lessons."

Which my mother gave to me and Esther and Samuel nearly every day, rain or shine, summer or winter, sick or well, and no argument about it, not that we were likely to give her one.

We could all read (though Samuel was just starting to get the hang of it) and speak the language of numbers, and we all knew about wars and presidents and the crash that had driven us from the gray, starving town into the green and generous mountain. But I pictured the bedlam when Esther found the snake, and I imagined coming back to something besides reading and writing and arithmetic.

I didn't see Samuel on the path up-mountain. "Samuel!" I called more than once, but he didn't answer. Surely he was somewhere back near the cabin, maybe trying to start his own little fire with a couple of hopeless rocks.

At the turn to the Andersons', I paused and looked up the path to where it dwindled into the undergrowth.

Nobody went up there, except to hunt.

Nobody lived up there, except the hag.

Samuel wouldn't have gone up there on his own.

I was sure he was somewhere down by home, maybe even in the yard by now, pestering my mother for a taste of butter straight from the churn. I pictured them all back in the cabin, Esther going along to check on my father, finding the snake, screaming like she'd been scalded, running from the room, her mouth a dark hole. My mother racing into the bedroom, the snake in a slick frenzy, thrashing toward escape, my mother slashing at it with her big knife.

I told the snake I was sorry. Hoped it reached the drain hole and through to safety.

And then I pictured Esther and my mother, trembling with fury, knowing that someone had shut that snake in with my father, knowing that it had to have been me, and I turned away from the Andersons' and went farther up the mountain instead, following the path that the wild ones had left, threading my way through the undergrowth as if I were a needle looking for something to mend.

———————

I expected to see the dog up there, and before long, I did.

I was navigating an especially steep, rocky place when I looked up and saw him above me, staring down. One tooth hung below his lip, but I decided that didn't mean anything. He wasn't growling. He wasn't snarling. But he didn't look very friendly, either. The tick on his face was revolting, and I made up my mind to yank it off when I could. If I could get close enough. If I could do it without dog-bite.

I said, "Hey, boy," in my calmest voice.

I could smell the fish in the pack that hung from my shoulder, so I knew he could, too. I had meant to trade it for eggs, but I was not in that world anymore.

"I have a fish for you," I said. "For you and . . ." But I didn't want to call her *the hag*. It didn't seem polite.

He took a step away and I took a step upward, and then another, turning my attention back to the climb, managing it carefully, slowly, mindful of the possibility of a fall.

When I reached easier ground, I found that the dog had retreated farther but was still near.

"Why don't you lead the way?" I said. "I'll follow. Go on."

Which he did, heading along what was surely his own trail, fewer trees up here, patches of green moss, gray moss, humps of rock everywhere, lichen and mushrooms, stray feathers, and, suddenly, an antler like a hard white flower blooming in a nest of ivy.

My father and I liked such things. The long, curved set of beaver teeth we'd found near the river. A snake skin, clear enough to see through; a matter of tiny diamonds and white lace that I wore in my hair until Esther plucked it out and threw it in the fire.

It had smelled like lightning as it burned.

A little farther along, the dog and I came through the stunted trees into a clearing, nearly flat, tucked against the topmost ledges of the mountain.

There was a fire ring in the clearing, but no fire. An iron spit stretched over it, with a cauldron hanging cold and empty above where there had once been a flame. Plenty of dead wood piled nearby. Nothing cut and split. Just old branches and sticks, fallen and gathered. Nearby, between two hemlocks, an old, tattered shawl hung from a line, dead leaves and a lone hawk feather caught in its weave.

There was a garden bed, too. A long, thin one with nothing in it. Just some weeds no one had bothered to pull.

At the far edge of the clearing, a little cabin nestled in a grove of red cedars. I could see that the door was open. There was no smoke coming from the chimney. No sound. No sign of life.

The dog trotted to the door and turned to wait for me.

Oddly, as I approached the door, he finally decided to growl.

"Which is it? Do you want me here or not?"

In answer, he disappeared into the cabin.

When I didn't follow, he stuck his head back out the door and looked at me curiously.

"All right," I said. "I'm coming."

Chapter Twenty-One

I peered cautiously through the door.

The cedars around the cabin greened the light coming through the windows, so it was dim inside. Like being in the woods.

But I could see enough.

I could see that there were clothes hanging from pegs on the wall. Some boots in the corner. A desk and a trunk with a humped lid.

Shelves on one wall sagged with jars and bottles.

There was an open-faced cupboard in one corner with more jars and some sacks, too. Grain and dried apples, from the looks of it.

In another corner, there was a cold fireplace. Alongside it sat a big copper bucket full of logs, and another smaller one with kindling.

And there were candles on every flat surface. One, on the floor, had melted into a puddle, its wick burned away.

I was amazed that it hadn't burned the whole place to the ground.

But I knew that if I were a flame I would rather fizzle out than ruin a place like this one.

For besides the ordinary, workaday business of clothes and boots and such, the little cabin was filled with other things as well.

On one wall: shelves of books in all colors and sizes, like the keys of a new instrument I wanted badly to play.

Hanging from the roof: dozens of faded bouquets dangling like an upside-down garden.

And there was a workbench and a back wall hung all over with tools that my father would have cried to see. Beautiful tools of all kinds, as if someone had made wonderful things here.

And . . . *wait*, there, just on the windowsill by the door, there *was* something wonderful. A tiny fawn, carved from red wood, its hooves more delicate than petals. And a mouse with his tail hanging down over the edge. And a tiny squirrel, its paws tucked under its chin, watching me as I edged farther into the room.

And that was when I realized the rumpled bed in the shadows along the back wall wasn't empty, as I'd thought.

I took a slow step forward, peering into the shadows, and saw that an old woman lay there, her face so pale it melted into the pillow and blended with the bedclothes, all of them faded and worn.

I looked again at the carvings on the windowsill, and for just a moment I thought this woman might have made such things for me, left them for me to find. But she was far too old to have the face I'd seen peering at me from the woods.

One of her hands, lying on the blanket, reminded me of the day I'd found a dead bird in the yard, its claws limp but curled up, like a baby's hands will curl when he's sleeping. Except there was nothing about babies here in this room. Nothing at all. Despite the books, despite the flowers overhead, despite the small wooden creatures and the handsome tools, everything here felt old and beaten and sad.

The air buzzed with flies.

The dog sat by the bed, waiting.

I put down my pack and walked slowly closer.

The woman who lay there was still, her eyes closed, but I could see that she was breathing.

A dead rabbit lay next to her head, flies drinking from its eyes.

I swallowed. Made myself breathe.

"That's the rabbit I saw in your mouth, down-mountain, isn't it?" I whispered to the dog. *"You were trying to feed her, weren't you, boy?"*

He watched me without blinking.

The woman looked clean but gray. Whole but broken.

"Ma'am," I said softly, and then again more loudly.

She didn't respond.

I touched her hand. I had expected cold. I got hot instead. Too hot. And I was suddenly filled with a terrible sadness and such longing that I felt empty and stricken and poor.

I touched her old-apple face. Even hotter. Even more like the end of a sad tale.

Something was very wrong with her.

There was a small cloth doll tucked up in the crook of her neck. It was made out of rags. The kind my father used to polish things.

I spent a moment looking at that, thinking about that, and then I pulled the blanket slowly down, past the hem of her nightdress, and saw that one of her thighs was swollen and purple but also oddly white and . . . almost *moving*, though her leg was still.

I leaned closer in the dim light and realized that I was looking at a clot of maggots feasting on her leg.

I dropped the blanket and stepped back, gasping.

Ran out into the yard.

Bent over, my hands on my knees, and swallowed hard, again and again, but I couldn't shake off the sight of that leg. The smell of it. The idea of her lying alone in that bed while her leg softened with rot and those hungry worms.

When I could, I stood up straight and wiped my face with my hands. Pushed my hair back and away. And went into the cabin again.

Into the terrible, raspy fizz of the flies.

I stood staring at the old woman. At the rabbit on her pillow.

What was I going to do?

I wanted her to wake up, but to what? The sight of her own leg rotting?

The dog lay down next to the bed and put his head on his forepaws, his eyes on me, his brows twitching.

"What am I supposed to do now?" I said to him.

But he didn't answer.

Chapter Twenty-Two

Fire, I thought. I would make a fire.

There was plenty of dried grass and moss and leaf litter near the cabin, all of which I gathered for tinder, carrying it inside to pile near the cold hearth. I made a nest of the best bits, tucked it between some cooking bricks, and went to work with my knife and flint until the sparks caught.

I had fire in moments.

Carefully, I blew on the small flame until it consumed the nest and easily lit the thin twigs I fed it, then the larger twigs, then a stick and another and another and then a small log until I had a strong fire burning.

I was as aware of the woman in the bed as I was of the mountain itself.

The dog watched me steadily.

The smoke from the fire fought off the smell of that leg, but I knew I would have to face it again soon.

I had once watched my father use a hot knife to seal a wound in the palm of his hand. It wasn't a very big cut, but it had begun to fester. "Best to kill a germ before it spreads," he had said, heating the blade of the knife on the kitchen stove and then taking it outside before pressing the tip of it hard against the wound.

He had bellowed like a moose, and I had cried at how much it had smelled like food cooking.

My mother had scolded him for doing that when he could have gone to the doctor instead. She had scolded him, too, for letting me watch.

But he had kissed her and told her that doctors cost money, that he'd heal faster this way besides. And that I'd be better off knowing such things.

Esther had wanted no part of it.

Samuel had been napping.

And I had been the one to learn that lesson.

But this was not a small cut on the hand of a strong and healthy man.

This was a serious wound, caked with maggots and pus.

I thought about how else to help her.

I could go get my mother. But what could she do?

Some things, she could do . . . and do well . . . without a second thought. And she was brave, too. Brave enough to give up town. To go with my father to the mountain. To start over in a place with no roads. No doctors. Almost no people. But her kind of courage had very little wild in it. Very little of the mountain. Which was all I had—wildness—though plenty of it. And of several sorts: not one vast thing, but as varied as trees. As flowers.

I looked around the cabin. There was a mangy dog, a tick as big as a lima bean hanging above his eye. There was an old woman lying in her bed, senseless, crawling with worms, in a fog of blowflies. And there was me. No one else.

I would begin. I would do what I could. And then I would do what I thought I couldn't do, before I went for a different kind of help.

The fire was starting to settle down, so I added more wood until the heat pushed me away.

The knife I carried with me wasn't big enough to do much good.

I went to the tools hanging above the workbench and chose a big chisel.

It would do.

I wedged its blade between the burning logs.

While it heated, I went to the old woman and had a good look at her.

Her skin had the lines and spots of a life spent in the sun.

Her hair was long and gray and tangled.

"I'm going to hurt you terribly," I whispered. *"I'm sorry."*

I didn't want to look at the wound again, but I knew I had no choice.

When I did, it took my breath away.

The maggots rolled and roiled as they feasted on the dead flesh around her wound.

I turned to fetch the hot chisel.

But that, right then, was when she woke.

Chapter Twenty-Three

"You didn't knock," she said. Her voice was dead-tree dry, but her eyes were so blue that for a moment I forgot she was old.

I gasped at them, at her, at the sound of her voice. It was weak and pale . . . but with a strong echo in it. Something that ignited a spark of memory.

"The door was open," I said as the echo faded and the spark winked out. "Your dog invited me in."

At which her eyebrows went up. "Him?" She looked around but stopped, wincing. It clearly hurt her to move.

I stepped aside so the dog could take my place.

"Ah," she said. "There you are." She reached out and laid her hand on his head. Closed her eyes. Sighed. And then grabbed the tick on his face and ripped it off with one quick jerk.

He yelped, pawed at his face for a moment, and then sat still again.

She held out the tick. "Put this in one of those jars over there. One of the empty ones. There, on the bottom shelf."

I had no idea what to say to that. So I fetched a jar, opened the wire bail, took off the lid, and held it out so she could drop in the tick. It bounced like a blueberry.

I put the lid back on and was about to lock the bail when she said, "Leave it loose. Air enough and all that blood will keep her for some time."

She hadn't even asked me my name, nor I hers, yet we were talking about ticks.

"But why do you want to keep her?" It was the first time I'd called a tick *her.*

"I might need her." She closed her eyes again.

I imagined her squeezing the blood from that tick. Making a potion with it.

Witch, I thought. *She's not a hag. She's a witch.* I took a step away from the bed.

"Don't be a ninny," she said, without opening her eyes.

As if she'd heard what I'd thought.

I put the jar on the shelf and then edged closer again, more curious than afraid. I had a hundred questions. Maybe more. I started with, "What's your name?"

She paused, as if to think. As if no one had asked her that question for a long time. "Cate," she said.

"Short for?"

"Cathrine. With a *c* and only one *e.*" She spelled it out. "After my mother, though she was never Cate. And you?"

"Ellie," I said.

"Short for?"

"Nothing. Long for Leigh."

"Leigh." The old woman nodded. "That's a good, strong name. Simple. With nice round edges. Like a pear."

We ran out of things to say about our names, so I said, "Why do you have a doll?"

She looked confused for a moment and then felt for the little doll and pulled it against her chest. "Why shouldn't I have her?"

I shrugged. "I didn't say you shouldn't. I just asked why you did."

She didn't answer, but I thought I understood. I had long since given my own doll to Samuel, who had lost it in the woods, but I still remembered how it had felt to hold her in my arms as I settled toward sleep.

"How did you hurt your leg?"

She gave me a hard look. "It's not good manners to come into my home and look at me while I'm sleeping."

Much of this situation was odd and surprising. That she would talk about manners was more of the same.

"I tried to rouse you. You wouldn't wake up. You have fever. There's a dead rabbit next to your head. Of course I looked at you."

She turned her head. Saw the rabbit next to her. Saw the flies. *"Oh Captan, my Captan,"* she whispered, reaching for the dog again.

I watched him relax under her hand. Watched his tail sweep the floor.

"Is that his name? Captain?"

"It is. But not Captain. Captan. No *i*."

I wanted to ask about that, but dog names and bottled ticks and everything else could wait. She still hadn't answered my question, so I asked it again.

"How did you hurt your leg? Did you cut yourself?"

She huffed. "I didn't get this old by cutting myself." To my great surprise, a single tear gathered itself in the corner of each eye and followed the map of her face. "It was a fisher cat. A big one. It went after Captan. Got me, instead."

I had seen a fisher cat only once, but once was enough. Far too many teeth for a critter not much bigger than a groundhog. And sharp. Like white knives.

Again, as if she could hear me thinking, the woman said, "Can't blame it, really, seeing as how it was not even half Cap's size and cornered, against a rock face. Nowhere to go."

"And you got between it and the dog?"

She stared at me. "Wouldn't you?"

I thought about Quiet, a dog I had known for only two days. Not even two days. "I would."

She nodded. "I thought so."

As if she knew me.

She peered down at her leg. "What a mess."

I nodded. "I was about to burn it."

She looked at me, startled. "Burn my grubs?"

Which startled me, too. "*Your* grubs?"

"Them!" she said, pointing at her leg.

I made a face. "I know what grubs are. But *yours*? You put them there?"

She closed her eyes. "They eat only what's dead."

"But there's pus, too. Can they stop the festering?"

She shook her head. "A fisher cat will eat something dead and get its mouth full of germ and then spread the germ into something else. Like it did to me. I tried burdock root. Pepper. I need honey. To kill the germ."

I thought of the hive I'd meant to raid.

"And witch hazel?" I said.

She looked at me sharply. "And witch hazel, I suppose. Though that alone won't make much difference. It's honey and grubs that will save my leg. Maybe save *me*. If I'm to be saved."

Chapter Twenty-Four

I rubbed the spot on my face where the bee had stung. "How much honey?"

"As much as you can get."

There. She expected me to get it. But I expected that, too. It was something I could do, so I would do it.

"I shouldn't burn it? Your leg?" And I confess that I was relieved about that.

She shook her head. "We open up the wound and pack it with honey."

I did not see any *we* about it. She could barely lift her head.

Her face suddenly changed. "Something's hot," she said. "What are you heating?"

"The chisel," I said. "For burning you."

She struggled up onto her elbows. "What chisel?"

"From over there," I said, pointing at the workbench.

"You put it in the fire?" She pushed herself up farther. "Get it out!"

Which I did, quick as I could, my hand wrapped in a hearth rag. The blade was black with smoke and heat.

"Hang it so it doesn't warp," she said quickly. "Don't lay it down. Hang it." She sounded like she might cry.

I did as she said, careful not to burn myself.

"I'm sorry," I said. "I was trying to help you."

"I know," she said, dragging one thin hand over her face. "I know. It's all right."

I watched her settle, settle, sigh herself calm.

"What do you make?" I said. "With all those tools?"

"They aren't mine," she said. "I don't make anything with them."

I wanted to ask something else, but before I could she craned her neck and said, "I would be obliged if you would bring me some water."

"Oh, I'm sorry." And I was. It must have been some time since she'd had anything to eat or drink.

"There's a spring just past the biggest spruce at the far edge of the clearing. Coming out under the rock there. Not much to it, so high up, but enough."

I took an empty jar from the shelf and went out into the yard, where I was surprised to see that the day was still just an ordinary spring day—night still waiting far beyond the curve of the world— that the trees were no taller than they'd been, that nothing much had changed while I was inside that cabin.

Such a lot had already happened on this one ordinary spring day—so much of it extraordinary—that I felt a little dizzy and unreal as I crossed the yard and went in search of the spring. And found it, just where she said it would be.

She was right—it wasn't much of a spring. But when I pushed the jar flat in the moss where the water bubbled out of the rock, a pool rose and flowed into its mouth, as if the jar were the thirsty one.

The water was cold and clear and, as I sampled it, delicious. Like poured winter. Fresh. Perfect.

I carried the jar into the cabin.

"Good," she said. "A girl who can tap a spring."

"Any girl can do that."

She looked at me for a long moment. "I know."

With one hand, I cradled her head and lifted it high enough so she could drink from the jar without choking.

Her tears came back as she drank, as if the well of her had dried but was now full again. And I felt some light in her now, too, where all I had felt before was darkness.

"So good," she said, sobbing a little, when it was all gone.

I laid her head back down and smoothed the hair off her hot forehead.

And asked her another of my hundred questions. "Did you carve that fawn? Or that squirrel?"

"Oh, child, if I could do that, I most certainly would. But I can't. And I didn't."

"Then who did?" I said.

She looked at me for another long moment, as if trying to decide something. "If you're lucky, he may come this way in time for you to see for yourself."

He. So my carver was a he. I had thought maybe so. "Come this way from where?"

"From somewhere else," she said, suddenly sharp.

So I asked something different. "Why do you have so many books?"

She squinted up at me. "Let me guess. You think an old woman living on a mountaintop can't possibly read."

I wasn't surprised by the bitterness in her voice, but I didn't much like it. "I don't think that. I just don't know anyone who has so many. Have you read them all?"

She looked past me at the books on their shelves. "Some of them many times. I don't know if I could have stayed here otherwise."

I thought about why she would choose to stay in such a place, books or not, though it was better than what we'd had when we first came to the mountain.

I figured any refuge could be a home if that's what it felt like.

"Do you want me to help you to the privy?" I said.

She huffed again. "Haven't got one."

Which startled me. "Everyone has a privy."

"Not up here. Not for me. Animals make water. Animals make dirt. So do I. Just like they do. In the woods." She lifted her chin. "And a person who says anything about that is a person I don't care to know."

She sounded queenlike.

"Do you want me to help you outside, then?"

"No need. I've eaten nothing. And that's the first I've had to drink since yesterday."

"You have fever."

"I know. My bones hurt with it. But it's no mistake and does more good than harm. Until it's high enough to kill me."

"Then I'll go get you the honey. And I'll come back as quick as I can." I looked at the rabbit alongside her head. "I can cook that up for you before I go."

She nodded. "For me and him both."

The dog smiled for the first time.

"And I brought you a fish," I said, remembering the trout.

She made a face. "Why would you come up the mountain with a fish for someone you'd never met before? And how did you even know I was up here?"

"My father told me about you. You saw him once, with a bad ear."

She squinted thoughtfully. "I remember him."

"And your dog. I thought he might be trying to tell me something."

"Good." She nodded briskly. "A girl who can understand dogs."

"Any girl can understand dogs."

This time, she shook her head. Closed her eyes.

For a moment, I thought she had more to say about that. But then she opened her eyes again and said, in a harder voice, "That rabbit's not going to cook itself, you know."

So I picked it up by its hind legs and carried the poor thing into the clearing, the trout along with it.

I'd butchered a rabbit before. My father had taught me how. And how to scrape the skin and stretch it in the sun to cure.

This one was no different, except I was alone. And the rising wind on the mountaintop spoke a different tongue than the wind down below. And that woman, Cate, was in terrible trouble.

I wanted to heal my father, and I would.

But I was suddenly the only one standing between that old woman and real danger. Maybe even the end of her.

At least she would not punish me for my troubles.

I could not say the same for my very own kin.

Chapter Twenty-Five

I expected to be punished as soon as I got home. But Samuel was still missing—and had been for two long hours—so finding him came first.

"No sign of him," my mother said, and I could tell that she was scared. "We hoped he was with you."

She and Esther were standing in the yard much as I'd left them, except now they looked grim and panicky.

"I said I'd send him home if I saw him." I could feel them blaming me again for something I hadn't done. It felt like horsehair inside my clothes.

But then I realized that this was about more than one kind of blame.

Esther looked like she wanted to claw me. "Why did you do that?" she hissed. "Why did you put a snake in with Father?"

I stood up as tall as I could. "I knew it would make you scream."

"Mercy," my mother said. "You really have lost your mind."

"Why would you want me to scream?" Esther said.

I couldn't remember the last time she had smiled at me, but I was sure that she smiled at our father every night before she went to bed, though he couldn't see her. "You think Daddy wouldn't do everything he could to help you if he heard that?"

I had decided I wouldn't cry, no matter what sort of punishment waited for me, but this kind of talk made me so sad that I struggled to keep my voice from shaking. "If anything is going to wake him up, don't you think his Esther, screaming, might?"

My mother and sister both stared at me with less fury than before, but not much more of anything good or kind.

"I'll deal with you later," my mother said. "Go find Samuel now, and be quick about it."

But as I turned away, she stopped me again. "Where are the eggs? You were gone long enough to lay some yourself."

"I don't have any."

"Then where's the fish?" Esther said. "And where were you, if you weren't at the Andersons' for eggs?"

"I was . . . looking for Samuel, up-mountain. And a dog ate the fish," I said, which was the truth. Or part of it.

My mother frowned at me. "That mutt?"

"What mutt?" Esther asked.

"I saw a mutt on the path," I said.

"And he took the fish?"

From my hand, yes. He had eaten eagerly, the fish steaming in the cool air. And I might have said something like that. I might have said, *Yes, he took it from me,* and told half the truth that way. But I wouldn't blame the dog for something *I* had done. So I said, "I gave it to him."

My mother shook her head. "You foolish girl. You want a wild dog coming around here, begging for more food?" She looked hard at my face. "What in the world is happening to you, Ellie?"

I wanted to tell her the truth: that I was not a good town girl trying hard to tame the mountain like she was. Like Esther was. That I had work to do. Honey to harvest. A hag to save. A father to save. And more besides.

But all I said was "He was hungry, too. And if he's wild, then so am I."

My mother sighed. "Which is exactly what I'm afraid of."

After searching everywhere, including the spot by the river where we'd fished just that morning—a spot I approached this time with a belly full of dread—I finally found Samuel in the cowshed, huddled in a corner behind the manger.

Quiet was in his arms.

"I waited until you went in the cabin, and then I took Quiet," he said. It was clear that he'd been crying.

"You were crying."

"I've been hiding here forever, and I fell asleep and got a crick in my neck, and I'm hungry, and Mother means to give your pup away. But I'm not crying," he said fiercely. "Not anymore."

I had no intention of teasing him. Certainly not for doing something so good and brave.

And in that instant I found myself thinking of how that terrible January day might have ended differently. Not with my father hurt, but with Samuel the one to be struck like a hammer on a nail, like a hammer on a nail of bone and blood, the air bursting from him as he hit the ground, his small, soft body lost to a jumble of wood and hard dirt.

"How in the world did you get Quiet out of there without Maisie noticing?" I said, my voice shaking a little.

"Oh, she noticed. And she didn't like it one bit. But she didn't bite me. I thought she might, but she didn't." He put Quiet into my hands. "Am I in trouble?"

"No," I said, tucking Quiet under my chin. Closing my eyes. "But I am. For giving one of the fish to that dog we saw on the trail. And for putting a black racer into Daddy's bed."

It was clear that Samuel didn't know which question to ask, so he asked three at once.

"Did you give him *my* fish? Did the snake bite Daddy?" He scrambled to his feet. "Why did you put a snake in his bed?"

I smiled. I couldn't help it.

"No. And no. And because I wanted Esther to scream so loud that she'd wake Daddy."

Samuel rolled his eyes. "Mother said loud noises won't wake him up."

I nodded. "I know. But hearing Esther afraid like that . . . I thought he would come back. To protect her."

Samuel thought about that. "Did he?"

I realized I didn't know the answer, though surely Esther and my mother would have told me if there'd been any change. Surely, they would have greeted me with such news.

"Let's go find out," I said.

I didn't want Samuel to get his hopes up, but I was pretty sure that amazing things happened all the time, partly because someone hoped they would.

Maisie was glad to have Quiet back. I didn't tell her how badly I had wanted to keep him. To take him back up the mountain to a place where he would be safe. I knew he was too young to leave his mother. And I knew I could not be the kind of mother he needed right now. But I was tempted to do as Samuel had done.

"Here he is," I said as I laid Quiet in the nest again. "Safe and sound."

Maisie licked him and pushed him around with her nose until she was sure he was all right, and then she looked up at me sternly, as if to say *Don't let that happen again.*

I didn't want to think about the look she would give me when Mr. Anderson came in a few weeks to take Quiet and all of her babies for his own.

Chapter Twenty-Six

"Samuel wouldn't tell us where he was," Esther said when I went into the cabin and found my mother flouring the fish for frying while my sister cut the whiskers off some wilted carrots from the root cellar.

I pictured Samuel huddled in the straw with Quiet in his arms, his face hot with sleep and crying. And I pictured Cate as well; remembered how it had felt to feed her bits of rabbit, how she had opened her mouth and waited for each bite like a child. And my father, lying so still in his bed. All of them waiting for me to do something.

"He was in the cowshed," I said.

"What was he doing in there?" my mother said.

I didn't tell her about Quiet. "He fell asleep."

Samuel came out of my father's room and joined us in the kitchen. *"He's just the same,"* he whispered to me. To Esther, he said, "I'm hungry."

"You'll have supper in a couple of hours."

"But I had no lunch."

"Which is your own fault, for disappearing like you did. You worried Mother, and me, too."

"But I'm hungry, Esther!"

"Oh, then sit down," my sister said, cutting him a wedge of corn bread.

She put it on a plate for him, the plate on the table. But when she saw me cutting some bread for myself, she snatched the pan away.

I had missed lunch, too. Had had none of the rabbit or the fish I'd fed to Cate and Captan. What was left, I'd left for them. Already today I had gone to the Petersons' for the venison, and then fishing, climbed the mountain up and down, and searched for Samuel high and low—all with nothing but a little porridge in my belly.

"You gave away your lunch," Esther said. "And your supper, as well."

My mother looked at me over her shoulder. I could see her regret, but something else, too. The same thing I saw on her face when any wild thing came too close to the cabin. "You'll spend the rest of the day doing chores, and you'll sleep in the woodshed with Maisie. Maybe with a snake of your own."

But she handed me a small bundle as I went out the door. A dried apple and a biscuit, folded up in a scrap of cloth. And a dish of cold venison scraps that I knew were for Maisie.

I felt a little better when she didn't explain that the meat was for the dog.

But I didn't say anything, either, as I left. My throat was too tight. And there was nothing to say that they should not have already known.

As it turned out, my punishment was exactly what I needed: the freedom to spend the rest of the afternoon collecting honey, and taking it to the top of the mountain, and looking for new ways to help my father come back to us.

I was sure that my mother had other chores in mind, but none of them was as important as those.

I took the venison to Maisie, fed her and gave her a drink, ate my own little lunch, and fetched the pack I'd hidden there. Then I made sure my flint was in my pocket and examined the jar with the soupy brew I'd made from river water and dew and balsam . . . and more than that.

The cold water I had thrown on my father had not been mine. It had belonged to the well, and before that the deep spring that fed the well, and before that the rain. I had come upon it by chance and seen in it a way to begin.

The snake had not been mine. It had been its own, entirely. A wild thing that came into our cabin without intending to serve any purpose at all. I had come upon it by chance, too, and seen in it a way forward.

But this brew: This was made from the river and cool night air drenching the grass in dew and the sap from an old, forgiving tree. But something of mine, too: my tears, which came from the memory of my father, hurt. And my own hurt, too.

I had not stumbled upon it. I had made it. And it was mine. Meant for my father, who was waiting for a way to wake up, just as Cate was waiting for some honey to help her heal.

I would try to help him first. And then I would try to help her.

I peeked out of the woodshed. There was no one in the yard.

I saw no one as I crossed the clearing and ducked around the back of the cabin, the jar in my hand.

When I looked through the window, I saw no one except my father.

Carefully, quietly, I pushed the window open, put the jar on the table just inside, and hauled myself up and through.

I could hear Esther and my mother in the kitchen, talking, but their words were jumbled. Just chatter. It had been some time since I had chatted like that with either of them.

I stood quietly for a moment, listening, and then turned to the bed.

My father was as he always was.

I unscrewed the lid of the jar.

The concoction inside smelled sweet and musky. I was suddenly very glad that I had never reached the stump below the cabin to gather skunk stink instead.

I screwed the lid back on tight and shook the jar for a minute or two until the balsam sludge had blended with the rest of the dark brew.

I wondered whether I should feed it to him. Or smear it on the scar where his head had split, though I didn't see what good that would do, since what ailed him went too deep for that. And the mess might make my mother work harder to keep me from trying what else I meant to try.

So I fed him what I could.

It was difficult to hold him up and drizzle the sticky potion into his mouth, and I could manage only a little at a time. Too much of it drooled down his chin. But I got some into him. Not much, but some.

I laid him down again and tipped the jar to gather some of the syrup onto the tip of my finger, and then I worked it into his mouth, lifting him again until he had swallowed it. I did that over and over until I'd fed him all I could. And then I cleaned his mouth with the hem of my shirt, screwed the lid back on the jar, and kissed him on the cheek.

As I stood up straight again, I saw his eyes roll behind their lids. Stop. Roll again.

"Daddy!" I whispered, close to his face. I shook his shoulder. *"Daddy, wake up!"*

But he didn't. His eyes went still again.

I pulled one eyelid up with the tip of my finger.

His eye was looking elsewhere. Nowhere I could see. And the thin, soft skin of his eyelid felt like a curtain to another world.

I could see stars there. Bright points in the darkness. But no sun rising. No waking yet.

I let his eye close.

I waited, watching him for the smallest movement.

But he didn't move again.

"Daddy," I said, close by his ear.

Nothing at all.

I said his name one more time, kissed him on the other cheek, watched for his eyes to move. And then I climbed back out the window with much more work to do.

Chapter Twenty-Seven

Down-mountain, at the hive where—just that morning—I'd meant to harvest honey for my brew, I reached into my pocket for my knife and flint, only to find the carved bee waiting for me.

I'd forgotten all about it.

Which astonished me, since every other carving had led me into endless curiosity and speculation and happiness . . . and made me grateful for the gift. Now I spent a long moment with the little bee, amazed at how fine it was, how perfect.

And this time I thanked the bee itself.

And all the other bees whose honey I had come to take.

I put the bee back in my pocket and opened my collecting jar. Put the lid in my pocket. Set my work gloves on a rock next to the trail.

Then I made another fire to stun the bees again, though it slowed me down. Time was short now, the day hurrying toward its end, but I knew the pain of even one sting and wanted nothing to do with a hundred.

I chose a good stick and laid it in the flames. Then I buttoned myself as much as I could, tucking my pants into my boots, my collar high around my ears.

But the morning's bee sting was still fresh on my mind, and I decided to do more, this time, to keep from being stung again.

When the stick was flaming well, I emptied my pack at the side of the trail and took a long look at the oak where the hive was waiting. Memorized the way to it through the undergrowth. Then I laid the torch on the path where it would slowly give up its flame and pulled the pack over my head, tucking the edges of it into my collar and buttoning my jacket up tight to hold the makeshift hood in place.

I felt for my gloves, pulled them on, pushed my sleeves down into them, felt for my collecting jar, carefully picked up the cold end of the smoky torch, and took a long breath.

Blind, my feet feeling the way, I navigated by sound, too. By the buzzing that came from the hive.

I knew the tree by its roots underfoot. Felt my way to its broad trunk. Took a breath. Closed my eyes for no good reason. And ran my hand along the bark until I felt the big hole where the bees were waiting.

I hated to take what was theirs.

I hated to leave them hungry and confused.

I hated the idea that more of them would die trying to stop me.

But there was a woman on top of the mountain who needed me. Needed what they had to give.

I poked the smoking stick into the hole, waited for it to do its work, and then cast it aside.

I reached slowly, slowly, into the hole.

I could feel the bees on my sleeve. One of them stung my wrist where there was a sliver of skin between glove and cuff. I tried hard not to yank my arm back, but it wasn't easy to keep still. The sting was like an acid fang in my skin. And I knew another bee had died.

The comb was like a soft, vibrating brick in my hand.

I broke off a chunk of it and pulled it out of the tree, jammed it into the jar, bees and all, and screwed the lid on as I stumbled away from the hive, falling into the bushes, bees attacking the pack that blinded me, their stingers catching in its weave, dying as they stung. I imagined their soft bodies embroidering the pack in yellow and black and blood.

Another one stung me on the ankle where my pant leg didn't quite meet my boot. Another on my neck where my hood had come loose.

And I felt besieged, suddenly, by the bees, by the need to steal from them, by the way I'd been banished from my own home, by the blame I carried with me like a harness, like a thorn in my hoof, like a puppy taken from his mother, from Maisie, from me.

But crying did no good at all.

When I could no longer hear the bees, I carefully pulled the pack from my head, a little at a time, and plucked the bits of bee from where they'd stung me, rubbing the awful stings and gulping the cool air, crying a little as I filled the pack with my things again, the jar fizzing with trapped bees.

Then I hurried up the trail.

Toward home.

And then past it, upward bound.

Chapter Twenty-Eight

This time, Cate was not alone.

A boy was standing by her bed.

"Well," she said when she saw me. She was breathing too hard for a woman lying down. "Larkin, this is the girl I told you about. The one who speaks dog."

And this was the boy whose face I'd seen in the woods.

He was about my age but a little older and a fair bit taller. Thin, winter-pale, with hair as thick and black as a bear's.

His clothes were ragged. Many times patched. His hands were covered with scratches, as if he'd been handling wild kittens. And his bootlaces bristled with burrs.

Even from across the room, just looking at this boy, I hurt all over.

I could feel his loneliness as if it were mine. And, in that moment, my own loneliness doubled . . . and then receded down to less than what it had been.

Which was when I learned that loneliness shared is loneliness halved.

He looked at me much as the dog had at first. Unblinking. Still.

"She's not going to bite you," Cate said, as if *I* were the dog.

"The rabbit. The fish," he said. "That was good of you."

I wanted to say, *You're my carver! You're the one who made the beautiful bee that's in my pocket right now! Right this minute! You're the one who's been watching me all this time!*

But he was part of a secret that was still mine to keep. It would have been wrong to blurt it out, especially when it was his secret, too.

"The dog caught the rabbit," I said. "And a slug caught the fish."

He seemed to like that. He lifted his head up and let his shoulders settle down. "I brought her some food and did some chores a few days ago. I would have come back sooner if I'd known she was sick."

Cate reached for his hand and gave it a little shake. "This one sneaks up to see me whenever he can."

I wondered about the *sneaks.* And about the *up,* too. Up from where?

Cate closed her eyes. "Not from the town side of the mountain," she said, as if she had read my mind. "From the other side."

The side that led nowhere except to more mountains and valleys and forest.

"You new people aren't the only ones who live on this mountain," Cate said.

Which I had always known but hadn't really believed: that there were people here who chose to keep their distance from us, though we were harmless. Although, come to think of it, a person might say that we had kept our distance, too.

And a person might not know we were harmless.

Except this one did. This boy who had been leaving me gifts for such a long time.

Surely he knew that I was a girl he could trust.

But if that were true, why had he never come closer? Why had he not just come straight up to me, this lonely boy who could make a knife sing? Why had he not just said, "Hello. My name is Larkin. I live on the other side of the mountain."

And that would have been that.

I turned to Cate. "I figured there were others, somewhere else. But nobody comes down past us to get to the river," I said. "Or to get to the road into town. We'd know if they did."

Cate frowned. "There's more than one way down a mountain, or up one, for that matter. More than one way across a river. More than one road into town. And more than one town, too."

In my mind, I flew up like a turkey buzzard to circle above the hills and valleys, looking at them with a new eye. "But why not come down to meet us?"

I was really asking Larkin, though I looked at Cate, who said, "Would you want to traipse down a slope you used to know, tree by tree, brook by brook, that's someone else's now?"

I felt bad about that—the idea that I had taken something that didn't belong to me—but I had no good answer.

Larkin stood by, watching us. I read a little bit of sorry in his eyes.

"But that's not your fault," Cate said, sighing. "So let's let that be. Did you find some honey?"

"I'm not sure *find* is the right word. More like, did I manage to collect it even though I got stung and some bees died and the rest of them will probably starve to death now."

She seemed to like that. "Spunk," she said, nodding. But then her face changed. "I am sorry about the bees. But I need their honey as much as they do."

"Why do you need honey?" Larkin asked her. "For your tea?"

As if she would have sent a stranger to get honey for sweetness alone. To ruin a hive for such a small reason. And I hoped this boy wasn't the kind of person who needed to be told everything.

"I hurt my leg," she said. "It's festering."

He frowned at her. "You said you were sick. Why didn't you tell me about your leg?"

"I just did. And the flies have been talking about it all along."

"I thought they were just spring-waking."

"And you didn't want to say 'Why is your cabin full of flies?'" She sighed tiredly. "Such a lad. Such manners. Now you can help her with the rest of it."

Larkin turned to me. "What's your name?"

Cate made a face. "Oh, mercy. Where are *my* manners?"

Again, talk of manners. So odd in this rough place.

"My name is Ellie." Which he had to know. Had to have heard my mother calling me through the trees.

Larkin nodded. Almost bowed a little. If he'd had a hat, he might have doffed it. More good manners.

"I'll help you with the honey," he said, his face serious.

"You'd better have a look first." Cate plucked at the edge of the blanket that covered her legs. "It's going to be a terrible business."

Larkin lifted the blanket away and gasped at the sight of the maggots churning and rolling on the wound. A smell rose from it.

"Oh," he said. It was part groan, as if he were the one who was hurt. And I knew, from that sound alone, that he was *not* one of those people who needed to be told everything.

Chapter Twenty-Nine

"It's awful bad," Larkin said when he saw the disaster of Cate's leg.

Honesty. Good manners and honesty. I liked those qualities in a person.

"Oh, now, you know better than that. There are things still to be tried," Cate said. She turned to me. "I've been teaching Larkin about healing. This and that. Now and then. Else it will all be wasted when I go."

She closed her eyes, clearly worn out by all the talk.

"First we clean it," Larkin said, swallowing. "Then the honey. Then we take care of the fever."

I was glad to have an order to things.

It had been just hours since I'd found this place, this woman, her wound. If I'd had an order to this day, it might have sent me back to bed instead of out into such a surprising world:

Eat breakfast.

Feed Maisie.

Find bee-gift on trail.

See wild dog on path to river.

Go fishing with Samuel.

Build fire.

Get bee stung.

Learn that Quiet isn't mine anymore.

Put snake in Daddy's bed.

Climb mountain.

Find dog again.

Find the hag.

Make fire.

Cook rabbit and trout.

Feed Cate and Captan.

Go back down-mountain.

Look for Samuel and Quiet.

Feed potion to Daddy.

Get honey.

Get stung some more.

Climb mountain again.

Meet Larkin.

And now there was more to come, all in this one same day:

Clean terrible wound.

Pack with honey.

And surely other things I could not predict.

But it all felt oddly perfect, so we lit the lamps as the day went dark and washed our hands with tallow soap and spring water. Then we pulled Cate's blanket down to her feet and stood staring at her poor leg.

My mother had taught me not to say the Lord's name in vain, so

I didn't. But I did send a prayer skyward before I took up my spoon, and Larkin his, and we began to carefully scrape the maggots off Cate's ruined skin, tapping our spoons against the lip of the jar so the maggots would fall, like dollops of oatmeal, to collect in the bottom.

We breathed through our mouths as we worked, the smell of her leg sweet and sour both.

Even Captan retreated to a far corner, though he watched us steadily from there, his eyes like small moons in the lamplight.

When we had removed the last of the maggots, I used my spoon to scrape away the pus welling up out of the holes that the fisher cat had made.

I decided that I would never again be able to eat custard without thinking of that pus.

"What does it look like?" Cate asked through her clenched teeth.

Larkin held the lantern close and peered at it.

"I need to cut you to get the honey in there."

She nodded. "Clean the knife first," she said, her whole body rigid, her feet arching with pain and the thought of more to come.

It didn't make much sense to clean the knife when her leg was already festering, but I didn't want to add insult to injury, and being clean was almost never a bad thing.

I took out my knife. "I'll put it in the fire."

Which I did, all of us quiet while the flames burned it clean.

Then Cate turned her face to the wall, tucked her little doll up between her shoulder and her ear, and waited for us to begin.

I handed the knife to Larkin. I could have done the cutting. I thought I could have done the cutting. But she had told him to do it, not me, and I confess that I was happy to let him do it. And not happy at the same time.

Larkin held the knife over the wound for a long moment, blinking and breathing hard, and then he made the cut with one hard, slow sweep, Cate jerking only a little, groaning only a little, the blood sweeping down as if Larkin had pulled a set of long red curtains across her leg.

When we pulled apart the edges of the wound, we could see that the infection had worked its way down into her muscle but not too far. I hoped not too far.

I took the honey jar from my pack and went out into the clearing, unscrewed the lid, tipped it quickly off, and waited, at a safe distance, for the trapped bees to fly away. When they did, I took the jar back inside.

Then, while Larkin held the wound open, I squeezed the comb like a wax sponge until the wound was full of honey. Then we pushed the wound closed with our fingers, the honey oozing up and gluing the seam mostly shut. For bandages, I cut the sleeves from my shirt—which my father had made for me with his own hands, which I hated to ruin, which I chose to ruin—and used them to bind up the wound, to keep it closed.

Oddly, it was only after we had finished, after the part that was hardest for someone awake, that Cate fainted. It was as if she had managed to be strong while she had to be strong but gave in to weakness as soon as she could.

And I felt much the same as we finished our work and finally sat down on the floor to rest.

Chapter Thirty

"We'll keep them, just in case, though they'll turn to flies soon," Larkin said, peering into the maggot jar at the terrible little nurses in their white uniforms. How odd that creatures so mixed up with mess could be so clean and tidy. "We can always get more if we need them later on."

"How do we do that?" I asked, watching Cate's face as she slept. I hoped she was dreaming about something pretty.

"We'll kill something—a rabbit maybe—and wait for the flies to find it. Lay their eggs. Wait for the eggs to hatch. It takes no time at all."

I imagined that. Cate, alone on the mountain, doing that.

"She said those weren't her tools." I nodded toward the workbench.

"They aren't," he said. It wasn't a sad thing to say, but it sounded sad.

"Then why are they here?"

He didn't answer for a long moment. "They were her son's."

"And he . . . ?"

"He died." Larkin looked away.

"Oh. Now I know why she didn't like it when I heated up a chisel."

He looked back at me curiously. "Why did you do that?"

"I thought I might try to kill the infection."

He raised his eyebrows. "You were going to burn her?"

"She was unconscious when I found her. I didn't know the maggots were there on purpose." I thought back to how it had felt to stand in that dim cabin with no one to teach me what to do. "I figured I would burn the cut clean."

He opened his eyes wide. "Do you think you could have done that?"

I lifted one shoulder. "I don't know. But I meant to try."

He seemed to like that. But he said, "Burning can lead to infection. You shouldn't try that unless someone's bleeding to death."

I thought back to my father, burning the cut on his hand. I remembered how he treated it afterward with vinegar. "I'm glad she woke up when she did. So, what now?"

Larkin used his knife to stab a hole in the lid and then put the jar of maggots on the shelf next to the one with the blood-fat tick. From the books on Cate's desk, he chose one as thick as three Bibles. "She likes this one."

I carried a lantern to the desk. *"Health and Longevity,"* I read. The cover was chapped and raw with handling.

"You know how to read?" he said.

I nodded. "Of course." But then I realized that not everyone had started life in a town. "I went to school before we came to live here," I said. "And my mother was a teacher, so we still have lessons every day."

Larkin stared at me. "Every day?"

I nodded, though lately I'd had lessons of another kind. "You can come down and get some whenever you want."

He thought about that. "If she's teaching you lessons, why did you say she *was* a teacher?"

I thought back. "*Is*, then."

He made no answer except to turn again to the book, which he opened to a section near the end. He turned the pages slowly, his lips moving, until he stopped and said, " 'Poisoned wounds.' " He stopped again and read to himself, then aloud: ". . . 'wounds sometimes received by butchers, cooks and fish-dealers, who handle—' " He paused. I looked over his shoulder.

"Putrefying," I said.

". . . 'putrefying animal matter,' " he continued. " 'Such wounds are particularly—' " He paused again.

"Virulent," I said.

He looked at me. "I'm not a very good reader." He tipped his head at Cate. "She's been teaching me."

"It will get easier, the more you do it."

He nodded. Turned back to the book. " 'A wound of this . . . character should be thoroughly washed,' " he read, " 'opened and swabbed with pure carbolic acid, then washed with' "—he skipped a word or two—" 'mercury solution, and wet antiseptic dressing. Bites by animals should be so treated, the human bite being one of the worst.' " He took a deep breath, as if he'd climbed something steep.

I thought about how snippy Samuel became if I helped him with a tough word. "I hope you don't mind that I helped you with that."

"Why would I mind?"

I shrugged. "My little brother thinks he should already be able to do things he doesn't know how to do."

Larkin frowned. "Why would he think that?"

To which I had no answer. I looked again at the book. "What does it say about fever?"

"I already know enough about fever."

"But I don't," I replied.

So he turned the pages one by one, past drawings of how to bandage and carry a wounded person, to a section called "Inflammation."

We read the section together. "We don't have what they say to use," he said. "But she taught me about willow bark, and there's some in that jar there." He pointed. "I'll build up the fire. You fetch some water from the spring. We'll make her a tea."

"And what do we use instead of carbolic acid or . . . those other things in the book? In case the honey doesn't work?"

He tipped his head again. "Why would you worry about what might not happen? The honey is good for now, and we can brew witch hazel for cleaning her. And if we need something else, we'll try something else."

I thought of my father. I thought of the *else*s I had tried and the others that were waiting their turn.

Larkin was reading more of the book, Captan watching Cate like a mother, while I went out into the night to tap the spring, so

I was alone when I saw that the stars had also come to be with us. They leaned down as if they thought I might have something to say. Or as if they did.

But the wind had a louder voice, and it told me to hurry now. To heat some water for willow bark tea. To wake Cate so she could drink it. To make enough to take down the mountain for my father, though he had no fever.

Willow bark was one of the *else*s I would try.

"What else?" I asked the stars, but they were silent on the matter.

"Star Peak," I said to them. "That's what this mountaintop is called now."

And I felt I had a perfect right to name it, as long as everyone else did, too. Like the river. Like the mountain itself, which someone else had named Echo, which was also Ellie's Mountain. Which was also Larkin's. Which was also Cate's. And my father's. And Samuel's, too.

But I didn't think my mother or Esther would want their names on any part of this mountain. And it made me sick and sad to think so.

We would need something else to bind us back to whole. All of us. To make them want to be where they were. To wake my father. To make me understand how I could be theirs and they mine and yet none of us the same, me least of all.

For all that, we would need another *else*.

And that was another *else* I meant to find.

Chapter Thirty-One

After we woke Cate and fed her the willow tea, I filled my honey jar with a cooled portion for my father and put it in my pack.

"Will you come back tomorrow?" Larkin asked.

But before I could answer, Cate said, "I'm grateful for your help, but I won't need you now with Larkin here . . . and close by when he's not."

There was nothing rude about what she'd said. And it made sense that she wouldn't need me, nearly a stranger, when she had this boy she'd taught how to read and how to make willow bark tea and how to pack a wound with honey. It made sense. But it also made me sad.

"*I* might need *you*, though," I said. "My father is in a coma. That means—"

Cate's eyes widened, bright with fever and . . . something else. "I know what that means," she snapped.

Which of course was true: that she knew about medicines from the wild but also the sicknesses and cures in those books on her desk.

"What's a coma?" Larkin asked, though if he'd been watching

me these last months he surely knew that something had happened to my father, whether he'd seen the accident or not.

"It means he's been unconscious for a long time," Cate said impatiently. "And this is something you're just now telling me?"

I took a step back. "I met you a few hours ago." Though it seemed like days. "You're sick and hurt. When was I supposed to tell you about my father?"

She flapped a hand tiredly. "Oh, well, all right then. But I know a thing or two about what ails a body. Come back if you want to, for help."

"And you can come get me if you need to," I told Larkin. I gave him a long look and told him what he already knew. "Straight down the deer path to a better path and then straight down some more to a cabin with a woodshed. But don't go near that. It's full of puppies, and their mother is nervous."

"Puppies?" Cate said in a somewhat stronger voice. "You didn't tell me that either."

"No," I said, confused by how changeable she was, sending me away one minute and then wanting to know me the next. "But you haven't told me anything much either." I turned to Larkin. "And I know nothing at all about you." Though I did.

The thought of not knowing him better, not knowing *them* better, felt like hunger.

Which was when, without warning, I felt as if I might start to cry.

I tried to say something else, but all that came out was a croak. More bird than frog, but animal regardless. A puny animal. One that was used to feeling small.

The two of them stared at me in the yellow lantern light. Captan stood up and watched me closely.

I put my jacket on over my shirt with its missing sleeves. Picked up my pack. Cleared my throat. "I hope you get better now, Miss Cate." I looked at Larkin. "I hope we never have to do any of this ever again." Though that wasn't entirely true.

And I took myself and my unspilled tears out the door.

I didn't get far.

The stars stopped me for a minute in the clearing outside Cate's cabin.

There aren't many hurts that a sky-meadow full of clean white blossoms can't make at least a little better.

But as I watched them, as my eyes became accustomed to the darkness, as the trees at the edge of the clearing slowly took shape, one from the next, I saw someone standing among them.

I felt my shoulders rise around my neck. My whole body went terribly hot.

It was a woman. Standing so still she might have been a tree herself. Except she wasn't. Everything about her said something else.

It was dark and she was some distance away, but something awful reached across that clearing and touched me.

And I felt what the fisher cat must have felt when faced with a hungry dog five times its size.

But as I stood there watching her, I realized that I wasn't just afraid. I was . . . shocked. By how dark she was. How bitter. Like something scorched.

And I could feel that bitterness even across the clearing.

I waited for her to move. To say something. But she just stood there.

The way home was to my left, close by, and I wondered if I could just go quickly and be away and gone. But it was a long way down to home, and it was dark enough and the path strange enough that I couldn't hurry without risking a fall.

So I turned, instead, and went back into Cate's little cabin and shut the door behind me.

"Third time you didn't knock," Cate said from her bed. Larkin looked up from the big book. Captan, lying on the floor by Cate, raised his head, looked at me, and began to growl.

"What's this, Cap?" Cate said. "She's—"

"There's a woman," I said. "At the edge of the clearing."

Captan stood up, stiff-legged, and growled some more, deep in his throat.

But Larkin surprised me by sighing. Closing the book. Rising from his chair and standing taller than he had before.

"You go on," he said to me, coming to open the cabin door. He led me outside.

The woman was closer now, halfway across the clearing.

"Go on," Larkin said again. "Go on home."

There was something urgent in his voice.

I looked at the woman, who had come closer still. "Who is that?"

Larkin took my arm and pushed me a little, toward the path. "My mother."

Chapter Thirty-Two

It's one thing to climb a mountain in daylight, quite another to climb down it in darkness, and I had to go so slowly and carefully that I wasn't far along when I heard shouting from above and stopped to listen.

Anger makes for loudness, but I still had trouble understanding much of what I heard as I stood among the trees. Something about Larkin coming home where he belonged.

Larkin yelling back. Something about him being old enough to make up his own mind.

After a while, the shouting stopped.

I imagined Larkin and his mother stomping down the other slope. All of us descending away from Star Peak. All of us except Cate and Captan, who stayed on that mountaintop alone together.

I had work to do, down-mountain. I had the chores I'd never done and my father to tend. But I decided I would come back soon to help Cate, too, whether she wanted me or not.

That was something I could do, so I would do it.

More than that, I *wanted* to do it. I wanted to do it like I wanted to be out in the spring air. To grow things. To grow up.

And I hoped that Larkin would come back soon, too, to see me and Cate both, no matter what his mother had to say about it.

I didn't care if he never left me another carving. Never again lingered close by the cabin to be a distant friend.

What I wanted now was to know him. Even if I already did.

And for him to know me.

It took some time to get back down that mountain, especially through the wildest parts. As I went, I carried my knife straight down alongside my leg, for comfort, my eyes drinking in as much starlight as they could hold. Breathing through my mouth so I could hear better. Watching for bears, though I didn't see anything of the sort. And I realized that I was more afraid of that woman from the other side of the mountain than I was of a bear.

Like the book had said: The human bite is one of the worst.

And I knew, all over again, that there was more than one kind of wild.

Maisie woke as I opened the door to the woodshed. She growled for a moment until she saw that it was just me, coming home, and then she got up to meet me, wagging her tail.

"Oh, my girl, my girl," I whispered. I knelt down and took her face in my hands, kissing the top of her soft head.

The puppies were sleeping, but I needed Quiet as much as he needed his rest.

"Hello, my sweetling," I murmured as I picked him up and held him against my chest, where he settled again into sleep almost immediately. Maisie wagged her tail harder, her whole body rocking, but she didn't seem to mind too much. And we lay down together in that messy, wonderful nest, warming each other, and slept hard until morning.

"Do you want breakfast or not?" my mother said.

She stood in the doorway of the woodshed, daybreak framing her in white.

I sat up, straw falling from my hair, and blinked at her. Maisie was already awake, and the puppies, too, staggering around their nest like sweet dopes.

"I do," I said, climbing to my feet, brushing myself off.

"Then come on inside."

As I followed her out, she reached for my hand and pulled me along behind her as if I were a little girl.

And I felt as if a thread of light bound her hand to mine.

I stumbled across the yard, paying too little attention to where I put my feet, and far more to the feel of my hand in hers.

She took me inside and sat me at the table by the kitchen stove.

"Get warm," she said.

It was early yet, Samuel and Esther still in bed.

I put my hands out toward the stove, yawning.

She brought me a plate of eggs and fried venison with a biscuit and some coffee.

I looked at her for a long moment.

"Eat it while it's hot," she said, turning to add more venison to the skillet.

I did that. It took me about one minute. I could have eaten as much again with no trouble at all.

When she turned back and saw my empty plate, she stood still. Looked at my face. Back at the plate.

"Will you stop all that business about your father, please?" she said in a voice not much bigger than a whisper.

I put down my mug. "Is that why you gave me such a good breakfast? So I would stop trying to wake Daddy?"

She sighed. "Have you ever known me to bribe my children, Ellie?"

"No."

"Then no, that's not why I gave you a good breakfast." She sat down next to me. "I know you mean well, but you're not helping. You're making things worse. Getting Samuel's hopes up. Playing a wild game with your father when Esther is terrified that you'll hurt him."

Again. She didn't say it, but I heard it anyway.

"And you think that, too?"

She looked at me intently. "I don't know. I want him to wake up. I want him to get well. Of course I do. And I almost think you might be right to do what you're doing. Almost. But I don't."

I was so sorry. I was so sad. But I had nothing to say to that except, "Doing something is more right than doing nothing."

I thought she might cry.

"And what if you do wake him up and he's still not well?"

I didn't know what she meant. "But there's nothing else wrong with him, except he won't wake up." It sounded more like a question than I'd intended.

"Nothing that we know of. But he wouldn't still be sleeping if he weren't hurt, Ellie."

I considered what she was saying. I pictured my father . . . changed. I pictured him unlike the father I'd known. And my heart hurt in a brand-new way.

"Maybe he'll be fine," I said, and I heard, in my voice, another thing about hope.

She nodded. "Maybe he will. But jarring him and shocking him might be the worst thing for him. Can you not see that?"

I remembered what had happened when I'd fed him my brew. "He rolled his eyes," I said, realizing, as I did, that I would now have to tell her about the other thing I'd done.

Chapter Thirty-Three

My mother sat up straighter. "What do you mean?"

"Yesterday," I said, though it felt like long ago. "I fed him some"—I couldn't say *brew* since it made me sound like a witch—"some broth. And after that his eyes rolled behind their lids."

She stared at me. "I made no fresh broth until last night, and I fed it to him myself. And he didn't roll his eyes." She grew still. "What kind of broth did you feed him, Ellie?"

"I made it. From river water and balsam." I didn't say anything about tears or dew, all of which made me feel more separate and apart from her than ever.

"And you thought it was all right to do that without asking me first?" She was angry but seemed sincerely curious, too.

"I would never do anything to hurt him. You know that, don't you?" I was as curious as she was. It was as if we were two dogs, facing each other for the first time, trying to figure each other out.

She sighed again. "Nonetheless. I want you to stop now. Do you understand me?"

I did. And I didn't.

"I can't," I said, my voice just as sad as hers. "And you've already punished me for anything I've done or might do." I thought about Quiet. How hard he would become, killing things to earn his keep. "You should have saved some of that for later. What's left now that could be any worse than taking Quiet away from me?"

Her face stiffened. Her whole body stiffened. "And if you kill your father, trying to wake him? Won't that be a far worse punishment? Have you thought of that?"

I hadn't. I hadn't for one moment thought of that.

She got up from the table to turn the venison, to crack the last two eggs into the grease. One for Esther. One for Samuel.

"I'm sorry," I said. And I was. I truly was.

She gave me a long look. "Does that mean you'll stop?"

But I didn't have a good answer to that, so I said, "What if I knew someone who might be able to help him?"

The eggs bubbled and popped. Esther came into the kitchen, rubbing her eyes. "How was it, sleeping with the dogs?" she said.

I ignored her.

I waited for my mother's reply.

She flipped the eggs, tended them, waited for them to be done, then slid one and some meat onto a fresh plate for Esther. She poured some coffee into a mug and put it on the table.

She said, "And who might that be?"

"Her name is Cate. She hurt her leg, but when she's well she could come down and see him."

"Come down? From up the mountain? You mean the hag?" And

her wide eyes narrowed, the curiosity on her face hardening into something else.

"What hag?" Esther said.

"What hag?" Samuel stood in the doorway. He was so sleep-tousled that he looked like he'd been caught in a storm.

"Sit down," my mother said, fetching another plate.

"What hag?" Samuel turned to me. "What's a hag, Ellie?"

"A witch," Esther said, her nightgown clean, her hair combed, her hands shiny with the tallow she rubbed on them before bed each night.

"She's not a witch," I said. "And she knows a lot of things about making people well. She has medicine she's made from the woods, and medicine she's learned from books, and ways to heal people from both" (though I said nothing about the maggots).

"And how is it that you know so much about this woman?" my mother said. She put Samuel's breakfast on the table.

"I saw that dog again and followed him up the mountain," I said. "She has a little cabin up there."

"That dog we saw?" Samuel said. "With the dead rabbit?"

"That's where you disappeared to yesterday? When you should have been doing your chores?" My mother shook her head. "You will not go near that woman again, do you hear me? Or that dog. Or up-mountain any farther than the turn to the Andersons'. Or I will lock you in the woodshed until you've found your wits."

Esther and Samuel had stopped eating. They stared at my mother. At me.

I got up from the table and took off my jacket. "I used my

shirtsleeves to tie up a wound on her leg," I said, my voice shaking a little. "A fisher cat bit her. And the bite festered. And she's sick with fever. And a boy from the other side of the mountain helped me clean the wound and pour honey in it and make willow bark tea for her fever. And his mother came and was angry with him for being there, just like you're angry with me now, though I don't know why, because Miss Cate isn't a bad person at all and she taught Larkin how to read, which is something you would have done, too, Mother. Or you, Esther." I turned to her. "And I *will* go back up there to help her again. And I *will* bring her back down here when she's well enough. And I *will* keep trying to wake Daddy up, because he has to get well. He has to," I said to my mother, to Esther. "Or you won't either."

I did not say, *And neither will I.* But I thought it. For the first time, I thought it.

No one said anything for a long moment.

"Who's Larkin?" Samuel said.

And just like that I could breathe again.

Just like that, the tears that had been ready to fall decided to wait.

I turned to him. "The boy who helped me help Miss Cate."

My mother ran her hands over her face.

She came and stood in front of me, bent down a little to look into my eyes, and took me by the shoulders. "You will not go near those people again, Ellie. I need you here. I don't need you hurt, too. I don't need Samuel following you into mischief. And I most certainly don't need a hag coming into my home to cast spells on your father."

"I told you," Esther said, returning to her breakfast. "That's what a hag is, Samuel. A witch."

"She's not," I said, shaking my head. "She's better than that doctor who did nothing at all."

"Because there's nothing to be done!" my mother said, letting go of my shoulders.

"I brought Daddy some willow bark tea. Which won't hurt him at all. Not a bit."

"And won't help him either, Ellie. Now, that's all I'm going to say about it. And that's all I want to hear."

She handed me my jacket. "Go do your chores. And if I find out that you've been back up to see her . . . I don't know what I'll do."

As I went out the door, I thought about all the ways my mother might punish me if I disobeyed her again. But I couldn't think of a single one that was worse than giving up on what I'd started.

Chapter Thirty-Four

The cows were eager to be milked, so I obliged them, soothed by the music we made in the process—the rhythm of the milk hitting the metal pail and then the wet *hush, hush* of its froth building.

All the while, I thought about my mother and my father, Cate and Larkin, his mother. All of it building toward something, though I knew not what.

I felt . . . tangled. Snarled up. Caught. Which made it hard to breathe. Hard to think straight. Hard to know where to turn next.

But chores helped.

They were simple. Straightforward. The same every day.

So I put the cows out to roam, carried the milk to the cabin, left it just inside the door, and went on with my chores.

The dogs came next. I mucked out their nest of straw, laid in fresh bedding, put Maisie out into the yard for a while.

The puppies cried for her, but I said, "She'll be back soon." When I picked Quiet up, he promptly peed down my arm.

"You little scamp," I said, putting him back in the straw.

I took off my jacket and put it aside for washing. Beyond wanting to be clean and dry, I knew that few things attract predators more quickly than a baby's scent.

While I worked in the kitchen garden, getting it ready for seeds, loving the feel of sun on my bare arms, I imagined Cate, her face pink with fever, her leg swollen and purple, Captan by her side.

I imagined her hungry, thirsty, wondering what might come through her door next. Wondering if she would ever go out that door again.

But she had to know that Larkin would be back soon, no matter what his mother said, and that her wound would heal, now that we'd tended to it. Surely she'd get better now that we'd done that.

I thought of my father. What my mother had said to me.

Surely I hadn't made things worse by trying to make them better.

"What have you done with your jacket?" my mother said when I came through the door and spent a moment taking off my boots.

"Quiet peed on it," I said, washing up at the kitchen pump. "I left it in the woodshed."

"Where it will not clean itself. See that you wash it when you do the rest of the laundry." She turned back to her work.

Another chore, then. One that Esther usually did. But I did not dare say so.

"I will," I said. "I came in to visit Daddy. But I'll do the wash straight after that."

She pulled a tray of venison jerky from the oven and slid in a fresh one. The venison had shrunk and blackened in the heat, but it would last long that way. Tough. Dry. Not given to rot.

I thought about Cate's leg again.

"Esther's in there with him now," my mother said. "And she'll be in there for as long as you are."

Even the heat from the oven did not warm me as I stood there, chilled by what she'd said.

"Is Esther standing guard?" My voice had too much mouse in it. "Because I fed him?"

"And threw cold water on him. And put a snake in there with him." She scraped the hot jerky onto a rack to cool. "And who knows what else."

What else.

Nothing yet, but I thought back to the other *else*s I'd considered. Horseradish, which had blown open every head cold I'd ever had. Skunk stink, which would surely tell him that something was amiss. The willow bark tea that was still waiting in my pack.

But Esther would never allow any of those *else*s to happen.

"Nothing else," I said. And now there was no mouse in my voice. No cat. Not much of anything. Not even me.

My mother must have heard that emptiness. That defeat. Because she suddenly turned and pulled me into her arms, her chin resting on the top of my head, and sobbed just once. And I could feel a softness I hadn't felt for a long time. *"He'll come back to us. Or he won't,"* she whispered. *"And what we'll do is wait for him."*

I nodded against her shoulder. She stepped back. "Go see him, then." She used her clean forearm to push strands of hair off her sweaty forehead.

I left her to her work.

Went into my father's room.

Found Esther in the rocking chair alongside his bed, reading aloud from the book in her lap.

Found Samuel sitting on the floor in the corner by the window, playing with a wooden top. Setting it on its pointed foot. Pulling the string to send it into a wobbly spin.

He looked up at me. Said, "Hi, Ellie." Slid under the bed to fetch his toy.

While I stood in the doorway, barely breathing, and looked at my father's thin, pale face.

And he looked calmly back at me.

Chapter Thirty-Five

I wasn't the one to call out for my mother to see that Daddy had awakened.

I was the one who went quietly to his bed, sat down on the edge of it, took his face in my hands, and cried the tears I'd been saving.

Esther looked up from her book and must have thought he'd died.

"Oh no!" she said at the sound of my sobbing. "Mother! Come quick!"

Which brought Samuel out from under the bed, pushing up alongside me to see what was going on. "Did you bring another snake, Ellie?"

And then my mother arrived like a summer storm in time to see my father's eyes, still open.

I didn't see her fall to her knees, though I heard her cry out.

I didn't see Esther's face when she realized that our father had not died after all, that he had come back to us. But I felt her put her arms around me from behind, so she was holding both me and him, too, and then my mother scrambled across the bed to kneel beside him, crying like a child, while Samuel said, "You're supposed to cry when you're sad, Mother."

I slipped aside so Esther could cling to his arm, smiling and crying, and Samuel could climb onto the bed and bounce into the happy fray like a puppy.

Through all of it, my father lay quietly.

"He might need us to calm down a little," I said, sounding a lot older than I was.

Esther turned to look at me and I thought she'd be angry, but she wasn't.

She let go of my father's arm, and she came to me all in a rush and hugged me like she hadn't hugged me since before the accident, back when she still loved me.

"Oh, Ellie," she whispered. *"You were right. You were right."*

But as I watched my father's slack face, I was afraid that my mother had been right, too.

He hadn't said a word. Hadn't smiled. And there was no light in those open eyes.

My mother pulled back from him, smiling, wiping the tears from her cheeks, and gave a long sigh. "You scared me," she said to him.

"Ellie put a snake in your bed," Samuel said.

And then my father closed his eyes and went to sleep again.

My mother knelt on the bed, her hand in his, until her legs began to cramp, and then she scooted slowly away, careful not to wake him.

I was amazed to see that. To see her try not to wake him.

She beckoned for us to follow her from the room.

"Go get Maisie and the puppies," she said softly.

I didn't ask why. I knew why.

"You better stay here," Samuel said to Esther. "Maisie is kinda nervous about the puppies."

"There's jerky in the oven," my mother said to her. "Go turn it and then fetch one of your father's work aprons and spread it next to him on the bed."

For the puppies, I imagined. For the mess they might make.

I was amazed, again, at such a thought in a moment like this, but my mother and Esther spent a lot of time trying to manage mess.

I couldn't imagine what they'd say if they knew that I had, just the night before, scooped pus and maggots from an old woman's wound.

"Come on, Ellie," Samuel said. "I'll help you get the puppies."

Which he did, carrying two of them, while I carried the other two and Maisie danced alongside us, rising up on her hind legs to butt us with her nose, singing with confusion and worry as we took them all into the cabin and along to where my father lay sleeping again.

I hoped that his sleep was just a simple sleep now.

Maisie looked surprised when I urged her up onto the bed, but as soon as I put Quiet and his sister on the apron and added Samuel's pair, she jumped eagerly up, herding them with her nose into a bundle next to my father and then circling three, four times before settling herself next to them. Without warning, she licked my father's face.

He didn't move at all.

"Good Maisie," I whispered to her. *"Good Quiet. Good pups."* I ran my hands over their neat little bodies, their perfect little coats, before leaving them all to their nap.

Chapter Thirty-Six

While the cabin sighed and settled toward noon, I sat at the kitchen table and poked new holes in my father's belt, now that he was so thin.

Then I got up and went to the door of his room to see if he was awake.

Then I used the tip of my knife to pry dried mud from the tread of his boots.

And went back to see if he had wakened.

After that, I worked dubbin into my father's work gloves to make the leather soft again and ready for his hands.

Then I went to see if he had opened his eyes.

"You're going to wear a track in the floor," my mother said.

She had started a pot of venison stew with potatoes, carrots still sweet, and a tune she sang under her breath as she worked.

I listened to that song with every kind of ear I had.

Esther had gone to fetch some firewood, something I usu-ally did, for which I was grateful, though I had not forgotten that standing guard over my father had been, just an hour earlier, her first purpose. That I had been, just an hour earlier, a threat.

Samuel had joined me at the kitchen table and was drawing a picture of a black snake. "So I can show Daddy what was in his bed while he was sleeping."

The snake looked about three times longer than the bed in the picture. It had a forked tongue and a wild eye.

"Whatever happened to that snake?" I asked my mother as she diced a yellow turnip for the stew.

She paused for a moment. "I would have put it in a soup. I would have chopped it up and put it in a soup . . . if I had caught it before it escaped down the drain."

She turned to look at me, the knife poised in her hand. "But I was glad I didn't kill it when I realized it could never have found its own way into your father's bed with the door shut as it was."

"Snake soup," Samuel muttered, his head low over his work. "That's silly, Mother." By now the snake in his picture had acquired a set of enormous fangs. "Nobody eats snake soup."

"Maybe not, if they have something better to eat," my mother said. "But some people don't, you know."

I thought of Cate and Captan.

"I'm going to show this to Daddy," Samuel said, hoisting the picture like a flag.

"Don't you wake him up," my mother said. "He needs his rest."

And I was amazed, once again, by the idea that she wanted him to sleep now that he had finally awakened. I wanted him up, on his feet, wearing that belt, those gloves and boots, a hat on his poor, battered head, ready for what came next.

"What will we do now?" I said.

My mother gave me a puzzled look. "That's a broad question, Ellie."

"I mean when he wakes again. Will we get him up so he can walk?"

"Oh, I don't think so. It's too soon for that." She sighed. "We have to be patient. It might take a long time for him to be well again. And he'll need all of us to help him. I know you'll do a lot of that work." She stirred the stew. "It's too bad you're not a boy, Ellie. You have all the makings of a fine doctor."

It wasn't possible to live without a heart that could beat, but I still managed to stay right where I was, upright, when she said that.

I'd never thought about being a *doctor*—that wasn't the word that had ever come to mind—but doing the work to wake my father and mend Cate had made me feel so very good that I wanted to be more like *that* girl. The one who tried to make people well. The one Cate needed. To help her heal. To be the reason she got better. Or one of the reasons.

One would be enough.

"I'm going back up the mountain to take care of Miss Cate," I said slowly.

I remembered the last words my mother had said on that subject: *If I find out that you've been back up to see her . . . I don't know what I'll do.*

This time, she spent a long moment looking at me before she

said, "I just told you that your father would need a lot of help. And you haven't had a lesson in days. You can't go without lessons. And—"

"Miss Cate taught Larkin to read. And she's already taught me how to heal a festering wound."

"You didn't let me finish," my mother said. "If you had, I would have said that I'm surprised you would rather help a stranger than your own father, especially since you worked so hard to wake him up. And you want to leave? *Now?* When he's only just come back?"

"But that's why I have to go," I said, learning the reason as I said it. "He's on his way home to us, and she's the one leaving. She's the one who needs help the most."

But my mother just shook her head. "You confuse me, Ellie. Every time I turn around, you're wearing a different face. One minute you're beating a path back and forth to your father's door, and now you want to go help a stranger when she already has that boy to help her."

"She's not a stranger," I said, which had been true from the moment I laid eyes on her. "And, even if she were, she'd be just as sick. And Larkin just as much one boy all alone with her."

"Nonetheless. It's not safe for you to go up there, Ellie." She put a lid on the stew. "Not on your own."

"Then come with me. Just to check on Miss Cate. Just to make sure she's all right."

She looked at me with wide eyes. "Do you honestly think I'm going to do that?"

"But she's sick, Mother."

Samuel said from the doorway, "One of the puppies peed on the apron."

My mother gave me a last look, filled with disappointment.

"That's what puppies do." She wiped her hands on a rag. "They don't know any better."

When she followed him toward the bedroom, I did, too. "Why can't he clean it up?"

"Who, Samuel?"

"Yes, Samuel. If a boy can be a doctor, why can't a boy clean up dog pee?"

"I don't want to be a doctor," Samuel said. "Who said I wanted to be a doctor?"

My father was still sleeping when we went into the room.

One of the puppies had found his neck and was nesting against it.

Another had draped itself over his arm.

A third was licking his hand, its tongue a tiny pink petal.

And Quiet, the dog who had started so much, was sound asleep on his chest.

"Oh, well, that's a sight," my mother whispered, smiling.

She folded the wet apron over on itself and gave it to me to take outside for washing. "Go get Esther," she said softly. "She should come see this."

My father was still deeply asleep, his mouth parted, his arms limp at his sides.

It could be hours before he woke again. And when he did, he would need me much less than he had before.

I went outside.

My sister was hanging laundry on the line, humming as she worked, her face happy.

"Mother says to go on in and see the puppies with Daddy," I said.

Esther looked up at me, smiling, as she pinned up the last of the wash and then headed for the cabin, the empty basket swinging in her hand.

I stood in the sun for a moment, thinking.

"What am I supposed to do?" I said aloud, though I was alone.

But the sky was busy being the sky. And the trees were busy being trees. And the birds, likewise, were busy being exactly who they were.

Which was, in itself, an answer.

So I made up my mind to listen to the flame in my chest, which sighed and roared and sighed again like a long piece of music I knew by heart but still seemed to be hearing fresh.

I went into the woodshed to fetch my jacket. Took the little wooden bee from the pocket and put it on the high shelf with the other gifts Larkin had given me.

Then I took the jacket with the apron to wash under the well pump. Wrung them out. And put the jacket back on, wet as it was. The cold was like a slap. but when the jacket dried, it would take the shape of me. Just so.

Then I hung the apron on the line, went back into the cabin, filled a jar with venison stew, and stirred in some cold water from the pump so I could add a lid. Took it out to the woodshed and switched it for the jar of willow bark tea in my pack.

And headed back up the mountain, with plenty of daylight left.

Chapter Thirty-Seven

Captan came to meet me at the steepest part of the path.

"How is she?" I asked as I climbed toward him.

He blinked an answer.

He came forward to sniff my boots. It was the first time he'd come so close to me.

When he looked up again, I read a bunch of questions in his eyes.

"Yes, that's puppy you smell. That's Quiet. When he's old enough, I'll bring him to meet you."

But then I remembered once again that Quiet was meant for Mr. Anderson.

"Maybe I'll bring him up here to live."

When I reached my hand out, palm up, Captan rested his soft jowl in it for just a moment and then turned to lead the way to Cate's cabin.

And I stood there on the path, ringing hard and loud with the feel of his face lingering on my hand, along with something more about loneliness and a sore heart and what a cabin feels like when the snow drifts so high around it that daylight is as thin and pale as whey. And the only sound is the wind sheering across the mountain-top. And the days are long and cold and hungry.

"You are a wonderful dog," I said to him when he turned to look back at me. "You are a wonderful young man of a dog."

Which seemed to please him, though he didn't smile.

When we got to the cabin, I paused at the open door.

Larkin was there, standing by her bed.

Cate had said she wouldn't need me if he was there to look after her, but I hoped there was still some work for me as well.

"Oh Captan, my Captan," Cate said when she saw us there. "What have you brought me now?"

I stepped inside.

Larkin turned.

And as my eyes adjusted to the light, I saw that he was hurt.

His left eye was swollen shut, the skin around it a mottled black and blue.

"What happened?" I said, walking close to peer at his eye. The lid above bulged out, balloon-like, and the skin below swelled to meet it, his lashes in between like little black teeth in a fat red mouth.

"He got a black eye for coming up to see me," Cate said. Her voice was dark and bitter but stronger than it had been, and there was some good color in her face.

I reached toward his eye, but he stepped away. "I'm fine," he said. "And she's getting better."

And I learned all over again, watching him, that it's possible to smile and look sad at the same time.

"I am," Cate said. "Not well, but better."

Larkin pulled the blanket down off her leg and untied the bandage so I could see for myself.

The wound was still swollen. It was still dark and looked awful. But it wasn't nearly as angry as it had been. No pus. And not much smell, either. And there was a fine crust of blood and honey where Larkin had made his cut, though the seam began to ease open as I watched, and Larkin quickly tied the bandage snug again.

"We should stitch that closed," I said, though I had never done such a thing.

"No," Cate said. "Not yet. We might still need to open it up. The bandage will be enough for now."

She pulled the blanket back over her leg. "I'll need your help to go outside," she said to me. "Not quite yet, but soon."

She still hadn't said hello.

Neither had Larkin.

Neither had I.

"How did you hurt your eye?" I asked.

Cate pulled the little doll out from under the blanket and set it to one side. "I told you," she said. "He came to see me."

"It was an accident," Larkin said.

Cate snorted. "Which happened because your mother was in a rage."

Larkin shrugged. "You're not wrong. But it was still an accident."

He turned to me. "She made me do my chores when we got home last night."

"In the dark," Cate muttered.

"And I was angry, too. And I split a log so hard that a piece of wood kicked back. Caught me in the eye." He smiled ruefully. "I won't do that again."

Cate flapped her hand impatiently. "But now it's done. So let's get on with things. Ellie, stir up the fire, will you? And heat your knife again."

"But the honey's working."

"Not for my leg," she said. "For his eye."

Larkin nodded. "She means to let off some of the blood." He didn't seem too alarmed at the idea. Trust lay calm on his face.

"And then a poultice," she said.

"I brought a potato for that," Larkin said.

Cate nodded. "Grate that into a bowl while Ellie heats the knife." She struggled to sit up.

We both helped her—Captan coming close to supervise—until we had her perched on the edge of the bed, weaving a little with dizziness, hanging on to both of us, her head low.

"Stars," she said. "Such a pretty warning."

We held her steady until she could raise her head.

Her bare feet, flat on the wood floor, were thin and white, woven through with blue veins, her toes tipped with thick yellow nails.

"Do you have socks?" I said.

She pointed. "In that trunk, there."

I fetched a pair, happy to see other warm things inside the trunk. A pair of good boots nearby, waiting.

I gave Larkin the socks. "Put these on her while I heat the knife."

He looked like he wanted to say something, but he didn't.

Cate watched us, smiling a little.

"And I brought some stew." I nodded at the pack by the door. "It should be warm enough still."

I held the blade of my knife in the flames and watched Larkin help her with the socks. Watched him dish out some stew. Watched her take a bite.

"Oh my," she said, her eyes closed. "In all my life, in all the world, nothing has ever tasted better than this."

"Do you want some?" I asked Larkin.

"I'm not hungry," he said, though he looked like he was. He fetched a bowl and a grater from the cupboard, and in no time he had turned the potato into shreds.

I liked a person who could do something well, without a lot of wasted motions, or time, or wondering how to do it. He just did it.

I said, "My father woke up this morning."

Cate stopped eating. Opened her eyes. "From a coma?"

I nodded.

"For how long was he gone?"

I thought back. "Since late in January. Since just before that big storm." We had been housebound for days, sitting in the dark, cold cabin, watching my father sleep while the world outside wore white and blue and gold.

"He was asleep for twelve weeks," I said. "Almost thirteen."

"And now he wakes, just like that?"

So I told them about the cold water and the snake and the potion I'd made. The twitching hand. The rolling eyes.

They listened as if to a bedtime story.

When I finished, Cate looked at me thoughtfully. "There was a time when I would have said *coincidence. Poppycock. Wishful thinking.* But that was a long time ago."

"Do you think it was something in the potion I fed him? Maybe the balsam?"

She shook her head. Went on eating. "Not in the least."

"The snake?"

She huffed. "Not that either."

"Then what?" Larkin said.

Cate shrugged. Tipped her head toward the big books on the desk. "Something else you won't find in those."

Chapter Thirty-Eight

"And now it's time for you to learn how to let blood," Cate said.

"What, me?"

"Hard for Larkin to lance his own eye. And I already know how." She looked at me thoughtfully. "It won't take but a minute."

"You want me to poke a knife into the skin by his eye?"

Larkin himself looked more than a little alarmed by the idea.

Captan did, too.

Cate smiled. "Aristotle said, 'For the things we have to learn before we can do them, we learn by doing them.'"

Which reminded me of my father and the day he'd taught me to make fire. And of Samuel as he caught his first fish.

"Who's Aristotle?"

"A dead Greek." She waved us both closer. Tapped Larkin gently, just below the corner of his bulging eye. "Not straight in. Not stabbing. Lay the blade flat against the most swollen part, here." She pointed with one ragged nail. "Away from the eye itself. Then push down a little so the knife tip is buried in the swell. And then slide it slowly until it pierces the skin. Just a bit."

I peered at her. "You're not kidding, are you?"

She shook her head. "I never kid when it comes to knives. Or eyes."

I looked at Larkin. He nodded.

I looked at Captan. If dogs could shrug, I believe he would have.

I followed Larkin as he dragged Cate's chair through the cabin door and out into the clearing. He sat in it and tipped his head back.

Captan came to sit next to him, leaning against his leg.

"And stand clear of where the blood will fly!" Cate yelled from inside the cabin.

I stood with the knife in my hand. "We don't have to do this, you know. You can just wait for the swelling to go down."

Larkin peered up at me. "Have you ever tried to follow a steep trail in poor light, half blind?"

I shook my head.

"I'd like to avoid a broken leg. So please, Ellie. Just cut me."

I sighed once. Twice. Did what Cate had said to do. Laid the knife blade flat against his skin, the tip pointed away from his eye, pressed until the flesh rose up around it, and slid it slowly, the pressure building around it, building around it, until it suddenly broke the thin skin and popped the blister.

I had forgotten to stand clear of the spray.

Larkin himself got the worst of it.

He looked like someone had swung a bat at his face.

"Yuck," I said, wiping his blood off my cheek. My jacket, still wet, was speckled with red that seeped out into little stars.

I helped Larkin to his feet and picked up the chair. We both followed Captan back into the cabin.

"Good sweet mother of souls," Cate said when she saw us. She beckoned Larkin closer and reached up for his chin, turning his face so she could see his bad eye better. She nodded. "Now the potato."

To me: "Fetch that, and a page from one of the books. Nothing important, though."

She told Larkin to lie flat on the floor.

I flipped through the biggest book until I found a page about chilblains. Not much to do about them except wear gloves. I tore out the page.

"Now heap the potato over his eye and top it with that page, folded over in half."

Which I did after wiping the blood from his face.

The grated potato was sloppy enough to soak the paper through. The edges of it stuck to his skin, holding it in place.

"Like this?" I said.

"Just like that. Now press gently to mold the poultice to the eye."

"I'll do that part," Larkin said, cupping his palm over it.

I stared at him lying there.

"Why potato?" I said.

"Takes down the swelling. Helps to prevent infection," he said.

"But why?" I sounded like Samuel.

"You want to know?" Cate nodded again at the books on her desk. "Find out."

The books contained, between their many covers, thousands of pages.

My father had always told me I had a choice, when faced with a giant task that would do me good: bellyache about how long it would take or be glad it would last.

"Can I come up whenever I want to read them?"

Cate nodded. "For a price."

I waited.

"Chores for lessons," Larkin said. The potato poultice had wept onto the floor near his head. It would leave a stain, but Cate didn't seem to care.

"I can do that," I said. "You mean like sweeping and cooking and doing your wash?"

"Yes. But right now, we'll start with putting on my boots and taking me outside."

I had helped Samuel put on his boots many times.

Helping Cate was nothing like that.

I wondered if my father would need this kind of help, too.

When her boots were on and laced, Cate grabbed my shoulders and pulled herself to her feet.

I helped steady her, and then we two hobbled out into the clearing.

"How long do I have to lie here like this?" Larkin called after us.

"Until we say otherwise," Cate called back.

I smiled at the *we*.

"What's so funny?" Cate said.

"Not a thing," I replied.

She steered us around the back of the cabin to a mossy spot between the cedars.

There was a big shed nearby. "What's that for?" I said.

She looked away. "This and that," she said, her voice . . . strange.

And I wondered what she kept in there.

She waited. "I usually do this alone," she said.

"Can you? With your leg like that?"

She stood, bent a little, holding on to my arm. "I think maybe not," she said quietly, looking around for a solution.

"Here," I said, peering into a hollow stump.

She looked at it, at me. "Necessity is the mother of invention."

I liked that, though I had to think about it as I helped her toward the stump. "Did you make that up?"

She shook her head. "Plato, maybe."

"Who?"

"Another dead Greek."

"How come you know so much about dead Greeks?"

She squinted at me thoughtfully. "You think an old hag like me has no proper learning, don't you?"

This was the second time she'd accused me of such a thing.

"I do not." I was annoyed and let her hear it. "And I don't much like you telling me what I think."

She raised an eyebrow. "Didn't tell," she said. "Asked."

The stump was the right height. Perfect, really, though she'd be sitting on a rough and spongy seat. Not very nice.

"It'll do," she said.

I fetched her again when she called me, and we both went slowly back into the cabin.

She was panting and sweating from the effort of being up, so I helped her lie back down again.

The crust on her leg must have broken some more, since there was a spot of blood on the bandage where there hadn't been one before. "What if it doesn't get better now?" I said.

She shrugged. "Why worry about something that hasn't happened yet?"

"Because I'd like to be ready to do what needs to be done, if it needs doing."

"Oh, if it hasn't improved enough by tomorrow, we'll clean it out and put in some fresh honey."

I chewed my lip. "We used it all, and I don't know how much is left in the hive. Probably not much."

"There's a hive right near where I live," Larkin said.

"And a mother who won't want you taking honey for me," Cate said, pulling the blanket up to her chin.

"If it does get better, will we just leave the honey that's in there now?" I asked.

Cate considered that. "Why not? Might make me even sweeter than I already am."

Which made Larkin laugh.

Cate said, "A boy who can laugh when he's lying on the floor with a potato poultice on his eye. What do you think, Captan? Is that some boy?"

Captan opened his eyes. He thumped the floor with his tail just once and closed his eyes again.

"Won't do me any good to cry," Larkin said, though he wasn't laughing anymore, either.

Chapter Thirty-Nine

"Did you make that stew you brought?" Cate asked.

"No," I said. "My mother did. And she'd have my head if she knew I'd put cold water in the jar so it would take a lid."

Cate said, "Oh, it was plenty good, even so."

I watched her trying to catch her breath, the doll again tucked up by her cheek. She seemed young and old at the same time.

"My father told me he saw you skinning a deer on that day he climbed up here."

Cate shrugged. "Maybe so. I do that when I kill one."

"You kill deer?"

She raised one eyebrow at me. Something I would have to try myself. "And why wouldn't I?"

I looked around the cabin. Saw no gun. No bow. Said as much.

"Have you never made a snare?" she said, clearly curious.

My father had. For rabbits. For other small game. And had taught me how, though I didn't like to snare things. The animals we caught tried too many hard things to get loose.

He had used a gun for deer. Taught me that, too. But I didn't like fast killing any better than slow. I did like to eat, though.

"I've made a snare," I said. "But not for deer."

She flapped a hand tiredly. "What works for small things, works for big ones. I do set a snare now and then. Bait it with corn. Sometimes I catch a raccoon. Sometimes a deer."

"You eat raccoon?"

"Don't you?"

"I do," Larkin said from the floor.

What a strange conversation we were having, we three. One abed. One lying on the floor. One standing. Talking about game.

"I haven't," I said. "But my father once made me a coonskin cap. The meat went to the dog."

Cate nodded. "If you cook it right, raccoon is quite tasty."

"Venison is better," Larkin said.

"But where are the skins?" I said.

"Pah. How many skins does one old woman need?" She held up her hand and turned it in the air. "I've got this one I was born with, which could use a hot iron. And I've got some deerskin leggings rolled up in that trunk. A coat, too, warm as any fur."

"Except bear," Larkin said.

"Except bear," she agreed. "But I cut the snare on the one bear I caught and ran for home as soon as I did."

I tried to imagine that.

"How did you kill the deer you snared?"

"I used a knife. Cut their throats."

Larkin nodded. "And she has a hoof scar to prove it."

The two of them sounded very . . . satisfied, but neither of them was smiling.

"And I gave away all the other skins." She held the doll closer against her cheek.

"Who did you give them to?" I asked.

For a moment, she didn't answer. Then, "To Larkin."

"How many skins does one boy need?" I said.

"And his father," Cate said, the doll clenched in her fist.

Which was the first thing either of them had said about his father.

I looked from one of them to the other.

Both had gone quiet. The kind of quiet that hurts the ear.

Something was very wrong, suddenly, and I was standing right in the middle of it.

I looked down at Larkin. "Why doesn't your mother like you coming up here?"

Larkin looked up at me through his one good eye.

"She doesn't know how to read."

Which was not a helpful answer.

"So what?"

"So I do."

Which wasn't any more helpful than what he'd already said.

"What's wrong with that?"

"Nothing's wrong with that," Cate said.

"She's scared I'll leave," Larkin said quietly.

"Leave?"

"Leave here," he said. "Leave the mountains."

I thought about Maisie and the things she might do to hold on to Quiet when Mr. Anderson came to take him away. But I couldn't imagine her doing Quiet himself any harm of any kind.

"What about your father?" I said. "Does he mind you coming here? Learning to read?"

Cate turned her face to the wall.

Larkin glanced at her. "He died when I was ten," he said quietly. "Right after you came here to live."

"Oh," I said. "I'm sorry, Larkin." I looked at Cate. The doll quivered in her hand. *"Did she know him?"* I whispered.

"She did," he replied. "Very well." I saw his throat working. "He was her son."

I looked from Larkin to Cate and back again.

And suddenly I saw what should have been obvious. In the way Larkin was lanky and lean. In the shape of his mouth. His hands.

"So Cate is—"

"My grandmother," he said.

Chapter Forty

It astonished me that neither of them had thought to mention that before now.

But I was not about to scold Cate, who was crying softly. Especially since I had told very little of my own story, and even that in fits and starts.

Nor would I scold Larkin, who had lost his father and, in a way, his mother, too.

So I simply let Cate cry herself to sleep while I bustled about, drying off the potato juice that ran down Larkin's cheek, fetching the deerskin leggings to make a pillow for his head, and taking the liberty of looking through what else was in the trunk.

I set aside a clean tunic and some britches for Cate to wear when she was ready for clothes.

First, I would help her bathe if she'd let me.

"Is there soap?" I whispered to Larkin.

"There is. In a box on the top shelf there."

"And washrags?"

"With the soap."

"And a towel?"

He cast a hand toward a canvas sack near the door. "Soiled. But she'll do her wash when she's better."

"Well, no. She won't," I replied. "You'll do her wash today."

He frowned at that. "I will?"

"While there's plenty of sun. What does she use?" I said, looking around.

"There's a tub in the shed behind the cabin."

Oh, I thought. *So that's what she keeps in there.* "Then when she wakes, you'll strip her bed and heat some water for the tub and soap everything up good, rinse it out, hang it to dry. Save the water for her bath."

"I will?" he said again. He sat up and let the poultice fall away into his palm.

I went to him and held out my hand. He gave me the wad of wet paper with the potato inside.

"Here, let me." I carefully plucked some stray potato off his lashes and gently smoothed the starchy mess from his cheek with the edge of my hand.

"Thank you," he said, patting his eye with his fingertips.

Enough of the swelling had gone to let him blink. But his face was still a wreck.

"Why didn't you tell me that Cate was your grandmother?"

"You're from town." He got to his feet. "You're new here."

"We're not new," I said. "We've lived here for three years."

"And my family has lived here for generations. Three years is birdsong."

I liked that birdsong bit, but I didn't like the way he'd said it. "What's wrong with people from town?"

"They're mean to her."

"Mean to Cate?"

He lowered his voice. "They think she's a witch."

I frowned at him. "Who's they?"

He made a face. "Maybe not everyone. But some." He thought back. "Do you have people called Lock something?"

"Lock something? The Lockharts? But I don't *have* them, Larkin. They aren't *my people.*"

He looked at me, puzzled. "What are they, then?"

I shrugged. "Neighbors. Friends. Okay, yes, my people, I guess. But they don't have any children, so I don't see them much. My sister and my brother and I are the only children on the mountain."

"On the town side."

"Yes, on the town side."

"And why do you think no one ever bothers with the other side?"

I remembered my father telling me to stay close to home. "My parents don't want us roaming too far. They say it's not safe. Because of coyotes and bears and steep places where we might fall."

"And mountain people like me. And a witch like her."

I huffed at him. "No one ever even talks about her, Larkin."

"Not even the Lockharts?"

I shook my head. "What would they have to tell?"

He sighed. "I was up here one day—a long time ago—when

the Lockhart woman came up. She said she had a bad pain here."
He put his hand on his belly. "Nothing helped, she said. The doctor
didn't help. The medicine he gave her didn't help. So she came up
here, and my grandma asked her a lot of questions and then went
in the cabin and came out with a jar of greens. Told the woman to
make it into a tea and drink it every day until she felt better. And
then my grandmother said what she always says to me, every time
I leave here."

I waited. "What does she say?"

Larkin paused. " '*Saol fada agus breac-shláinte chugat.*' Or maybe
it was '*Slainte mhor agus a h-uile beannachd duibh.*' One or the
other."

I stared at him. "What?"

He repeated himself.

"Is that a spell?"

"No, it's not a spell. You see what I mean? Words don't make
people witches, Ellie."

I was bothered by that. Him talking to me like that. "Then what
is it?"

"It's Gaelic. Her mother, my great-grandmother, came from
Scotland. It means 'Good health to you and every blessing.' Not a
spell. A blessing."

"Well, that's not much of a reason to call her a witch."

"No, but the Lockhart woman didn't get better. She got worse."

"How do you know that?" I asked.

Larkin shrugged. "I know a lot about what happens on this
mountain."

I remembered, then, some fuss about Mrs. Lockhart having a stone in her belly. Having it cut out. I remember wondering how it got in there in the first place.

"So one person thinks she's a witch," I said. "That's enough for you to think bad things about people from town?"

He shrugged. "They tend to take things that don't belong to them."

As before, I was glad he'd said *they* and not *you*. But not very glad.

"What things?"

"Mountains," he said.

I thought back to how we'd come up from town. How we'd built our cabin. "My mother and father spent the last money they had to buy our land," I said.

He sighed. "I'm not talking about you."

"Sounds like you are."

"No, I'm not. I'm talking about people who decide they own something just so they can sell it."

And I remembered having a similar conversation with my father.

And how I'd had a similar thought: A mountain didn't seem like something that could be owned.

But I had said *our* land. Just now, I had said that. And I had meant it.

And I'd stood just outside Cate's cabin, in the clearing, and named it Star Peak. And named the mountain Ellie's Mountain. Though not *just* Ellie's Mountain.

If I had felt tangled before, I felt even more tangled now.

I opened my mouth to sputter something, I don't know what, when he said, "It's all right. I don't think of you that way."

I looked at his face and was torn between hating how his poor eye looked and loving the colors that bloomed around it.

"Then why didn't you just come right out in the open?" I said.

I watched as his one good eye grew big. "What do you mean?"

"When you left those things for me to find. Why didn't you just come to meet me?"

"What things?"

"A lamb. A dog. A cow. A chickadee. A full moon and an inchworm. A snowdrop." I thought back. "An acorn. And a honeybee."

He looked at the floor. Looked back at me. "And you," he said.

Chapter Forty-One

I glanced at Cate. Led Larkin out into the clearing.

"Why did you just leave them for me like that?" I said. "Why didn't you answer me when I called to you? Why not show yourself?"

He shrugged with just one shoulder. "I didn't know you."

"Then why give gifts to someone you didn't know?" I asked. "And to a girl like me?"

He looked confused. "What's a girl like you?"

I crossed my arms. "You just said some pretty bad things about people from town."

He shook his head. "I could tell you weren't like that."

I waited.

"I could just tell," he said.

I waited some more.

"And you were all so . . . poor," he said, which really meant something, coming from a boy whose clothes were a matter of patches held together by burrs. "Sad," he said, which was the truth of it. "You were hard to watch when you first got here."

It had been hard to *be* those people, so I knew it must have been hard to watch us, too.

"That little lamb you sent on Capricorn's collar . . ."

"I meant it for the boy," he said. "That little boy."

"Samuel." It hurt to know that it had not been meant for me after all.

"If the wind was right, I could hear him crying from a long way off." He shook his head. "At first I thought he was a lamb."

"There are sheep on this mountain?"

"No," he said. "That's why I went looking."

I thought back to that muddy day as I had stood outside the tent, skinny and cold. "Were you watching when I found it?"

He nodded. "I was."

His smile told me what I needed to know.

"And the others?" I said. "The dog? The chickadee?"

"They were for you, Ellie. All of them."

Which was when I smiled, too. "I saw you, you know. One time. In a thicket of bushes."

"I remember. You looked my way. But I didn't know you saw me."

"I did," I said. "But just your face." I looked into that face. "I still don't understand why you didn't show yourself."

At which he ducked his head. "I've been sad for a long time." He glanced at me and away again. "Making those little carvings. Leaving them for you." He sighed. "Made me happy."

I waited. I thought I understood. "So is it all right?" I said. "Or is it ruined now? Knowing me without the trees in between."

He looked up at me, startled. "It's not ruined."

When we went back into the cabin, Cate was as she'd been, her face turned to the wall.

"I should have known she was your grandmother," I said softly. "You're so much the same."

He liked that, I could tell.

I had already pried a lot out of him, and I didn't want to push too hard, but there was a lot here that I still didn't understand. "You said your mother's afraid you'll leave here, if you learn too much, if Cate teaches you too much."

He nodded.

"But you actually get in trouble because you come up here? You have to sneak around, to see your own grandmother?" I said. "It sounds like your mother—" I stopped.

Larkin sighed. "She doesn't like Cate."

"But why not? Cate's . . . *wonderful*."

"It's complicated." He looked at the floor. "My grandmother grew up on this mountain, but she left to go to school, to become a nurse, and married a doctor and had a baby: my daddy." Larkin glanced at Cate. "She brought him here a lot when he was a boy, and he loved the mountain, but he grew up in town and he went to college and he lived in a city and had a job in an office. All that. For a few years. Until he got sick of it."

"The city?"

"And the job, too. And that life." He looked around the cabin. "He liked it here. And he decided to come here to live."

"By himself?"

"Yes, at first. He wanted to be a luthier, and he wanted to live with trees all around him. He—"

"What's a luthier?" I said.

He looked surprised. "A luthier makes instruments."

"What kind of instruments?"

"The kinds with strings. Guitars. Fiddles."

"Mandolins?" I said, thinking of the one gathering dust in the corner near my father's bed. I remembered the sound it had made in my mother's hands. There was no finer sound. No better music than that, except her voice, which had also gathered far too much dust since my father's accident.

"Especially mandolins," Larkin said. "He was famous for his mandolins. He named them for my mother. Keavy. Every music shop for a hundred miles had them." He looked proud, despite the bruises on his face.

"My mother has a mandolin."

He raised his eyebrows. "Maybe my father made it."

I thought about that. Pictured Larkin's father up on this mountain, living with trees all around him. "He made them out of trees?"

Larkin nodded. "Sugar maple. Red spruce."

I imagined his father waking the memory of wind and rain and sun and snow and starlight from wood otherwise mute.

I thought of my mother sitting by the fire, playing her mandolin, releasing all that rain and snow and sun and starlight. The thought made my bones hum.

"He must have been a very good musician," I said.

Larkin sighed again. "Of all the things I miss about him, that may be what I miss the most. How he played. Which was why he was able to make such beautiful instruments. Because he understood what they could do, in the right hands."

I looked at Larkin's long, slender fingers. "Did he teach you?"

At which Larkin bowed his head. He didn't look at me when he answered. "Of all the things I wish I'd done before he died, that's the biggest thing. To spend more time at my lessons, learning to play. Though yes, he did teach me."

I tipped my head toward the tools hanging on the wall. "He used those?"

"He did. And he made the glue out of deer hide."

"Deer hide!?"

"Sometimes rabbit. Mostly deer. You cut it up and add a little water and boil it and it makes the strongest glue you could want."

Which sounded awful to me. But if that was what it took to make a mandolin, then it couldn't be all bad.

And that explained why Cate had given deer skins to his daddy. But it didn't explain the rest.

Chapter Forty-Two

"That still doesn't explain why your mother doesn't *like* Cate."

He thought back. "I guess that's the wrong way to put it." He paused. "My grandfather died a few months before the crash. He had a heart attack." Larkin paused again, thinking back. "I didn't know him all that well. I told you, he was a doctor. And that's most of what he was, being a doctor. When my grandmother came up here to see us, he stayed in town. He didn't like to leave his patients."

Which was something I understood: how a sick stranger might count more than a grandson, even.

"We went to town sometimes," he said. "And I saw him then, but he was a serious man. I don't think I ever saw him in anything but a suit and waistcoat. Always very proper . . . and a little cold . . . and it was always my grandmother who was the big, warm, jolly one." He looked over at her in her little bed. "Not like she is now." He sighed. "She's changed a lot." The look on his face made my heart hurt. "After he died, she waited too long to come out of her grief and decide how she would live. She waited too long to sell the house. The crash came and no one wanted to buy a big house like that. So she locked it up and left it behind and kept nothing much but her books, really, when she came to live with us."

"Almost like we did," I said, thoughtful, though the house we'd left behind was no longer ours.

"A season before you." He gave me a sad little smile. "And not quite as you did. She was from these mountains. From *this* one. And she came to *us*, who had made our home here because we wanted to. Not because we had to."

I looked at my boots. "You said it before. How hard it was to watch us in the beginning. How sad that was."

He nodded. "But it was different for her. For us. When she first arrived, everything was fine. Everything was really good." He looked at nothing in particular. "But then, a few weeks before you came here to live, my daddy took sick." He swallowed hard. "I don't know what it was. Something terrible. And he was dead before we could do anything about it."

I waited.

"My mother thought . . . well, she didn't see how my grandmother, who had so much learning and had been a nurse and lived with a doctor for all those years, could be so . . . useless."

I thought about Esther. How much she needed someone to blame for what had happened to *our* father. I looked around the little cabin. "And Cate ended up here, by herself?"

Larkin nodded. "It was just awful after my daddy died. My mother was like a wild woman." He shook his head. "Three years it's been, and she's still not right."

I thought about that—how Larkin had lost his father just weeks before he stood in the trees and watched us come to live on the mountain. Watched our pitiful start. Listened to Samuel bleating like a lamb in the cold, gray time before the wilderness greened again.

"You carved that little lamb for Samuel when your father had just died," I said, wanting to touch his wonderful hair, his battered face.

"I did," he said. "But for me as much as him."

"And treasures for her, too," I said, nodding at the tiny fawn on the windowsill. The little squirrel. The perfect mouse.

When he looked at Cate, his face softened. "I think about how my grandmother lived before she came to us. In a fine, big house in town. And now . . ." He looked around the sad little cabin. "But she won't leave me."

I looked at his black eye. The sadness in it. "And your own mother doesn't want you coming up here?"

He shook his head.

"Just because your grandma is teaching you to read?"

"That." He sighed. "And other things, too."

I tried to put myself in his mother's shoes. They were far too small. But I knew more than I had before. "She's worried you'll go off to school and become a doctor and she'll never see you again."

He chewed his lip. "I think so."

We looked at each other.

"And be useless," I said.

"Hard to know how she can feel that way." Larkin wiped a clot of muck from the corner of his eye. Cleared his throat. "I keep hoping she'll get better. But I don't know what to do about that."

At which Cate turned from the wall.

I wondered how much she'd heard.

She reached for Larkin, who went to her.

"None of that is your fault," she said, and I knew she'd heard it all.

Thoughts of my own father, my own mother, rose up like bread. "I should be getting home."

Cate nodded. "You'll do your father good, being there."

I turned to go.

She said, "You never said how he ended up in a coma."

And I didn't much want to tell the story now. But after what Larkin had just told me . . .

"He was cutting down a tree. It hit him on the way down." I didn't bother telling them the rest. It had nothing to do with how long my father had been asleep.

"Where did the tree hit him?"

"In the garden," I replied. "We were—"

"No, not *that* where," she said impatiently. "Where on his head did it hit him?"

"Oh. Here." I tapped the top of my head.

She nodded. "He may be right as rain after a while. The body is sometimes its own best doctor. But you may need to teach him how to talk again. And walk. And he may be . . . different now. Not quite who he was before. And he may not remember some things."

Four *may*s, and only one of them good. The other three were a mountain range I did not want to climb.

"How do you know that?" I said in a voice far too small for any business involving mountains.

"Larkin just told you. I was a nurse." She frowned thoughtfully. "The brain's like the world. Every part of it has a way of doing things. But you won't know what you know until you know it," she said. "Your father will come back to himself slowly, and along the way you'll find out how to help him."

"Like with your leg?" I said. "We just wait and see and figure out what to do when the time comes?"

She nodded. "Exactly right." She pushed away her blanket and laid her hand on the bandage. "It's not too hot. And my fever is gone. So we'll let it be for now."

"I'll come back tomorrow and help you with a bath, if you like," I said. "Larkin is going to do your wash now, and I told him to leave the water after. I'll come back and add some hot when you're ready."

If I'd wanted to surprise Cate, I'd succeeded. I could tell from the look on her face. But she didn't say a word.

Larkin said, "You can rest in a chair while I change your bedding."

Which made Cate gaze at him fondly. "You'll need a good bit of water, and hot, for the wash."

"I'll get some going."

"And I'll bring bread when I come back," I said. "Mother makes good corn bread."

"Which she won't want to share with an old witch like me," Cate said, some thistles in her voice.

I thought she might be wrong.

Now that I had a story to share with my mother, she was sure to find in it a reason to be generous with what little we had.

Especially now that my father was awake, and her own wound surely healing.

When I got back home, I stopped in at the woodshed and found the puppies all back in their nest and sleeping alongside Maisie, who scrambled to her feet when she saw me.

"Are you a very fine girl?" I said, rubbing her ears and kissing her on the head. "Are you my very fine girl?" She answered with a whimper, her tongue just kissing the tip of my nose before she returned to the nest and curled up again with her litter.

"Wake up soon, Quiet," I whispered. *"We don't have much time left."*

But with my father awake again, I found myself hoping that other things might have changed as well.

Chapter Forty-Three

I expected the cabin to be as I'd left it.

My mother smiling again. Singing again as she worked. Esther on her way back to kindness. Samuel that much farther from the boy who had chased a rabbit into such long, sad trouble.

But when I went through the door, I found the kitchen empty, the cabin quiet but for the sound of Esther's voice.

I followed it to find everyone clustered around my father as he lay sleeping.

Samuel was curled up beside him, my mother by the window, watching. Both of them listening as Esther read a book out loud.

Which was when I began to be afraid again.

My mother wasn't hushing anyone.

She wasn't telling them to let my father get his rest.

And the look on her face had no song in it.

"'Generally, by the time you are Real, most of your hair has been loved off,'" Esther read, "'and your eyes drop out and you get loose in the joints and very shabby. But these things don't matter at all, because once you are Real you can't be ugly, except to people who don't understand.' "

I knew that book. I knew that story. *The Velveteen Rabbit.* One of my favorites. It brought to mind the little doll clutched in Cate's hand.

When my mother saw me standing in the doorway, she let out a breath and said, "It's high time you came in." Esther stopped reading, and everyone turned to look at me. "No reason on earth why you should want to be anywhere but here."

And it was, truly, at first glance, a scene from a storybook, my family all together, their cheeks rosy with the warmth they'd breathed into the little room. All except my father, who was still as pale and thin as a parsnip.

And he was still sleeping.

I wanted to tell them about where I'd been and how much Cate had liked the stew and how she was Larkin's grandmother and all the rest, but I wanted to be part of this story, too. The one right here in this room.

It would take a lot of work to be a character in both stories without becoming two characters. Or one, split in half.

But it was work I could do, so I would do it, even if I felt tangled and torn along the way.

For a long time, I'd thought that people simply were who they were and became who they became. But I didn't think that anymore.

"Hasn't he woken up again?" I asked.

My mother shook her head. "Not yet."

I went to the side of the bed, looked at my father's still face, and said, "Wake up, Daddy."

But he didn't wake. Or move at all.

I looked over my shoulder. Met my mother's eyes.

I reached out and shook my father by the shoulder.

It was like shaking a bag of seed.

"Ellie, don't," my mother said. "Let him be."

"Daddy, wake up," I said again.

But he didn't.

My mother left the room.

Esther started to read again. "'"I suppose you are real?" said the Rabbit. And then he wished he had not said it, for he thought the Skin Horse might be sensitive. But the Skin Horse only smiled. "The Boy's Uncle made me Real," he said. "That was a great many years ago; but once you are Real you can't become unreal again. It lasts for always."'"

Which was the only thing I wanted in that moment. For some things to last for always. And other things to end.

I found my mother in the kitchen, at the stove, doing nothing.

"He'll wake up again," I said. "I know he will."

She turned to look at me.

Her eyes narrowed. "What's that?" she said, coming to finger the blood splattered on the jacket I was wearing. "Is that blood?"

"It's—"

"Take it off," she said roughly, working the buttons free. "Take it off this minute."

Which I did, quick as I could.

She snatched it away and thrust it under the pump, drenching it with cold water again, working tallow soap into it, her hands turning red as she worked.

I didn't say, *It will come clean*. I didn't say, *Daddy will make me another one*. I didn't say, *I can learn to stitch ivy like that*.

I thought of Cate as she smelled the hot chisel I'd meant to use on her wound. The alarm on her face. The relief when I hung it straight to cool.

"I'm sorry," I said again, as tangled up as I'd ever been, and went out into the yard to look at the sky and try to know what I couldn't know.

The sun was slipping down the far side of the day, and the shadows were slowly unspooling like black ribbons across the yard.

I wanted to follow them.

I wanted to stay where I was.

But I found myself in a third place altogether when Larkin's mother suddenly appeared through the trees.

Chapter Forty-Four

She was a small woman, which should have made me feel better, but she was like the centipedes that sometimes raced in a frenzy across the cabin floor, their legs like brittle hair, so fast and shivery that I'd leap in terror at the sight of them.

"Stay away from my boy," she said.

And I yelled, "Mother!" as loud as I could. And then again, "Mother!" more loudly still.

Maisie appeared at the door of the woodshed, growling.

Samuel came out into the yard.

He took one look at the woman and seemed to be split, as I had, between wanting to stay and wanting to go.

I loved him more than ever when he scampered to my side and took hold of my hand.

"Who's that?" Samuel said.

"That's Larkin's mother."

He peered at her. "I don't like Larkin's mother."

"Where's your own mother at?" she said.

"Mother!" I called again, more loudly.

And she came through the cabin door all at once.

Esther, who followed behind her, took one look at the situation and stopped short, wavering in place, like a dress pinned to a line.

My mother didn't slow for one moment.

"And what's this about?" she said firmly, taking her place at my side.

But just then Larkin came down the path, too, yelling, "Mother! Mother, wait!"

We all stayed in place, like game pieces on a board.

Larkin slowed as he came into the yard.

I tried to see him through my mother's eyes, this lean boy with his dark, dark hair and his worn-out clothes, and his half-this-half-that face. From one side: just a boy. From the other: a boy hurt.

But we were looking at him straight on, and he was both of those things and more besides. "I'm sorry if she scared you," he said. "Mother, what are you doing?"

"Who's that boy?" Samuel said.

"That's Larkin," I said.

"I didn't scare them," his mother said, though she had.

But, up close, I could see that this was no centipede.

Looking at Larkin's mother was like looking at a broken bowl. Jagged. A woman in pieces.

And I didn't see how she could ever be whole again.

Or hold anything properly ever again.

Not with that look on her face.

As on the mountaintop, I could feel the mad-sorrow coming off her like a stink.

"I don't know you," my mother said. "I'm Evelyn."

"You don't need to know me. Or my boy either."

My mother looked at Larkin's battered face. "Did you do that to him?"

"Of course not. He did that himself, paying no attention to what he was doing. But *she's* the one who cut him."

My mother turned to me.

"I only let off the blood so he could see better!"

"That blood," my mother said. "On your jacket." She put her hand on her forehead. "Esther, take Samuel into the cabin." To me, she said. "Is that something else the hag taught you?"

"No," I said carefully. "*Miss Cate* taught me to do that. And how to fill a wound with honey. And how to use maggots to eat away dead flesh. And how to make a potato poultice. And—"

"What's a poultice?" Samuel said over his shoulder as Esther dragged him toward the cabin.

"All right," my mother said, holding up her hand. "That's more than enough." She turned to Larkin's mother. "What is it you want?"

"I want your girl to stay away from my son. She has no business telling him to wash an old woman's underthings."

Which might have sounded comical if someone else had said it. But there was nothing funny about Larkin's mother.

"They needed washing," I said.

She nodded. "Then you're the girl to do it."

My mother held up both hands now. "You came all the way down here because your son had to do the wash?"

"I came down here to tell you that Larkin already knows his business," she said, looking not at my mother but at me. "Without you telling it to him. You and his grandmother. Teaching him things that won't do anyone a bit of good. Telling him to scrub her sour bedsheets when there's work to be done at home." She leaned closer. "I'll thank you for seeing to your own business and letting us see to ours."

Larkin shook his head. "I'm sorry," he said again.

"No need to apologize," my mother said mildly. "You haven't done anything wrong."

"You don't know a thing about it," his mother said. "Or about your own girl. Out in the night alone, roaming around in trousers, telling Larkin what to do. When *she's* the one who needs a strong hand but no man at home to give it."

My mother stared. "Whatever gave you the idea that there was no man here?"

"You mean that little boy?"

My mother snorted like a spring horse. "I mean my husband, who built this cabin and made these clothes we're wearing and cut a notch in this mountain for our garden there and a great deal more. None of which is any of your affair. So, as you said before, I'll thank you for seeing to your business and letting us see to ours."

She lifted her chin and looked down her nose, as if she had royal blood running in her veins. Which, as far as I was concerned, she did. "And unless you own this mountain, my daughter will climb it whenever the spirit moves her. And she will visit Miss Cate whenever Miss Cate wants her to."

"You'll be sorry. I know more about it than you do."

"Oh, now, look," my mother said impatiently. "This is easy. My daughter is a kid. Your son is a kid. They are kids on a mountain that has very few kids. Is it really such a terrible thing that your son knows how to wash a bedsheet? That he has a friend in my Ellie, here?"

I liked that, but Larkin's mother didn't, and she said so.

"Friends now, and I hope that's all they'll be. But when things get better in town, you'll all go back again. And she won't be taking Larkin with her." She looked at me. "So don't think you will."

I felt myself pink up.

Larkin looked like he had swallowed a bug.

His mother glared back at mine. "We know what we need to know, and we have what we need to have." She turned and headed toward the path up-mountain. "Come on now, Larkin."

Larkin sighed. "I'm sorry," he said yet again.

"I'll come up tomorrow," I said softly.

Then I realized what I'd done.

"I'll come up tomorrow," I called after him—loud and clear—as he followed his mother out of the yard.

But only his mother looked back.

I didn't like what I saw on her face.

And when we went inside the cabin again, I locked the door behind us.

Chapter Forty-Five

"Now, tell me what just happened," my mother said when we were back in the kitchen.

Esther and Samuel sat waiting for us, clearly eager to know more about Larkin and his mother and Cate.

It had been a long time since Esther, especially, had seemed interested in anything I had to say.

Samuel was most curious—and alarmed—about the maggots. "What's a maggot?" he said, his eyes big. "And, Ellie, what did you mean, they eat dead flesh? Do they eat alive flesh, too? How big are they? Do they eat boys? Have you ever seen a maggot?"

"Oh, for pity's sake," Esther said, looking a little green around the gills. "A maggot is just a worm, Samuel. About as big as an oat."

"But how can a worm as big as an oat eat a boy?"

"Hush now," my mother said. "Go on, Ellie."

So I told them the story of what I'd done over the days since Quiet's birth.

It took me a long time.

Samuel interrupted to ask why Cate had saved the tick from Captain's ear.

The rest they listened to in silence.

I felt almost as good telling it as I had felt living it.

"So that poor woman lost her husband," my mother said, clearing her throat. "And that poor boy lost his father."

Esther got up from the table and went to the window.

"You left out a few things," my mother said. "Like how I made you sleep in the woodshed. And how I had Esther stand guard over your father before he woke up."

"But how were we supposed to know that all her weird business might help Daddy?" Esther said. "She's not a doctor. She's just a girl. And she's too wild and willful. You know she is. If she weren't, she wouldn't have been under that tree when it fell and none of this would have happened in the first place."

I took a step back.

I couldn't help it. I was amazed by how ugly a pretty girl could look.

Samuel said, "You're as nasty as a rat, Esther. Ellie didn't mean to be in the way of that tree."

Which brought me up short.

"I'm not nasty," Esther said. "You just wait until *you're* fifteen and all *you* want to do is get off this mountain."

Nobody said a word.

My mother looked away.

I thought back to town. For me, that life was hazy. Not only because I'd been so much younger then, but because I'd given myself instead to the here and now.

Esther surely had strong, clear memories of that time. That home. And I knew that, for her, life on the mountain was the thing she'd rather forget.

For the first time, I realized that town wasn't just a place where Esther wanted to be.

Town was Esther's mountain.

And I felt newly sorry for my sister, who had once held me in her lap with a doll and a book.

But mean was mean. And it wasn't any more useful to Esther than it was to me.

"I won't," I said. "I won't want to get off this mountain. And if I do, I'll find a way to go."

"Now hush, the both of you," my mother said. "Nobody's going anywhere. Esther, what's gotten into you? Ellie didn't make us poor. And Samuel, Esther's not mean. She's just mad. Because she's fifteen. And don't ask me to explain that, but you'll understand when you get there."

"Then I don't want to be fifteen," Samuel said.

"That has nothing to do with it," Esther said. "It's this place. It's snakes that come up in the washroom. And mice in the grain. And spiders in the privy. And everything, Mother. And you know it, too."

"I know no such thing," my mother said.

"But you do! You know Daddy's gone again. Because of a stupid tree that he shouldn't have had to cut down. For what? To make a bigger garden? When we should be able to go to market and buy whatever we need?"

"He woke up once. He'll wake up again."

"And if he doesn't? No matter what kind of potion Ellie tries next?"

"Esther, stop." My mother looked as if she might cry. "You're just cold from a long winter."

"And the one before that," Esther said. "And the one before that. But that doesn't make me wrong."

She went back to the room where my father lay sleeping.

I thought of Cate in the midst of a blizzard, shaken by the screams and wails of a storm as it rolled over the mountain.

"Maybe I should take Esther up to Miss Cate's cabin," I said. "Maybe she'll like ours better after that."

"She's just upset." My mother sighed. "We're all just upset. To have your father back for such a short time. Almost worse than if he hadn't woken up at all."

I disagreed. "He woke up once. He'll wake up again, just like you said."

My mother nodded. "I hope so."

"And tomorrow I'm going back to see Miss Cate. She knows a lot about how to make people well, and she has books. There are plenty of other things we can try."

Samuel said, "I want to go see Larkin."

"You'll stay right here," my mother said. "Now fetch some potatoes from the root cellar. I'll mash them for supper."

She had not said that I couldn't go back up to Cate's. She had not said anything about locking me in the woodshed. She had not said that I was entirely too wild and willful.

Something was changing. I could feel it.

Chapter Forty-Six

When Samuel had left the kitchen, I said, "You miss town, too."

My mother looked at her hands. They were rough and red and split at the knuckles.

After a long moment, she said, "I do, Ellie. Every day."

"The house we had?"

"That." She took her apron off its hook and put it on. "Lots of things." She closed her eyes. "I miss being a teacher."

I remembered what Larkin had said. "You're still a teacher."

Which made her smile for a moment. "I suppose I am. But I miss the people. Molly Peterson is nice enough, but I had *real* friends in town, Ellie. The other teachers at the school. The choir at the church. We had neighbors close by. Even the people I didn't know well, I still knew. Mr. Turner, the butcher, used to tell me a new joke every time I went into his shop. That nurse, in Bethel. Mrs. Cleary: I liked her a lot. She used to call you Rapunzel, for all that long hair you used to have. Remember all those trips to Bethel when Esther had her earaches? Mrs. Cleary was so kind to Esther. To all of us."

At which a seed began to sprout in my startled brain, and I sat up straighter in my chair.

"And so was Mrs. Stark," she said, pulling me back. "The grocer's wife. So kind. Did you know she lost four babies, one right after the other? But she still smiled every time I walked in the door with you children."

"I remember," I said slowly. Distracted. "She gave us peppermints."

"She did. Every time she saw you." My mother thrust a log into the stove.

She pulled a mug from the cupboard and measured some balsam chips into a scrap of rag. Dropped the pouch into the mug and stood quietly, gathering wool, as the kettle began to tick and rumble.

"Yes, I miss town," my mother said quietly, after a bit. "But I have people here, too."

She poured water in the mug, and the steam rose from it like wet, white fire.

I watched her as if she were a bird perched on my finger. "I wish Daddy could have seen you out there."

My mother looked at me through the steam. "Out where?"

"In the yard. Standing up to Larkin's mother like that. Talking about Daddy and all he's done."

My mother made a face that was part rue, part something else. "If he'd been there to hear all that, I wouldn't have had to say it in the first place."

Which was true enough but not the whole story. "You might have added a thing or two about us, still here and all right no matter how long Daddy's been asleep." I paused, but she didn't say anything. "How you yourself have managed." I swallowed. "And Esther, too."

And Larkin's mother, I thought, years beyond when her own husband had gone to his rest.

I wondered if my mother would well up with the same kind of darkness if, years from now, my daddy still hadn't come back to us or, worse, left us altogether.

As Esther had once said: *If* was quite a word.

My mother nodded thoughtfully.

I waited for her to say something about how I, too, had managed since my father's accident.

"We have done our best," she said. "But I fear that Esther and I are not meant for this kind of life." She met my eye. "Not like you seem to be."

Which was both praise and accusation. Not just what she said but how she said it. Enough bitterness to spoil the sweet.

"And that's it?" I said. "We're born to one thing and that's it?" Of all the things she'd ever said to me, this was the most confounding.

"Of course not, Ellie. I hope we all have at least a little chameleon in us. But chameleons change to suit what's around them, and it was the other way around in town." She looked at her ruined hands. "I feel like a stranger in this new skin. I left behind too much of who I've always been, with not enough new to fill up what's empty now. Not enough new that suits me."

I thought about that.

"So it's not just Daddy being asleep that makes you feel that way?"

She shook her head. "I'm stronger now because I have to be, and I suppose I should find some satisfaction in that." She picked up her mug with both hands. "And I do, Ellie. But satisfaction doesn't hold a candle to what I had before."

I watched her drink her tea, her eyes closed.

"What would you call that?" I said.

"What I had before?"

I nodded.

"I don't think there's a word for it." She paused. "I was who I was, without thinking too much about it."

And I realized that she must have forgotten how it felt to be a girl untying a new ribbon, opening a new box every day, and finding, again and again, what it meant to change, to grow, all of it troubling and exciting and true.

Surely Esther knew how that felt.

As if she'd heard my thoughts, my mother said, "Esther is like me. Holding fast to who she's always been. And what's wrong with that?"

"Nothing," I said. "Except . . . what about the other things she might become?"

"That's Esther's business." My mother rose to her feet. "Not mine. Not yours."

And I had no argument with that. Not if it was really true.

"Now go find out what's taking your brother so long," she said, turning away. "He could have grown those potatoes by now."

Chapter Forty-Seven

I sat on the cabin step, lost in thought until Samuel came up from the root cellar, a basket of potatoes over his arm and a grin on his face.

"I saw a white spider as big as my hand. It was disgusting. Kinda squishy."

"You didn't kill it, did you?" I pictured the spider smashed into the root cellar floor like a spent star, dingy and dark.

"Don't be foolish. Of course I didn't kill it. I just touched it to see how it felt. It was disgusting." He grinned some more. "I might want one for a pet."

"Hmm. I bet Mother and Esther would love that."

"No, they wouldn't, Ellie," he said, shaking his little head. "Mother's right. You have lost your wits."

"Do you want me to teach you how to make a potato poultice?" I said. "To make Daddy's sores better?"

Samuel made a face. "A what?"

"Come inside. I'll show you."

Which I did, though I ended up doing most of the work myself while he told me how to do it.

As I squeezed off some of the potato juice, he said, "Why isn't Daddy awake?"

I stopped what I was doing. "He's tired, is all. He needs a lot more sleep before he wakes up again."

"But he's already been sleeping for a long time."

I nodded. "I know that. But he'll wake up soon." I set aside the potato. "Now we'll collect some witch hazel twigs."

"Some what?"

By answer I took him out again into the yard and across to where the witch hazel grew. "The bark makes a good skin cleaner." I yanked off some twigs.

Samuel spent some time on one of the bigger branches before he gave up and dedicated himself to a twig as thick as his little finger. But even that was too much for him.

"It would be easier if these were dead," I said. "But they're alive, so they bend a lot before they break."

Which made me think of Cate, and my father. And mother. And Larkin. And his mother.

The list was long.

"Here," I said. "Let me."

But he shrugged me off and used both hands, bending the twig back and forth until he'd sawed through the raw green of it.

He held the twig up like a trophy. "Do you want some more?"

"No, that's perfect," I said. "We'll boil this up and mix some with the potato."

Which we did. The result was a goopy mess, but I had learned to have quite a lot of faith in goopy messes.

"Just lay this onto his sores," I told my mother, holding out the bowl. "And cover them with something. The witch hazel might sting, but it won't be as bad as vinegar."

My mother didn't take the bowl. "Don't you think you should do this yourself?"

I thought about how I had managed to squeeze honey into Cate's wound but had not imagined treating my own father's sores.

"Won't you?" I said in a small voice.

She considered me for a long moment, chewing her lip, before she reached for the bowl. "Yes. I'll do this part, Ellie. You go on and help Samuel with his lessons."

Except that wasn't right. That didn't feel right. Or good at all. When she said that, my gut—the spot at the top of my belly, just below my heart—swung off-kilter.

I remembered teaching Samuel to catch the trout. How I had been the one to club it over the head. But he was just small, and I wasn't. And if I was to be the one to start something, I would be the one to finish it.

So, "No," I said slowly, swinging back toward true. "I don't mind. I'll do it."

"I don't want to do my lessons," Samuel said. "And I made the potato thing, so I should get to help, too."

"Esther needs someone to read to while we take care of your father," my mother told him. "Let that be you."

He wasn't entirely convinced, but my mother's face gave him no choice in the matter, so he went with us toward my father's room to fetch Esther.

When she heard what we meant to do, she stood up so quickly that her book fell to the floor.

"Come on," Samuel said, picking it up. "You can read to me now."

For a long moment she stayed where she was, looking at me and the bowl of potato in my hand, looking at my mother, a fair amount of regret plain on her face. But she didn't say a thing.

It was clear that she wanted no part of what we were doing, though I would have thought some messes worth making, even for Esther.

Maybe if I could help my father all the way to well again, she would come back to me, too, as she had for a little while, not so long before. But that would be up to her.

When Esther and Samuel had left, my mother turned my father over and used clean rags to cover him everywhere except the sores themselves so I was looking at a landscape of white cloth and red flesh.

All the while, he lay still and showed no signs of waking.

Nonetheless, I talked to him as I had for months now, hoping he could hear me.

"I'm sorry if this hurts," I said as I spooned the potato mixture onto the wounds and laid more rags over the poultices.

My mother stood out of the way while I worked, holding her

own hands, but as soon as I was through, she covered my father with a blanket and pulled the rocking chair up close beside him.

"I'll stay with him," she said. "You go and finish getting supper ready." She stroked his hair.

At the door, I turned back to see her lay her head next to his, her whole body shaking.

But then Samuel came running, shouting. "Come see! That big dog is at the door, Ellie. And he has a doll in his mouth."

Chapter Forty-Eight

My mother wanted me to wait until morning to go see if Cate was all right.

"But that's her doll," I said at the cabin door, Esther and my mother on either side of me. "Captan wouldn't have left her alone at night, and he wouldn't have taken her doll unless something was wrong."

"What's an old hag doing with a doll?" Esther said. "I'll bet it's a poppet. For making spells. Or cursing someone."

I thought about the blessing Larkin had taught me. The one Cate said to him whenever he left her. *Saol fada agus breac-shláinte chugat.*

"Shame on you," I said.

But Esther didn't look ashamed. "And why would her dog come to you? You've only known her for a little while. Why wouldn't he have gone to Larkin?"

I didn't know the answer to that, but I pictured him there, too. Trying to help her but needing help himself.

I said as much.

"Then I'll go with you," my mother said, though she sounded a little uncertain.

"You will?" I turned to stare at her.

She looked like the same mother I'd had that morning, but something was different, and I thought back to what she'd said about emptiness.

Maybe she saw—in the shape of a dog with a doll in his mouth—a chance to do something about that.

"I will," she said. "If it's more trouble than the two of them can handle, they'll need both of us. Esther, you'll take care of Samuel and your father while we're gone." She glanced down at her dress. "But let me do something about this first."

I didn't know what she intended, but then she came back wearing a pair of my father's trousers, cinched with his belt at the waist and rolled into cuffs at the ankle.

"You'll have to clean off those poultices in a while," she told Esther, who looked like a child for the first time in years.

"I'll help you, Esther," Samuel said. "I'm good with poultices."

His face reminded me of when he had helped Mr. Peterson with the thorn in Scotch's hoof.

But Esther just looked hard at me and then my mother and back again before turning away toward my father's room.

"Now what did I do?" I said softly.

"Nothing," my mother replied. "I think she's upset with me this time."

"For going to Miss Cate's with me?"

She sighed. "For both those things."

I had said only one thing, though I now saw it was two.

I pulled on my boots while my mother fetched hers. We buttoned up our jackets, mine still damp but warm from hanging by the stove.

"Should we take something along?" my mother said.

"Me," Samuel said. "I want to go, too."

"No, Esther needs you to stay here," my mother said. "To help with your father."

"We should take some jerky," I replied. "And a lantern." We would need light on the trail, and quick fire when we got there.

"And bread." She put the food in a sack while I fetched a lantern and lit it at the stove.

I felt in my pockets for my knife. My flint.

"You should wear a cap," I told her. "So the branches on the path don't get caught in your hair."

She stared at me. "Is that why you cut yours off?"

I nodded. "The trees kept trying to comb it."

My mother reached out to touch my hair for a moment. Then she put on a cap and gathered her things.

Captan was still waiting, but as soon as we joined him he dropped the doll at my feet and then loped off across the yard toward the path up.

It wasn't quite dusk yet, though the woods were full of shadows and I was glad to have my mother close beside me, better than a knife in my hand.

But before we had gone very far, I heard Esther calling, "Wait, Mother! Wait!"

We stopped. Captan stopped.

Up the path Esther ran, panting.

"Let me," she said. "Mother, if something happens and you're not back soon . . . I don't know . . . I won't know what to do with Daddy and Samuel. Let me go instead."

She looked very young standing there.

"But we're already on our way," my mother said, and I heard, in her voice, something just as young. A thread pulling her back toward a time when she was a girl on an adventure. The same thread pulling her forward. "And we'll be back before you know it."

But Esther was pulling on a similar thread, and she was much closer to the spool than my mother was, the thread less likely to break. "Please," she said. "I'll help Ellie. I promise I will. And I'll look after her."

As if I needed her to look after me. The idea was just plain silly. And it made me mad. But I stood still and waited for the two of them to sort themselves out. Captan did likewise, though his whole body yearned to be gone, uphill, to home.

My mother looked past Esther, toward the cabin. "You left Samuel alone."

"I did," Esther said, nodding. "I told him you'd be down soon."

Which seemed to decide things.

My mother sighed. Pulled the cap from her head and handed it to Esther. Handed her the bag with the bread and jerky.

She gave me a long look. "Take care of your sister," she said.

And I loved her more than ever.

I had wanted her with me. To meet Cate. To look into those blue eyes and realize everything I'd realized, and maybe more.

But I wanted Esther to know just as much.

As it turned out, I had plenty more to learn, too.

Chapter Forty-Nine

The climb was easy for me, but Esther had a hard time with the pace, the rocky path, the darkness as it deepened, and the way the branches batted at her face as she struggled up the deer trail.

To her credit, she didn't say a word.

Not even when she fell. Once. Twice.

"You can go back if you want." I waited as she struggled to her feet, clapping the dirt off her hands.

"Just go on." She was a little short of breath. Her hair had come loose and hung from her cap in soft, fair loops.

I stepped to one side so she could go first. "Give me that sack," I said, handing her the lantern. "And go on ahead. I'll be right behind you. When we get to the steep part, don't let go of one tree until you've got a grip on another."

"How, when I have to hold the lantern, too?"

Which made me impatient, that she would ask me such a thing when the only answer was to manage it, difficult or not. But I said, "I'll help you." And when it came to that, I did.

When we arrived at the cabin, Cate wasn't there.

"Where is she, boy?" I asked Captan when I opened the door and found her bed empty. But he stayed out in the yard and didn't answer.

Esther crept in behind me, swatting at a fly come to taste her lips. *"What an awful place,"* she whispered, and I saw it fresh through her eyes.

The narrow bed, one hard chair, a table, the shelves with jars full of oddments and potions and worms. The nubs of spent candles squatting like toadstools all over the place.

But then I swung the lantern so she could see the fistful of snow-drops in a mug next to her bed, which meant Larkin. The tiny fawn and the mouse and the squirrel. And those tools, which were in their own way beautiful. But it was only when I held the lantern high to cast light on the shelves full of books, the hanging garden, that I saw her face change.

"Oh," she said.

I laid the little doll on the bed.

There was a stain on the blanket.

"I wonder if her wound opened up." I bent to sniff the blanket for pus or honey, pulled back at the idea of what that would look like to Esther, then leaned closer, inhaling the scent of Cate's wound.

It was chilly in the cabin, and a wind had kicked up to push the cabin door wide and follow us inside.

"Maybe she fell," I said.

I ducked past Esther and into the yard, pausing at the sight of

Cate's clean wash hung to dry, waving and dancing at the edge of the yard.

Larkin. He had done her wash and left water for her bath.

And I wondered if she had decided not to wait for my help.

"This way," I said, following Captan around the side of the cabin toward the shed behind it.

We found her lying outside the shed, wrapped in a blanket that was red where it covered her leg.

I rushed to gather her up. "Help me!" I yelled when Esther stood back watching.

So Esther did help me, though with such a look of distaste that I wanted to slap her.

Cate was heavy despite how thin she was, but we managed to carry her back into the cabin while Captan danced along beside us, whining darkly.

She moaned a little as we laid her on the bed and covered her up. "There's firewood in the yard, Esther. Go get some."

Which she did while I ripped pages from the big book on the desk and shredded them on the hearth. I hoped they taught nothing more important than the benefits of fresh air and clean water, which I already knew.

When Esther came back, I twisted a whole page into a wick and lit it in the lantern, laying it gently on the hearth.

"Careful," I said, as she reached out with a handful of twigs. "You'll smother it. Just one at a time to start. Like this." I laid a single twig across the bricks I'd pushed into place on either side of the flame. "It's not like the oven at home." Which could handle a heavy hand.

In this way, I taught my sister how to build a fire on a cold hearth.

Before long, we had a good blaze going, and I opened the cabin door just a crack so the smoke would rise straight up into the wide mouth of the chimney.

Then I fetched a clean nightdress from the wash line and took it inside to warm by the fire.

While Esther stood and watched, I went to Cate and pulled the blankets away from her leg.

The wound gaped like a terrible red mouth, but it wasn't bleeding much anymore.

"The bath must have melted the honey, opened the cut. Maybe she fell. Maybe she fainted. We'll know when she tells us," I said. "But I don't know why she let it get wet in the first place."

Captan stood beside the bed and laid his head next to Cate's.

"Why did you open the door if you're trying to warm her up?" Esther said.

"To increase the draw, for the fire," I replied. "The draft. The flow of air."

"I don't know what that means." She sounded cranky and subdued at the same time.

"When the fire eats the air inside, the smoke comes back down the chimney instead of going up it." My father had taught me that. I wondered why he hadn't taught Esther, but I knew that it was easier to teach a thing to someone who wants to know it.

"I thought you said she was getting better."

"She was. But she's stubborn. And she's used to doing for herself. And she didn't wait for me to help with her bath."

I pulled the blanket back over her leg. Then I fetched the deerskin coat from the trunk and laid that over her, too. It was so heavy that I knew it would keep her heat in where it belonged and make her feel safe, besides.

"Heat up some jerky. In that skillet, there. On the wall," I told Esther. "Just lay it across the bricks."

She did what I said without question, tending the fire and the jerky both. The smell of the venison softening made Captan go toward her and sit nearby.

"What an ugly dog," Esther said.

"Oh, hush," I said. "You're a beauty, Captan. A beauty."

At which Cate stirred.

She peered at me in confusion.

"Captan came down to fetch me," I told her. "He had your doll in his mouth."

She looked at me, blinking, slow to wake.

I said, "I don't know why he came for me instead of Larkin."

She closed her eyes again. "Larkin's mother isn't so fond of Captan."

I pushed Cate's hair away from her face. "How could she not be fond of a dog like that?"

"He was my son's dog." She closed her eyes again. "First mine, as a puppy, but he took to my son like a bird to the sky. So . . ."

"Shouldn't that make her love Captan even more?"

Cate didn't reply.

After a while, she opened her eyes again and said, "You must be a very strong girl, to carry me back in here."

"Oh," I said, realizing suddenly that Esther was still standing quietly by the fire where Cate couldn't see her. "My sister came up with me."

"And we should be getting back now," Esther said. "Mother will be worried."

Cate craned her neck around. "A sister?"

Esther came forward a bit, though she still kept her distance.

Cate stared at her. "You can come closer, child. I won't bite."

After a long moment, Esther came to stand next to me by the bed, though she looked like she wanted to be somewhere else altogether.

"Ellie, fetch the lantern," Cate said, frowning. Which I did, hoisting it so the light fell on Esther's face.

"Oh my," Cate said, her eyes growing wide. She reached for my sister's hand, though Esther clearly did not want to give it. "You look nearly the same," she said. "Older, but the same."

And I smiled at what was coming.

Then she looked harder at me. At my face. My hair.

"You, though, have changed quite a lot. You're thinner than you were. Taller. And your hair used to be so long." She reached up with her other hand, and I bent lower so she could touch the soft short-ness of it. "I used to call you Rapunzel."

And I felt, in that touch, the big, jolly nurse we'd once known. The one who had called me Rapunzel and tended to Esther's earaches.

Cate was not big. Nor was she jolly. But as I looked into her blue eyes, I knew both what she was and what she had once been, which were really the same thing, though they weren't.

Here, beside me, was another soul both split in two and doubled.

She looked at Esther again. "Do you not know me?"

Esther shook her head. But then she bent closer. And her own eyes grew big. "Nobody called Ellie Rapunzel except Mrs. Cleary," she said slowly.

And it wasn't the lantern that lit my sister's eyes as she sat down on the edge of the bed and said, "But Mrs. Cleary was a big woman. She was a big, round woman with rosy cheeks and hair in a braid down her back and blue eyes"—she leaned closer—"like yours, but . . . you can't be her. You can't be."

And then Esther was crying, wrapped in the arms of a woman who had wanted nothing at all but to make Esther well when she was sick. To make her stop hurting so much.

I felt like a bystander, which made me sad. But I felt joyful, too.

The Esther I'd once known was right there, close enough to touch. And so was the hag who had once been Mrs. Cleary. And still was.

Chapter Fifty

After that it was different.

My sister wanted to stay, to look after Cate while I went home again.

It was clear that Esther didn't want to go back out into the dark. But it was also clear that she wanted to be with Mrs. Cleary.

"All right," I said. "You stay. I'll go back." Though I felt sad, even a little annoyed, to be leaving Cate in Esther's hands . . . and to see that they were content to stay there together without me. First Larkin, which I had found easy to understand, and now Esther, which I found . . . unfair.

But I had been the one to wish for Esther to wake up a little. To open her eyes. So I could not very well blame her for doing just that.

"Mother will be in a state, wondering what's become of us," I said, as matter of fact as I could be. "So I'll go home now and then to Larkin in the morning, and we'll fetch you some more honey in case that leg festers again."

Cate nodded. "I could use some more." She pushed the deer

hide away. Saw that the blanket was bloody where it covered her wound.

"Where are the bandages we wrapped it in before?" I said.

"I washed them in the bath. I had them with me. But I remember feeling dizzy on my way back here." She frowned. "Nothing after that."

"I'm surprised you let your leg get wet," I said, and I could hear the disapproval in my voice.

She sighed. "I didn't mean to. I was clumsy. And all for something that might have waited till you got back." She gave me a rueful smile. "I'm used to doing things for myself."

"The bandages are somewhere on the ground near where we found her," I told Esther. "Go find them. And if they're dirty, wash them out again."

She stayed right where she was for a long moment of *no* and then went out into the night.

When she returned, I pointed at the fire and watched as she draped the wet bandages over the back of Cate's one hard chair and dragged it close to the flames.

Cate looked from me to Esther and back again.

"What's wrong between you two?" she said. "You used to be like peas in a pod."

I thought about everything I might say, then chose the simplest. "We're different."

Cate scoffed at that. "So are ink and paper, but they get along very well indeed."

"She's mad at me," I said.

"Not mad," Esther said.

"She thinks I'm the reason our daddy got hurt."

Cate scoffed again. "You're a girl. You're not a tree."

"She was in the way," Esther said.

Cate shook her head. "*Blame* comes from the Greek for 'curse.' That's the root of it. A curse. Against the sacred. Which is what sisters are. Or should be. To each other." She glared at us both. "Sacred."

I looked at Esther. She looked at me.

"It's all right that you were in the way," Esther said. "You're just a kid."

Which made me mad, but I held my tongue.

I found Cate watching me carefully. "Captan fetched the right person," she said.

And, just like that, I wasn't mad anymore.

"In the morning," she said, "look for Larkin down the path alongside the spring, down over the rocks and around and down until you reach the cabin."

"I will." To Esther, I said, "Wait until those bandages are bone-dry, cooked clean, and then wrap her leg up again. Clean as you can. And light that lantern there before I go," I said, since I would need my own for the hike back down to home.

And, along with it, a good bit of courage, besides.

Chapter Fifty-One

My lantern ran out of oil before I ran out of path.

I stopped then and there, the woods dark and windy, and wanted badly to go back the way I'd come. But I'd heard my father say many times that wild animals were more afraid of people than people were of wild animals, so I wasn't much more than nervous as I continued on in darkness.

The bear I saw as I rounded a bend in the path was several shades blacker than the night.

When I saw him, I froze.

He did, too, when he saw me.

And for a long moment, we stared at each other in the darkness, and I was glad that he was not a big, burly summer bear.

Not a wounded bear, since I knew that a bear hurt was a bear mean.

Not a mother bear, her cubs bleating with fear at a girl in the woods.

Just a thin spring bear who was surely as scared of me as I was of him. My father had said so, and I had believed him.

But then I made the mistake of reading, in his eyes, a wildness I admired. Of feeling, in him, a love of things I loved: like lying in a meadow with the grass rising high all around, hiding me from everything but the sky and the bee-heavy blossoms nodding down toward me, springing up again as the bees flew. Or a pink end-of-day sky. Or the clear whistle-ring of a wood thrush.

And I leaned—just a little—toward the bear as he stood there, stiff-legged, his head up, his eyes on me . . .

. . . and he decided to prove my father wrong.

When he started toward me, growling, I dropped the dead lantern and ran.

I knew better.

I knew that a bear would chase someone who ran.

I knew that he could run faster than me.

I knew that he could manage the trail far better with his night-eyes than I could with my day-eyes.

I knew that I would be smarter to play dead.

But I ran anyway.

And he would have been on me in no time if I hadn't fallen and suddenly found the good sense to tuck my hands up under my chin and lie still.

I had already done a few hard things in my life, but one of the hardest, then or since, was lying with my face in the dirt, without moving at all, not at all, while the bear snuffed me and kicked my legs, still angry but puzzled and winded from the uphill run, more interested, it seemed, in new grass and grubs than in girl.

But when he plucked the cap off my head, I learned a new kind of fear.

And when he finally turned and left me, I said a new kind of thanks.

For my life.

For my unscarred skin.

And especially for the fact that Esther had stayed with Cate.

I tried to imagine her meeting up with the bear. Then I tried not to imagine that.

I lay there, unmoving, for some time.

And then I got up slowly, in chapters, and quietly brushed myself off, retrieved my cap and my lantern, and went carefully down the path, stopping often, listening as hard as I could, hoping we wouldn't meet again. Only a small part of me wishing that we would.

When I walked through the door of our cabin, I found my mother waiting inside by the window, and for just a moment I thought maybe my father had woken up again.

She took one look at my face and said, "What happened? Where's Esther?"

I didn't know what to say first. "Is Daddy awake?"

She shook her head.

So I told her everything in order. Ending with the plan to go find Larkin and get more honey for Cate's leg, first thing in the morning.

I left out the part about the bear. Otherwise she would never again let me go back up that mountain in darkness, doll or no doll.

And I left out the part about Cate being Mrs. Cleary.

I would let Esther tell that part, though I'd miss the chance to make my mother smile.

Ever since I'd imagined Esther being mauled by a bear, I had cared much less about other hurts, however real they might have been.

"Esther stayed there? Instead of you?" my mother said.

"She didn't much like being in the woods, and she didn't want to come home in the dark." Which was true. I didn't say that she had wanted to stay with Mrs. Cleary. That they were most likely chatting, at this very moment. Or maybe Esther was reading Cate a story from one of her many books. "She'll come home as soon as I go back."

"After you fetch honey with Larkin? I don't like that at all, Ellie. You going near his mother. That woman's far too angry."

My mother was in her nightgown, her hair down around her shoulders, but she still managed to look fierce.

"You would go, too, if you saw that wound on Miss Cate's leg."

She pursed her lips. "Not near Larkin's mother. And neither will you."

I squinted at her thoughtfully. "Wait right here," I said.

She gave me a puzzled look but stayed put while I went through the kitchen and along to the bedroom where my father and her mandolin were both sleeping.

I picked it up and carried it to my mother. What I felt as I held it in my arm made me lonely.

"Wait," I said again when she began to speak.

I held the mandolin up to the lantern light and peered past the strings to the mark burned into the back of its belly, a label pasted below that.

The mark said KEAVY.

And I knew that Larkin's father had made this mandolin. And named it for his wife.

I held it out to my mother.

She gave me the lantern and took the mandolin in her arms as if it were a baby.

"What?" she said.

I held the lantern up.

"Look inside."

"I don't need to," she said. "I know what's inside. A maker's mark. Keavy. It's a Keavy mandolin. The best."

"Which is her name."

"Whose name?"

"Larkin's mother. That's her name. Keavy."

My mother peered into the mandolin. Looked back at me, her eyes wide.

I said, "His father was a luthier." The new word tasted heavy and good on my tongue. "He made mandolins. He made that one."

"He was a luthier," she said softly. "He made my Keavy."

She seemed confused, and I thought I knew why.

I said, "It's hard to imagine him naming his mandolins for someone so mean."

She nodded. "It is."

"Larkin says she wasn't mean before his father died. Maybe she'll wake up soon and come back to what she used to be."

My mother looked me in the eye. "Or what she'll be next."

Chapter Fifty-Two

It was odd being in the cabin without Esther.

I could breathe more easily. But the cabin also felt emptier.

I fell asleep almost as soon as I lay down, the day catching up with me. And the day before that. And the one before that.

As I slept, I dreamed a different version of the memory that had so often kept me awake.

As always, I was with my father, clearing trees by the frozen garden.

As always, Samuel came running after the rabbit, my father and Esther and my mother all busy with their work.

But in this dream, I didn't see my little brother in time.

In this dream, I rushed toward him too late. And then I tripped and fell as he ran, the tree sweeping through the air, spinning on its stump.

This time, my father saw only me, sprawled in the dirt.

And Samuel, this time, was the one felled by the tree.

In my dream, I saw him dying. I saw his small body go still. I saw his head loose on its neck, tipping toward its rest.

I saw Esther's face. The panic in it. And I knew what she was feeling. That there had to be a way to stop everything and wind it back. Wind it back to before she had strayed too far into the trees in search of kindling while Samuel went on his silly way, chasing a rabbit toward an end to everything, toward a stillness that would never warm, never wake, never change no matter how much we hoped and prayed it would.

I woke before the dream had a chance to show me my mother's face. Or my father's. Or my own.

I woke to tears and a terrible need to know that Samuel was all right.

"What are you doing, Ellie?" he mumbled as I climbed into his bed and took him in my arms. He was warm and soft. Nothing but warm and soft, which was everything. "Your feet are cold and your face is wet. I'm *sleeping*, Ellie."

So I hushed him and told him it wasn't morning yet. To go back to sleep.

Which he did.

It took me much longer to follow him, though I was as tired as I'd ever been.

I woke the next morning to the sound of Samuel in the kitchen, asking why I was in his bed and what was wrong with my own bed and where was Esther.

"I don't know why Ellie is in your bed," my mother said. "We'll ask her when she wakes up. And Esther is up on the top of the mountain with Miss Cate, helping to look after her for a bit. Now, sit down and eat your porridge."

"Porridge? I'd rather eat a giant spider."

"I traded Mrs. Lockhart a pair of slippers for some maple syrup to sweeten it up," my mother said, "but if you'd rather eat a spider, you can do that."

It sounded like a good morning. Better than most since my father's accident. And I wanted to lie still and listen to it unfold before anything else came along to drag me away.

But then I remembered my father, who needed waking, too.

And Cate's leg. And Esther, waiting.

"I think I'll keep this bed for my own," I called out, eager to be roused by my small, rumpled brother before I set out once again to make myself useful.

"That's my bed!" Samuel cried, racing in to wrestle me out onto the floor. He shoved his legs under the covers and pulled them up to his chin.

"Then that's my maple syrup," I said, heading for the kitchen while he scrambled to beat me to the table.

"What's for Maisie?" I said as I pulled on my boots.

"I'm stewing up the last of the venison, but I saved some for her."

I dragged my jacket on over my nightdress. "Will you come with me this time?"

"To see Maisie?" She handed me an old, battered skillet that had lost its handle. "I added some gravy. But it's time for her to be hunting again. Put her out after she eats. The puppies will be fine without her for a while."

I stared at her. "Is that your way of telling me I'll be fine on my own, too?"

She stared back at me. "Oh. You meant go with you up-mountain?"

"It won't take long. It's not so far."

She turned back to the stove. "No, Ellie. Your father needs me here."

"But you were ready to go last night when Captan came down with that doll."

"I know. But your father could wake up again while we're gone and I can't very well leave Samuel alone with him. Besides, she has family of her own."

"She has one boy only."

"And you're one girl, doing more for her than anyone. And now Esther, too. And you want me to get involved as well?"

"What about Larkin's mother?"

She threw a log in the stove and latched the door. "What about her?"

"She's Keavy," I said.

"Which is just a name, Ellie. She's not actually a mandolin." She began to pump water into the kettle. "I've never seen a person with less music in her."

Which I understood. Which was true. For now, that was true. But I thought my mother was being hard-hearted.

Especially when, just the night before, she had seemed newly soft.

"Since Daddy got hurt, you haven't played once or sung really at all," I said carefully.

My mother put the kettle on the stove, too hard, and stood with her back to me for a long moment.

Then she said the same thing Samuel had said not so many days before. "You're twelve, Ellie. What do you know about it?"

I spent some time thinking about what she meant by *it* while she stood warming her hands over the kettle.

Then I said, "I know what it's like to try to change something sad and awful."

She turned from the stove and looked at me.

"I suppose you do," she said, too much weariness in her voice. "But I won't leave your father to go up that mountain with you."

Which was all right, really. Going back to Cate's alone was something I could do, so I would do it. But I would miss the chance to unspool the thread that kept my mother bound to where she was.

And then she said the thing that made me sorry for pushing so hard: "I already have enough sad and awful as it is."

"I'll go with you, Ellie," Samuel said from the doorway.

And I loved him even more.

"You'll do no such thing," my mother said. "You, at least, will do your lessons and your chores today. That's what you'll do. You"— she looked back at me—"you do whatever you want. But send your sister down here again. Miss Cate isn't the only one who needs some help."

"I'll feed Maisie," Samuel said, still watching us. "And I'll look after the puppies."

I handed him the skillet. "She'll be glad to see you. And tell Quiet I'll be back soon."

Before I left, I went to see my father.

My mother had turned him onto his side and propped him there to take the weight off his back for a while.

I knelt next to the bed and looked straight into his slack face.

The pillow by his mouth was wet with his drool.

"You woke up once," I said. "You need to wake up again." I kissed his forehead. It should have been warmer. "When I come back, we're going to start all over again. Not just me. You, too."

But if he heard me, he showed no sign of it.

Chapter Fifty-Three

I got dressed. Ate my porridge in a few big bites. Packed a fresh jar for gathering honey. Made sure I had my work gloves. My flint. My knife.

My mother watched me. "Does she have any food up there?"

"Some. I don't know. But I saw grain. Some dried apples. And there's the bread and jerky I took up yesterday, if they haven't eaten it all. She must have more, stored somewhere."

I thought of the shed behind the cabin and what might be in it. Larkin bringing her what he could. That garden, and what might have grown there. The snares she set.

"Even so, put the last of that porridge in a crock."

There. That was what I needed. To hear her say such things.

I packed everything in my pack and hung it from my shoulder.

I looked at Samuel, who had come back in from the woodshed and was humming and swinging his feet as he finished his breakfast.

"Keep Daddy company while I'm gone."

"I will," he said solemnly.

"And don't forget to check on the puppies, too, and give Maisie plenty of water."

He shook his head. "I won't."

"And don't go wandering off anywhere."

"Ellie, stop being so bossy," he said, glaring at me. "You sound like Esther."

Which set me back a step or two.

"I have to go now," I said slowly, my mind already on its way. I started to say *Be good* but stopped myself and said, "Goodbye," instead.

"I'm going to bring Frank in to visit with Daddy." Samuel scraped the last bit of porridge up and into his mouth.

"Who's Frank?"

"The puppy with the white paw," Samuel said.

I opened my mouth to ask why he had chosen *Frank*, but instead I said, "It's not a good idea to name puppies we have to give up."

At which he gave me his usual scowl. "You got to name Quiet."

I nodded. "Yes, I did. That's how I know."

And my mother turned to look at me before I went out the door.

I had intended to stay away from Quiet, since spending time with him would just make it harder to let him go, but I stopped in the woodshed before heading up the mountain again.

"Hey, little one," I said as I picked him up and held his nose against mine.

Maisie had licked the skillet clean and was grooming her paws, the other puppies staggering around the nest in search of her. She looked at them fondly but stayed right where she was.

I didn't know how she managed to be such a good mother with no one to teach her how.

"Go on out for a bit," I told her. "Go on. Go have a run. They'll be all right."

I opened the door and coaxed her outside, where the sunlight made her sneeze and yawn.

Quiet had wrapped his soft legs around my hand and was trying to suck on my finger.

"How in the world am I going to give you up?" I whispered.

One more thing I didn't know how to do. One more thing I would have to do in order to learn how to do it.

I didn't see Captan on my climb.

I had thought to go straight down the other side of the mountain to find Larkin and, with him, the honey we might need if Cate's leg festered again. But I went to check on Cate first, to see how she and Esther had fared while I was gone, hoping she was enough improved that we could leave the honey to the bees.

The yard was empty when I got there, but for its dead garden and its cold firepit and those empty clothes hanging limp on the line.

I pictured Cate as I'd first found her. Her long, ratty hair. Her thick yellow nails. The candle stubs burned out on her floor. The maggots and the blowflies. Such sad company.

And I felt tired just thinking about her life alone.

But when I went into the cabin this time, it was nothing like that.

Now, on the hearth that had been black and cold, there was an orange-and-yellow fire having a spirited conversation with a birch log.

A skillet bridging the hearth bricks sizzled with jerky and what smelled like pumpkin seeds browning.

The books on the desk stood in tidy stacks, the jars on the shelves were lined up from small to large, and Captan sat by the fire, his coat smooth. No burrs at all.

Cate lay propped up in her bed, in her clean nightdress, her blanket smooth and straight, her hair in a neat braid that wound its way over her shoulder to flaunt a bow fashioned from a strip of rag.

Her hands gleamed with oil in the firelight, their nails short again.

"Doesn't she look better?" Esther said, going to sit on the edge of the bed.

"Civilized," Cate said, smiling tiredly. "She's made me tidy again."

And for a moment, I felt stupid and small as I looked around at what Esther had managed while I was gone.

But then I looked more closely at Cate lying so still and calm and clean in her bed.

Her collarbone—the cleft in it just there, at the base of her neck—looked so fragile that I thought of songbirds and mice and rabbits, but old ones. Thin ones. The ones who, in fairy tales, always had important things to say.

Except she wasn't saying anything as she lay there and gazed up at me.

Her cheeks were too rosy. Her eyes too bright.

And there was something about her smile that worried me. It looked like a lot of work, that smile.

I laid my hand on her cheek.

"Can you move away?" I said to Esther, who stayed where she was, frowning. "Please, let me see her leg."

"Ellie, she's fine," Esther said. "Look at her."

"Are you fine?" I said.

"I don't know," Cate said. "Perhaps not as fine as I look."

"She has a fever again," I said, pushing Esther aside. I drew the blanket down and worked open the knots holding the bandages in place.

The cloth, inside where it was knotted, was still damp.

"Bone-dry," I said. "These should have been *bone-dry.*"

"Why?" Esther snapped. "What does it matter?"

"What happens to a bedsheet left wet?"

She grew still. "It molders."

When I pulled the bandages away, Cate's wound gaped open like a little swamp, just as green and foul.

"Oh dear Lord," Esther said, her hand over her mouth. She stepped back from the bed so suddenly that she nearly tripped over a chair.

And I rushed to the shelf of jars, searching for the one that held the maggots, but when I found it and carried it to the fire I could see only a cluster of cocoons inside. Flies inside those, waiting to emerge.

"No grubs," I said.

I handed the jar to Esther, who nearly dropped it.

I went back to kneel by Cate's bed.

"Is it so bad?" she said, craning her neck to look down along her body.

"It is. I don't know how, so quickly, but it is."

"The germ was still there," she said. "The honey was working, but the germ was still there." She closed her eyes.

"So what do we do?" I asked, trying to keep my face calm.

"Perhaps you need to cut all that part away," she said, swallowing hard. "If you think you can do that."

"Cut it away?" I tried to picture that. "But I was on my way for honey when I stopped here. I'll go for it now, straightaway. Before we try anything else."

She gave me a sad look. "I'm sorry I wrecked what you and Larkin did. Bathing like that. Falling like that." She turned to Esther. "You didn't do this, child. Wet bandages didn't do this."

"I'm still sorry," Esther whispered. She stood away from us, her hands tucked under her chin.

For the first time I noticed that her hair was untidy, her face tired. I imagined her sleeping on the floor, getting up to tend the fire, afraid of whatever was beyond the cabin door.

"She's right," I said. "You're not a fisher cat, Esther. You didn't do this."

I turned back to Cate. "So will we try honey again?" I hated the thought of cutting her. I hated the thought of being the one to do that, though I would if I had to.

She sighed. "I wouldn't mind that, if the bees can spare some."

"Not a doctor?"

She closed her eyes. After a long moment, she said, "If we sent someone right this minute, it would still be a day or more before he could get here."

Her lips quivered and I could feel her trembling as I pulled the blanket back up to her chin.

I wondered if she was thinking of her husband, the doctor. Or her son, who had died so quickly.

"Clean up her leg," I said to Esther. "I'll be back as soon as I can."

Chapter Fifty-Four

I hurried past the spring and down a path made as much by boy as deer, down and around until, through the trees, I saw where Larkin lived.

The cabin was a big one, with a stone chimney, ringed with gardens in patches like someone had sewn them there, just so, and old maple trees that would cast green shade in the heat of summer, red and gold when autumn came.

I hadn't expected anything so fine.

But as I came out of the trees, I saw a grave under one of the maples.

Larkin was chopping wood at the far edge of the yard.

As I went toward him, he looked up, saw me, and put down his ax.

He glanced toward the cabin and came quickly across the clearing to meet me.

His face was yellow and green now, along with the black and blue.

"I thought I'd see you at my grandmother's again, not here," he said, looking over his shoulder.

"You would have, if you'd been there. I've gone back twice."

"I was there last night. I spent some time with her. And Esther. She seemed fine."

I didn't know which *she* he meant, but the thought of him and Esther and Cate together in the firelight, talking and laughing, made me sad and sore.

He ducked his head. "My mother has had a lot of work for me to do, but I planned to go back up soon."

"She's not fine, Larkin. She's sick again. Her leg is festering again and she has fever. We need more honey."

Which was when his mother came out of the cabin and across the yard toward us, saying, "I thought I told you to stay away from my boy."

But I wasn't scared of her anymore. No matter how dark her eye.

"My mother has a mandolin named for you," I said. "She hasn't played it since my father got hurt. Did you know that? That my father was hurt? That he's been asleep for months now? No, I didn't think so. But you don't want to know about things like that. Or that Miss Cate is sick up there. Or that Larkin here is just as sad as you are. Except he's not mean. Not at all."

Which stopped her in her tracks, though it didn't shut her mouth. "You think I'm mean?" she said, though she didn't yell it and there wasn't quite as much darkness in her eye.

"I need honey," I said. "For Miss Cate's leg. Which is festering terribly. And I don't want to have to cut off the bad part, and she doesn't want that either, so can Larkin please take me to the hive to get what we need?"

She pinched her lips shut for a moment. "There's some justice in that," she finally said. "If she dies of something she can't fix."

And I knew she was talking about how Larkin's father had died. "See, that's what I'm talking about," I said impatiently. "That's just mean. When that's not what we need right now."

She glared at me for a long moment. Then she sighed. "There's no honey. Not in our hive. I was just there, not two days ago, and it's dead. Every bee."

I was shocked at the idea of that. A whole hive dying. "But, *why*?"

I sounded like Samuel.

She looked at me in surprise. "Things die. No reason to it."

"Maybe too wet," Larkin said. "Maybe mites. Maybe something robbed them and they starved."

I thought of the honey I'd taken from the hive by the river.

"Don't you have any of your own?" I said. "From last summer?"

"We might," Larkin said, his eyes wide. And off he ran, into the cabin, then came slowly back again with a jar in his hand.

"Nowhere near enough," he said, tipping the jar into the sun so we could see the thin golden film in the bottom of it.

I knew that our own honey was much the same, spent on Christmas.

I couldn't imagine Cate dying for lack of honey, though maybe any reason, even that one, was better than none. "We could go for the doctor," I said.

"Who will want to be paid," Larkin's mother said. "In real money. Do you have any of that?"

To which I said nothing.

"Nor do I," she said. "Not enough."

"We could offer something in trade," I said. "When my father got hurt, my mother paid the doctor with a silver locket."

She lifted her chin. "Do you see a silver locket?"

I looked at the fine cabin. "You must have something you could trade. A mandolin?"

"No," she barked. "I have just one left and I'll not trade it away." Though I knew she would, in an instant, if it were Larkin who was sick. "Besides, it would take too long for a doctor to get here." Something she clearly knew, as Cate had known. Something that brought the darkness back to her face.

She turned and went into the cabin.

But she did not drag Larkin with her.

"Will you come with me?" I said.

"To the other hive? The one where you went before?"

I shook my head. "I already took most of what they had."

"Then where?"

"Maybe the other families have some."

He frowned. "And if they don't?"

I thought of the pail of cold water on the cabin step. The bear on the path. Captan. And everything else that had brought me to this moment. This fresh chance to be of use.

"I don't know. But I'd rather ask for it and get none than cut Miss Cate's leg without ever asking."

Larkin must have heard something in my voice. Something that echoed what he was surely telling himself.

With a last glance at the cabin, he said, "Then let's be quick about it, or it will be for nothing."

Chapter Fifty-Five

We stopped first at the Andersons', where Mrs. Anderson came rushing to the door when I banged, perhaps too hard, and asked her for honey without saying why.

She looked past me at Larkin, who stood in the yard, a little distance away, his face hidden in the shadow of his hat.

"Who's that?" she whispered. Mrs. Anderson was so thin that she'd once traded five blueberry pies to my father to make a Sunday smock that didn't swallow her whole.

I remembered thinking she should have just eaten the pies herself and filled out the smock she had, but I was happy with any arrangement that let me eat pie for days on end.

"That's Larkin," I said.

"Who?"

"He's from the other side."

"The other side of what?" As if we lived on the moon and could not fathom the side we couldn't see.

"The mountain," I said, as patiently as I could.

"Oh." She looked a little confused. "And what will you give me for the honey?"

I hadn't expected to pay for it, even in trade, and I had no time to bicker, so "My thanks," I said. "And whatever I have to give that's mine, down the road. But I need the honey now. As much as you've got."

Which wasn't much, in the end, but more than I had.

I watched as she spooned perhaps a smidgen, no more than a dollop, from her own jar into mine.

"I'll have you muck out the chicken coop for that," she called as we hurried off down the path.

"I will," I called back. "I promise."

The Petersons came next, with much the same result. No more than a tablespoon.

"The honey's a fair trade for the balsam that sealed Scotch's hoof," Mr. Peterson said thoughtfully. "So consider us even."

He looked at Larkin, who stood a little away.

"You're from here?" Mr. Peterson asked him.

To which Larkin said, "Since before your grandfather was born."

I expected some feathers to ruffle at that, though none did.

"Smart of you to start out where so many of us are ending up," Mr. Peterson said.

Which apparently sat well with Larkin, who said, "Thank you for the honey."

"Don't thank me," Mr. Peterson said. "It's her honey now. Though why it merits a visit from the pair of you I do not know."

"It's for a good reason," I said, heading off the porch and down the path, Larkin at my heels.

Next, we stopped at the Lockharts', where Mrs. Lockhart said she did, indeed, have some honey but was also the most reluctant to part with it.

"What do you want it for?" she said.

Of all the families on Echo Mountain, the Lockharts were the ones we knew the least. They were farther away, where there was little reason for us to cross paths, and they seldom wanted to barter.

Larkin had said nothing about payment for the tea that Cate had given Mrs. Lockhart for her stomach problems, and I imagined that Mrs. Lockhart had given her nothing in exchange.

Just as she had given nothing in payment to my father when he had mended her feathered church hat, which was molting.

I was surprised, then, when she looked at me standing there on her porch and said, "Honey's not free, you know."

"I need it to heal something," I said.

Larkin stood in the yard near the step to the porch and stared at the ground.

Mrs. Lockhart looked me up and down. "You seem to be in one piece," she said. "And so does he. Is he some kin of yours?"

I almost said no, but I didn't want to say that he was the grandson of the "witch" who had cursed her with a belly stone—though part of me wanted to put that notion to rest. And I felt the time ticking more quickly the longer we were away. So I said, "Yes, he is. Come to visit."

"To help with your father?" she whispered.

I nodded. "So will you share some honey, Mrs. Lockhart?"

"It's for him, isn't it? Your father?" she said, somewhat softer now.

"For his bedsores," I said, hoping that would turn the key.

But all she said was, "Share? No, I'll not share. But I'll sell."

"For how much?" I said, as if I had money to spend.

"Five trout," she said. "I hear you're quite the fisher-girl."

"Done," I said, holding out my jar.

But she stepped back inside and said, "You'll have my honey when I have the trout," and closed the door in my face.

I stood on the porch, amazed beyond words.

"I told you," Larkin said. "She's one of them."

"One of who?"

"One of them who decide they own something just so they can sell it."

I looked at the too-little honey in the jar. "Just one more family," I said, heading down the path again. "The Neills. Closest to the river."

"No. We're taking too long and the Neills aren't likely to have any honey. But the bees still do."

"Larkin, I told you. I already took what they had to spare."

When he stopped, I stopped.

"Here's the thing about bees," he said. "They die. Winter's too cold, they die. Too wet, they die. We take their honey, they die. It's all the same."

I shook my head. "My father told me I should always leave some for the bees."

"And if he were awake to ask, he'd say maybe not this time. Especially when it's springtime and the flowers are in bloom and, with them, more honey."

"If the bees live long enough to make more."

"Which they might. Which they probably will, Ellie."

And there was something so sad in his eyes, so broken, that I felt broken, too.

"All right," I finally said. "As long as we spend it on Cate, we should take what honey we can."

Chapter Fifty-Six

"That's quite a flint," Larkin said when I took the spearhead from my pocket and opened my knife.

I held it up. "It sure is," I said. "Used to be bigger, but I've worn it down some. I'd like to know who made it."

"People here long before us."

I liked that. That he had said *us*.

He watched as I collected some tinder and showered it with sparks until there, a thread of smoke. I bent low and blew gently, gently until a small flame leaped out of the smoke like a bright tongue from a gray beard.

We watched as it caught, grew, consumed the twigs we fed it and asked for more.

I tended it carefully until it was big enough to handle a stick we'd use to smoke the hive.

"That's good work," Larkin said to me.

"Thank you," I said. "The hive's pretty close to the ground, but since you're taller, would you mind being the one to reach in?"

At which he smiled ruefully. "Oh, the curse of tallness."

"Except you have no gloves," I said. I pulled mine from my pack. "And I don't think these will fit you."

He tried to pull them on.

"Not quite," he said.

I sighed. "Oh, the curse of smallness."

Which made him smile again.

But I wasn't smiling when I did as I had done before, emptying my pack so I could wear it as a hood.

Larkin helped me tuck my sleeves into my gloves, my pant legs into my boots, the hood into my collar.

I'm sure I looked stupid and funny, but neither of us laughed.

Larkin directed me toward the tree and then told me to wait while he slipped the hot branch into the hole and filled the hive with smoke, and then he rushed away to wait up the path at a safe distance.

It went much as it had the other times.

I stumbled back with all the comb that was left in the hive, most of the bees stunned by the smoke but some dying as they attacked my thick gloves and a few coming after me, dying on my clothes, my hood, though some made their way through a gap in my collar to die on my neck as they stung me.

And I cried as I had before. From all that hard, unnecessary pain. Mine. Theirs. Except it *was* necessary. We had decided that it was necessary, Larkin and I. But that didn't mean I couldn't cry as I lurched out of the undergrowth, saying *sorry sorry sorry*, and huddled on the path, waiting for the bees to give up and go home to what was left of their hive.

I felt their misery, which was much too big for such tiny animals, and their fury and their confusion. But, most of all, I felt their hunger.

And I was determined all over again to make Cate well.

When I finally pulled off the hood, I found Larkin coming cautiously back down the path toward me.

"Are you all right?" he said.

And I would have said yes if a last bee had not just then come to spin a halo around my head and kill itself on my neck where three other stings were already swelling.

"No," I sobbed, swiping the bee away. "I'm not all right."

So he put his arms around me while I cried some more.

As it turned out, a boy like Larkin was a fine antidote to bee venom.

"Okay," I said after a bit. "I'm okay now." I put the honey jar and everything else back in my pack. Smoothed my wild hair and wiped my wet face.

I rubbed the tears on my neck.

They did little to soothe the hot, bumpy terrain of my poor skin, though their cool saltiness helped for a moment.

Bee venom, even in a bee-sized dose, was a sharp and painful business, more shocking than a burn or a hard slap.

But it also infused, in me, a good kind of sharpness. A keenness. As if the poison were medicine as well, brewed from the best the mountain had to offer: something ancient and pure and perfect.

Larkin looked at me curiously as I smiled.

He didn't know what I'd just decided to do.

And then we hurried off toward home with a jar full of honeycomb and a few furious bees trying their best to bore straight through the glass.

Chapter Fifty-Seven

To get to the hive, we had taken a path from the Lockharts' that cut through the woods well below home, but we were now on the one that took us straight there.

"We'll stop there for a minute before we go back up," I said.

"No time for that. We should be getting back."

"I know, but my mother won't forgive me if we go straight past without stopping. And there's something I need to do for my father."

"Ellie, we need to get back up-mountain. And I expect your mother won't thank you for bringing home a stranger."

"Don't worry. This will only take a minute. Besides, you're not a stranger."

"Even worse. One meeting, and it was a bad one."

"Not because of anything you did."

He shrugged. "Even so."

I wasn't likely to knock on my own door, but I wanted to give my mother some warning that I had brought Larkin home with me, so I called out, "Mother!" as soon as we got there and then waited just inside the door until she came.

"Oh!" she said at the sight of him. "Larkin. Come in." And then, before he had a chance to say a word, she blurted, "I have one of your father's mandolins."

He smiled. "My father never knew what became of them, after they left him."

I thought that was a very lonely thing to say.

"She used to play it all the time," I said.

He raised his eyebrows at the *used to*.

"Oh, I've just been busy lately," my mother said. She didn't seem aware of how her fingers plucked at her skirt. The collapse of her face.

And then Samuel came running out of nowhere, yelling, "He opened his eyes, Ellie!"

And I felt myself swell like a blossom.

But my mother put up her hand, her own eyes closed, and said, "He means Quiet."

I could not recall ever feeling so disappointed over something I'd wanted so badly.

"Not Daddy?"

She shook her head. "He's the same."

"I went out to the shed to give Maisie some water and Quiet looked up at me!" Samuel was fairly dancing. "Come see."

"That's awfully soon for a puppy to open his eyes," I said doubtfully.

Samuel made a face. "He wanted to see us, Ellie. And Quiet's different from the others."

Something I'd known since I'd pulled him, dripping and squirming, from a bucket of well water just days before.

"Where's Esther?" my mother said, looking past us and through the open door.

"Still up there," I said. "Miss Cate's leg is worse and we had to come down for honey again."

"I don't understand." She looked more and more confused. "Esther stayed on?"

I said, "Yes, Mother. She wanted to."

Which made her sigh and shake her head.

Samuel pulled on my hand. "Come see Quiet!"

"Just for a minute," I said. "Miss Cate's waiting."

He led us out to the woodshed and pointed at Quiet, who was the only one of the litter to raise his head toward us, blinking, as we came in from the sunlight.

Maisie, standing over the pups, stared at us uncertainly.

"It's all right, girl," I said. "It's just Larkin."

Who got down slowly onto his knees and held out his hand.

Maisie looked at me. I nodded. So she went to him, sniffed his hand, looked at me again.

He peered at the pups. "They're much like Captan was as a puppy. Do you know who their sire is?"

I shook my head.

"I believe I do," he said thoughtfully. "Unless there's some other brindled dog on this mountain."

"Huh," I said. "You think Captan is Quiet's daddy?" I liked that.

"Who's Captan?" Samuel said.

"Do you remember that dog on the path? The one with the rabbit in his mouth?"

"Yes, I do," Samuel said. "Is he Quiet's daddy?"

"Maybe so." I picked Quiet up and looked him in the eye. "You do have some of Captan in you, I think. I bet you'll look a lot like him when you grow up." But then I remembered, all over again, that Quiet was not to be mine. That I would not see him grow up, except perhaps from a distance. "I hope you'll be like him."

"Brindled?" Samuel said.

"Strong enough," I said.

Larkin climbed to his feet. "For what?"

"For anything," I said, holding Quiet closer.

While Samuel was busy with the other puppies, I pulled the footstool below the high shelf where I'd hidden Larkin's carvings.

"Look," I whispered to him, tipping my head up toward the shelf.

So he stepped onto the stool and looked at what I'd hidden there. For a long moment, he simply looked.

Then he climbed down and pushed the stool away.

"You missed a few," he said.

"What? I didn't find them all?"

He shook his head. "I made a fox. And a bear cub." He thought back. "And a box turtle."

"But where?" I hated to think that he'd made me such things and I'd missed them. That they were out there in harm's way when they should have been with the others, safe. Mine.

"You'll have to find them yourself," he said. He sounded . . . unhappy.

"What's wrong?" I said, leading him out of the woodshed, Quiet asleep in my arms.

He shrugged. "Why are you hiding them?"

Which surprised me a little, coming from a boy who had given those gifts in secret, much as I had kept them that way.

I thought about how it had felt to find them, one by one, and to think that they were meant for me. To think that someone understood what they would mean to me. To think that someone understood *me*.

"Finding those carvings, keeping them to myself, how mysterious it all was . . . made me . . . happy," I said, looking away.

I waited.

"So is it all right?" he said. "Or is it ruined now? Knowing me without the trees in between."

I smiled at him. "It's not ruined," I said. "Let's go see my father."

Chapter Fifty-Eight

"Where are you going?" my mother said as I led Larkin past the kitchen table where she'd laid out two buns stuffed with jerky and dried apples.

"Just for a minute, to see Daddy," I said, the bees buzzing in my pack, Quiet nesting in my arms.

Larkin gave her an apologetic look. "If that's all right with you, ma'am."

"I, well . . . it's just . . ." She gave me a stern look. "I thought you were in a hurry, Ellie?"

"We are, but this won't take more than a minute. I want to introduce them, is all."

To which she said nothing. But she went along with us as we headed toward the bedroom.

I led Larkin through the door.

When he followed me in, he went not to the bed but, after a moment, straight to the corner of the room where he picked up my mother's mandolin as if it were made of glass.

He carried it to the window. Tipped it in the light and looked inside for the maker's mark.

When he turned to my mother, I had a hard time deciding which of their faces was the more stricken.

"If you don't want this anymore, I'll trade you anything for it." He sounded as if he had something stuck in his throat.

My mother went to him. Took the mandolin in her arms and held it against her chest.

"What in the world makes you think I don't want it anymore?"

"You don't play it."

"That doesn't mean I don't want it."

She put the mandolin back in the corner.

And then she left without another word.

Larkin watched her go. Then he turned to my father.

Since the doctor had come months earlier, no one else outside my family had been allowed to see my father, and it was odd to watch Larkin as he went curiously toward the bed.

"Daddy, this is Larkin, who lives on the mountain. On the other side. He's helping me help that woman who told you to put a leech on your ear."

I didn't expect an answer, and I didn't get one. His face was as pale as a candle, his skin just as waxy, and he was more still than a stump.

"I'm sorry I haven't been to see you lately," I said. I was sorry, too, that I had tried nothing to wake him since he'd rolled his eyes. But I would do something now, though it frightened me.

I tucked Quiet alongside my father's neck.

It was amazing how different the little dog looked now that his eyes were open.

Larkin moved around me so he could see the place where the tree had hit my father's head. "That's quite a scar."

I glanced up and found him looking not at my father but at me, as if I were the one who'd been hurt.

"Yes."

He didn't take his eyes off my face. "Trees don't usually fall on the person cutting them down."

I blinked too many times. "Not usually," I said.

I pulled the blanket up over Quiet and my father. To Quiet, I whispered, *"Teach Daddy how to open his eyes while we're gone."*

Which sounded too much like a lullaby, such gentle talk.

I put my hand on my father's scar. "Everyone thinks I'm the one who caused this," I said, without looking at Larkin. "They think I was in the way when the tree fell. They think my father ran to save me. That *he* got hurt instead of me." I swallowed, but my throat stayed just as tight. "I'm pretty sure my sister would have preferred that I was the one hit by the tree."

"Oh, that's not likely," Larkin said.

I shook my head. "It doesn't matter. He's hurt, all the same."

Larkin frowned at me. "You said people think you were in the way of that tree."

"They do."

"You didn't say that you really were in the way."

I wiped the tears from my eyes before they could fall. "But I wasn't. Samuel was. And my sister was supposed to be watching him." I looked up at Larkin. "Imagine Esther knowing she's the reason Samuel was in harm's way."

Larkin didn't move. Didn't blink. He looked at me steadily, his face serious.

I said, "Imagine Samuel knowing he's the reason his daddy got hurt."

But Larkin shook his head. "Imagine a girl deciding to take a blame that isn't hers."

I turned back to my father. I hated the way his skin pulled hard across the bones of his face, as if someone were making him into a drum. As if he were hollow. As if someone was supposed to hit him to make any music at all.

I thought of things like skunk stink and horseradish.

I went to the pack I'd left by the door.

The bees inside the honey jar were pulsing quietly on the comb, their feelers sweeping the air as I looked at them through the glass.

"What are you doing?" Larkin asked.

"No more lullabies," I said, shaking the jar as I went back to stand beside my poor father.

And then I unscrewed the lid and quickly put the mouth of the jar up against his temple where there was nothing between the bees and his brain but flesh and blood.

Chapter Fifty-Nine

At first, the bees simply tumbled across my father's temple, looking for a way past the rim of the jar where it pressed against his skin, but when I rapped my knuckles against the glass and bent low with a quick shout, they both stung my father and died doing it, protecting a comb they'd already lost, their church-window wings going still, their fuzzy bodies broken, poor little unlucky things that they were.

"I'm sorry," I whispered as I pulled the jar free and gently swept them away with my fingertip.

And, just like that, twin lumps rose up on my father's temple.

I watched my father's eyes, hoping they would roll, hoping they would open.

And that was when he groaned.

Not loudly. He didn't wail. But the sound that came up out of him was the first one he'd made since the accident.

"Daddy!" I said, patting his cheek lightly. "Daddy, wake up."

He groaned again as my mother came through the door.

"What was that?" she said as she hurried to the bed.

Which was when my father groaned again and turned his head just a little.

"What did you do?" she whispered.

"Bee sting." Though it was more than those two words. It was every single thing I'd learned along the way.

I pressed the back of my hand against his cheek. He was not as cold as he'd been.

"Good Lord," my mother said. "Good Lord, Ellie. I should be angry."

I moved aside so she could come close to lay her hand on my father's forehead. And then she kissed it and said, "Ethan? Ethan?"

But he was still and quiet again, though his eyes were crimped a little at the corners.

We waited, watching, barely breathing, but my father didn't surface again.

I put the lid back on the honey jar.

Larkin looked at me.

"One more minute," I said.

Nothing.

"I don't know why he won't wake up all the way. I don't understand."

My mother sighed. "It's what the doctor said, Ellie. His body knows what it needs."

But I knew that a person was more than just a body.

We waited.

Larkin said, "I'm sorry, Ellie, but we need to go now. Or I can take the honey and you can stay."

I imagined Esther pulling apart the edges of the rotten wound while Larkin squeezed the honey into it.

"No, I'll go with you."

My mother frowned at me, clearly confused. "Just like before. You do something meant to wake him and then you leave."

"Miss Cate's sick." I plucked Quiet out from the shadow of my father's chin and handed him to Larkin. "But I have other some-things to try when I get back."

I put the honey jar back in my pack, my pack on my shoulder, and took a long, last look at my father.

Then we all returned to the kitchen in time to see Samuel fin-ishing the last of my sandwich.

"Here," I said, nodding at Quiet, who was trying to gnaw a but-ton off Larkin's shirt. "Take him back to Maisie."

"But I want to keep him here for a while," he said, pulling Quiet up against his cheek.

"And Maisie wants him back."

Larkin picked up his sandwich, tore it in half, and gave some to me. "A pup will be more yours if you let him choose to be."

"Aw, it doesn't matter. Quiet is Ellie's dog until he's old enough to be Mr. Anderson's."

Larkin squinted at me. "The Anderson woman was the one who gave you honey for chores?"

I nodded.

"And Quiet's to be theirs?"

"For hunting," I said. "All of the puppies. In exchange for a milk cow."

"A fair trade," my mother said.

"It is not," I said, flaring like a new wick.

"Either way," Larkin said, "Quiet will decide whose dog he is. Just like his daddy did."

Chapter Sixty

We ate our small lunch as we walked.

"What did you mean back there?" Larkin said. "No more lullabies?"

I knew that the answer would make me sound mean, but it was the truth, so I said, "My mother and my sister thought the best way to wake my father was to be gentle and quiet and calm. Like they could tempt him awake with flowers and soft talk."

"But you thought otherwise?"

I nodded. "I imagined myself in his place, hearing nothing but good things. If it were me, I'd come back faster if I thought something was wrong. If somebody needed something."

"Or if someone hurt you?"

That took me aback. "The bee stings were the first hurt I gave him." I reminded Larkin about the other things I'd tried so far.

"You really put a snake in his bed?" There was some admiration in his voice.

"I thought if he heard Esther screaming about the snake, he might come back to save her."

He made a little *I see* sound. "The way he tried to save Samuel from the treefall."

"Yes." We walked for a while in silence. Then, "Has your mother ever been inside Cate's cabin?"

He thought for a moment. "Not since my grandma went to live there. But before that, yes. All the time." He kept climbing as he talked, and his voice was tired. "That little cabin was where my daddy made his mandolins."

I stopped.

After a moment, he did, too. He turned to look at me.

"Why would he have a place up there when he could have made them right close by where you lived?"

"He tried that, but his luthing got all mixed up with everything else. And he liked the idea of a place that was for nothing but one thing." He smiled sadly. "Plus, my mother hated the smell of the hide glue. Even when it was hot, though it wasn't so bad then. I think she hated the thought that it was made from deer. She loved deer coming through the trees below the cabin."

"So he made his mandolins on the mountaintop?" I loved that. The very thought of it.

Larkin nodded. "The cabin was left over from when my grandma lived up there, when she was a little girl. Before her people built something better."

He turned and started to climb again.

"I used to love spending time with my father in that little cabin. Watching him work. He would let me help when little fingers worked better than big ones."

"And that's where Cate went, after your father died?"

He nodded. "After we buried him. I went looking for her. And I found her sitting among his tools. Just sitting there. The hide glue had rotted and the place stank. But she just sat there in that stink, crying like a baby."

I tried to imagine that. Then I tried not to.

"I asked her to come back. But she said she'd be fine, and I think she really did want to be alone." He was silent for a while. "No, my mother has never gone back in that cabin since my father died. I took all my grandma's books and other things up there, one box at a time." He paused again. "And Captan chose her, so she had him, too."

We made the rest of the climb in silence.

Captan met us in Cate's yard.

He didn't make a sound, either.

"How is she?" I asked him.

At which he turned and led us to the cabin so we could see for ourselves.

Chapter Sixty-One

She was worse.

"What took you so long?" Esther said the moment we walked through the door.

She was sitting next to the bed, holding Cate's hand.

"We had to go to a lot of places for the honey," I said. "And we stopped at home on the way back, to see Daddy." I wasn't going to lie about that. "But we're here now and we have enough for her leg."

Esther stood up. "I cleaned it out with the old bandages." She swallowed hard. "And then I burned them."

Which explained the smell in the cabin. Part good hot fire. Part corruption.

I thought of those bandages, which had once been sleeves my father had made and, before that, bolted muslin, and, before that, cotton on a loom, from a plant known to draw blood from the hands that picked it.

"Her fever's bad," Esther said. She frowned at Larkin. "Why didn't you come up before now? Ellie could have gone for honey without you."

Before he could reply, I said, "Stop that, Esther. You only came here yourself because you were scared to be home without Mother."

"But he's her grandson! And I didn't know she was Mrs. Cleary."

"What difference does that make?"

"Hush now," Cate said. She was trembling, her face white and dry. "It doesn't matter."

Larkin said, "You knew her when she was Mrs. Cleary? From town?"

"From when she was a nurse. In Bethel," I said. "But I've changed so much, and she has, too, that we didn't recognize each other."

"But you haven't," Larkin said, looking at Esther.

"Haven't what?"

"Changed."

"Yes, she has," I said, looking steadily at my sister. "She cleaned out that wound with no one here to teach her how."

I took the honey jar from my pack.

"You found some honey?" Cate said.

"Yes." I nodded. "If, by *found*, you mean wrangled some in exchange for cleaning a chicken coop and then stole the rest from a hive." I craned my neck so she could see where I'd been stung.

"More spunk," she said. "That's good."

Larkin pulled the blanket off Cate's leg.

The wound, clean now, was still a dirty mess and, despite myself, I wished again for maggots.

I gave the honey to my sister. "I'll pull back the edges," I said, nodding at the wound. "You squeeze the honey in, Esther."

After a long moment of *no*, Esther slowly dumped the whole

comb out into her hand and carefully squeezed it over the wound. "Like this?"

"Just like that," I said.

While we worked, Cate trembled and flinched, but she didn't make a sound.

From the corner of my eye, I saw Larkin take her hand.

When I glanced up at his face, I was stunned by the grief I saw there.

I looked around the cabin. "We'll need more bandages. The wash that was on the line. Where is it?"

Esther said, "I put it in the trunk."

I went, found a clean sheet, used my knife to notch it at one end, ripped away three long strips, brought them back to the bed, and wrapped them around Cate's leg, under and around, again and again until I ran out of cloth.

"I took some honeybees to my father so they could sting him," I told her.

"What?" Esther said, looking at me sharply.

Cate looked at me, too, wide-eyed. "To wake him up?"

I nodded.

"Did it work?"

"Some. Not enough."

She settled back against the pillow. "Step by step. That's the way out of something hard."

I smoothed Cate's bandage in place and pulled her blanket over it.

To Esther, I said, "Will you brew some willow bark tea? For her fever?"

"She's already had some," Esther said, wiping her sticky hand on a rag.

"Then give her some more," I said.

"There aren't any more twigs."

"Then go find the tree," I said, trying not to sound impatient. "Willows are thirsty. Look near the spring."

When she'd gone, Larkin said, "Your sister isn't much like you."

Which was true, though it wasn't.

I watched Cate reach out tiredly to run her hand down Captan's back.

"Do you really think Captan is Quiet's daddy?" I asked Larkin.

He nodded. "I do believe he is."

Cate, hearing this for the first time, said, "Who's Quiet?"

I almost said, *My pup.*

"One of the pups at home."

"They look like Captan did when he was young," Larkin said.

Cate smiled. "Must be handsome then."

"They are," he replied. "And spoken for, or I'd ask for one."

"Spoken for?"

"To be hunters," I said. "In exchange for a milk cow."

Which was when Esther came through the door, her fist full of willow twigs like a Quaker bouquet.

Which led Larkin to add another log to the fire.

Which made the kettle hum.

"Last time, the honey worked in a day," I said to Cate, who nodded.

"And it may do the same this time. If not, you'll have to cut me after all." She tried and failed to look brave about that.

"But you can't cut her," Esther said to me, her own voice trembling a little. "You won't need to do that. Will you?"

"Oh, child," Cate said, "it might not come to that."

But then the kettle began to scream.

And Esther turned toward the fire.

And Larkin scraped willow bark into a mug, where the hot water would soften it into medicine.

And I thought of the dead honeybees. And the terror of the snake. And the willow buds withering on the floor, just there by Larkin's feet. And my mother's mandolin, its strings sagging. How lonely Esther seemed. My Quiet, racing after a fawn, his teeth bared. Cate sitting alone in a fog of stink. And Larkin, standing by, appalled, while his father died.

And then Samuel coming out of nowhere, suddenly, the rabbit intent on the trees ahead, Samuel intent on the rabbit, as my father's ax chocked and chocked against the tree, as the tree began to shake and crack, leaning, leaning, its branches frantic as it began to fall, my father stepping back and back, the tree spinning as I began to run, too slowly, toward my sweet, small brother, the tree thrashing overhead as I reached for him . . .

. . . and I felt, more clearly than ever before, my father's hand on my back, pushing me hard. Felt him shove me clear as I swept Samuel into my arms and fell with him, the tree's smallest branches sweeping across us as we fell, my father crashing to the ground behind us, and—

"Ellie, did you hear me?" Esther said, and I came back to myself, to the little cabin, to Esther saying something about going home soon.

"I really was in the way," I whispered.

I looked up to find Cate's eyes on me.

"We have to go home now," I said slowly, standing up, looking around for my things.

Esther said, "I just told you that, Ellie. We need to go."

"No. Not just us," I said. "Cate, too."

Larkin looked at me sharply. "What, sick as she is?"

"And hurt. Yes, I know." I went to the trunk where Cate kept her leggings. Gathered them up. "Which is why we should do every last thing there is to do. Not just what we know to do. And not just what we *think* we know." I thought of my mother on the morning of Quiet's birth. How she had held Maisie's head in her lap and stroked her ears through the long labor. How tenderly she had gathered Quiet up and put him into my hands. And I wondered for the first time if that was how I'd known what to call him: how quietly he had filled her hands, not yet breathing.

Which was when Cate said, "It's a good idea. To take me down the mountain with you."

"But why?" Larkin said. "If you're going anywhere, it should be home with me."

"With Ellie," she said firmly. "To be of use."

We both knew there were many ways to be of use.

I could see a fire in her tired eyes, burning stronger at the very thought of it.

And mine, as well, reflected in her eyes.

Chapter Sixty-Two

I made more bandages from Larkin's sleeves, this time, tied them tight around Cate's wound, and dressed her in leggings and a tunic. Laced up her boots.

She took nothing else with her except the little doll, which she clutched as if it were part of her.

With Larkin on one side of her and me on the other, we managed the path slowly, carefully, stopping often to rest.

At the roughest spots, we had to ease her down as if she were made of glass, bit by bit, careful of her leg.

She trembled like a dog does when thunder's near, but she was clear-headed and clear-eyed and . . . excited.

I could feel that. Her eagerness. And my own fire burning hotter with every step we took toward home.

Esther seemed confused about things in general and said nothing at all as she followed us down the mountain, clutching Cate's biggest book to her chest.

My own pack was filled with other things Cate had told us to bring, like bits cut from the upside-down garden hanging from the roof of her cabin. Things I couldn't name. Not yet.

There were no bears or fisher cats or other wild creatures on the path this time, though I imagined that there would be some wildness in my mother's face when we appeared at the cabin door.

I didn't know where we would put Cate, what we would feed her, but I didn't much care.

I would happily sleep with the dogs in the woodshed. Give up what jerky or eggs or bread were meant for me and eat, instead, what I could harvest from the forest floor: mushrooms and fiddleheads; lamb's-quarters and dandelion leaves; chives and acorns; the taproots of wild carrots.

For I knew, with great clarity and certainty, that there was more I could do to help Cate. I just didn't yet know what that might be.

Nor did I know what next to try for my father.

But I felt that helping one would help the other.

And that we would wake my father, Cate and I. What scared me now was what might come after the waking.

I imagined my father changed. Unable to walk. Confused by who we were.

And I didn't think there was anything in Cate's book that would bring him back from that.

But the closer we got to the cabin, the more I was able to see what the bear saw in the eye of the purple aster, what the crow saw from her topmost nest, what any untamed creature knew from the moment it first opened its eyes: that life is a matter of moments, strung together like rain. To try to touch just one drop at a time, to try to count them or order them or reckon their worth—each by each—was impossible.

To stand in the rain was the thing. To be in it.

Which I would do.

Which I would do to make my father well . . . and to learn him all over again if I had to.

And I wouldn't move from that spot until I did.

There was a reason why I could feel the tree roots wince as we trod on them. Why I had been able to hear the cry of that tree as my father swung his ax, as it fell toward my sweet Samuel, just there, in its twisting shadow, chasing a rabbit across the cold ground.

There had to be.

All I had to do was find it.

Chapter Sixty-Three

We told Captan to stay outside by the cabin door, so he reluctantly lay down and put his head on his paws.

"When we come back, I'll take you to see Maisie," I told him. "And Quiet."

He answered me by raising his eyebrows.

And then we helped Cate inside.

"Who's that?" Samuel whispered when he came around the corner and saw Cate for the first time.

"This is Cate," I said. To Cate, I said, "And this is my brother, Samuel."

"Which is a fine name," Cate said, sagging against me. "For a fine boy. Who I hope will lead me to the nearest chair."

My mother seemed to speak a new language as we filed into the kitchen and sat Cate down at the table.

"What is . . . Can you . . . Ellie, how did . . . ," she said, backing and shifting around us much as Maisie had when I had first touched Quiet.

"I'm sorry we came down uninvited," Cate said.

"Came down?" my mother said, which was an odd question since there we were, in her kitchen, come from above, and no doubt about it.

"From up-mountain," Cate said, and I saw her through my mother's eyes. A shriveled, gray, hunched woman in a tunic and leggings made of deer hide and a pair of worn-out boots, a tattered rag doll in one hand.

"Thank you for the food you sent up," she said to my mother. "Especially the venison stew," though my mother didn't know I'd taken some. "But more than that, thank you for sending your daughters," though we all knew I'd gone of my own accord.

"Ellie's the only one who deserves your gratitude," my mother said, still jangled from our sudden arrival, but also by a new confusion I saw on her face, in the way she clenched her hands.

"And she has it," Cate said, though she hadn't yet told me so.

"I helped," Esther said too loudly. "Didn't I?"

Cate nodded. "You did. And brought me such lovely remembrances."

"Remembrances?" my mother said.

Cate nodded, smiling. She paused. In the silence, nobody said a word. We all watched Cate curiously, as if she were the only one of her kind. And then she said, "Do you not know me?"

My mother leaned closer and looked into those blue old eyes, much as Esther had done.

And then she must have recognized the woman she'd known from Bethel. Who couldn't possibly be this hag, sitting here in our kitchen as if she, too, had come up through the drain hole like a cold snake or fluttered down through the chimney like a lost bird or threaded her way from a stray seed in the floorboards to sprout branches and leaves above the table and through the window into the sunlight.

I watched as my mother reached out a hand and touched Cate's shoulder. *"Mrs. Cleary?"* she said softly.

Cate put her hand over my mother's. "Not much like I was when you knew me, am I?"

My mother smiled, though there were suddenly tears in her eyes. "No, you're not."

"Quite a hag now. Oh, it's all right," she said at the look on my mother's face. "No harm in calling me that. You weren't wrong. It's what I am. Nothing at all wrong with being a hag." She gave me a look. "Nothing wrong with being smart that way. And anyone who thinks otherwise needs to think again." She held out a hand to me, which I took. "I've come to help Ellie. Who is also a hag, you know."

And I, in that moment, became an oak. A snake. A bright bird.

But then Samuel said, "Why can't I be a hag?" and I was a girl again, just like that.

She smiled at him. "I didn't say you couldn't."

"What's a hag?" he said again, just days after Esther had answered with *a witch*.

"I'm a hag," she said.

"Oh." Samuel looked at her for a long moment. "Is there some other kind of hag I could be?"

"Of course," Cate said. "But you might need to grow up for a while first."

He shook his head. "You said Ellie's a hag and she's only twelve."

At which Cate nodded. "Well, some people are born to it. Others, like me, need to work at it for a long time."

When she struggled to rise from her chair, I held out my arm and Larkin came to help. "Now, if you wouldn't mind, I'd like to meet your father, Ellie."

So we slowly made our way back to the bedroom where my father lay sleeping no matter how hard the jonquils outside the window blew their yellow horns.

Cate stopped in the doorway.

I thought she'd been brought up short by the sight of my father.

But after a moment she started forward again, leading us not to him but to my mother's mandolin.

Which Cate picked up carefully. Tenderly.

She smiled at me, my mother. "My son made this."

She hadn't needed to look inside to know that.

I nodded. "Larkin told me."

Cate looked at me, amazed. "Do you play?"

"A little," I said. "My mother does."

Cate turned to her, holding out the mandolin. "And will you?"

"Oh, perhaps later," my mother said, taking the mandolin and setting it aside. "It needs tuning and—"

"Oh, it's all right. I understand," Cate said. I'd never heard her sound so sad.

I pulled the rocking chair close to my father. Larkin settled her in it carefully.

The rest of us took up stations around the bed.

My father was as he'd been. Pale. Still. Thin enough to break.

"You said he's been asleep since January?" Cate said.

"He has," I said.

"Then where's his beard?"

"We shave him, every day," Esther said proudly.

"You shave him?" Cate looked at my mother.

My mother nodded. "Should we not?"

"Oh, it's not a matter of should or should not. I just don't know why you'd bother."

My mother looked confused again. "He has always been a clean-shaven man," she said. "In the beginning, when we didn't shave him, he began to look too—"

"Dirty?" Cate said.

"Wild," my mother said.

Cate shrugged. "Nothing wrong with wild."

It was odd to be in the room with so many people, all of us clustered around the bed looking at my father, as if he were a bug in a jar.

Esther put the big book on the bed. "What do you want to try first?"

But Cate shook her head. "Nothing written down."

She turned to Larkin. "Thank you for taking such good care of me for so long."

And there, in those twelve words, I heard the beginning of some kind of goodbye.

Larkin must have heard the same thing. "I didn't take care of you," he said, his voice trembling. "You took care of me."

She nodded. "Then we're even." Her lips twisted. "But now I wonder if you would go home and look after your mother for a while. I have some things to do here, and they are things best done alone."

Larkin looked stricken. "Without me?"

"I think so." And the tears she'd been holding spilled down her cheeks all at once.

"But I can help."

"Not this time. But, oh, my sweet boy, don't you ever forget how much you've already done. And so much more to come." She held her little doll out toward him.

He took the doll. Thrust it into his pocket and left his hand there with it.

The others must have heard the goodbye now, too, since they all, even Samuel, looked much as Larkin did, though we were not all kin. Though we were.

Then Cate said her old blessing. And again. And a third time, her tears like rain.

Which was when Larkin began to cry, too, bending to hold her in his arms.

"What's that she said?" Samuel whispered.

"That was Gaelic," I said, my throat tight. "It means 'Good health to you and every blessing.'"

"Come along now," my mother said, herding everyone toward the door. "Let's let her work."

When I turned to follow, Cate said, "Not you," and we all turned back.

She beckoned to me. "Not you," she said. "You stay."

Chapter Sixty-Four

When everyone else had left, Cate and I looked at each other for a long time without saying a word.

From beyond the bedroom door, I could hear Samuel yammering away, my mother answering him softly.

Then, from the near distance, came a long, lingering howl.

It was as mournful and wild as any coyote I'd ever heard, but I recognized the voice. And I imagined little Quiet nearby in the woodshed, hearing his father for the first time.

"Oh Captan, my Captan," Cate whispered.

Then a second howl, longer and louder than the first.

I listened to it with every kind of ear I had. "What does that mean?"

"My boy is calling me," she said, her tears starting again.

But I knew what the howl meant. "His name, I meant. *Captan.* Without an *i.* What does that mean?"

"Ah," she said. "I was wondering when you'd ask that. It means 'song.' In the old language of my family, it means song."

An apt name for the dog of a luthier with Gaelic blood in his veins.

"But you know, Ellie . . . and I haven't thought of this in a long time . . . there's a book up in my cabin, something called *Girls Who Became Famous* . . . about, among others, a girl named Florence Nightingale. Do you know who she was?"

"I don't." And I didn't see what that had to do with Captan's name, either.

"She was a nurse. Maybe the most famous nurse, though there aren't that many famous nurses." She closed one eye. "Can't think of a second one, to tell you the truth, and I should know." She opened her eye again. "Her first patient was a sheepdog whose master meant to hang him, over a broken leg." At the look on my face, she said, "Oh, not because he was mean. The thought of hanging that dog brought him to his knees. But because the dog was in such misery, you see."

And I did see that. I saw it clearly. Though I was still waiting to see what any of this had to do with Captan.

"Miss Florence Nightingale, who was not yet a nurse . . . or didn't yet *know* she was a nurse . . . loved animals so much that she decided the dog mustn't hang. And, in the end, he didn't. Because she brought in a doctor, and the broken leg turned out to be a bruised leg, nothing more, which healed rather quickly when Florence dressed it with warm compresses."

Cate looked at me expectantly.

"That's a nice story," I said.

"Isn't it, though?"

She waited.

"But what does it have to do with Captan and his name?"

At which Cate smiled, though she was weary and worn and feverish and hurt. "His name was Cap. The sheepdog. His name was Cap, too, though I learned it long after I'd named Captan."

I smiled, too. "I like that."

She nodded. "Sometimes things seem to happen out of order, or in an order of their own, but they make perfect sense if you don't worry too much about how they ought to line up."

We both spent a moment pondering that.

"And why do you always say 'Oh Captan, my Captan'?"

Cate sighed sadly. "It's from a poem about a great man dying. Only in that case it was Captain. With an *i*."

I thought about that. "Do you think you'll ever feel better?"

Cate wiped the tears off her face. *"Ever,"* she said. "Such a word."

But I didn't want to think about what she was saying. That *ever*, for her, might not be a long time, even if she got well.

Thinking about that would do me no good.

Do her no good.

Wouldn't help my father at all.

"Not your leg," I said. "I mean you."

She sighed. "I know what you mean."

"I'm sorry," my mother said, opening the door. "But he wouldn't go with Larkin, and—"

"Oh, there he is," Cate said as Captan barged into the room and went immediately to lay his head in her lap. "There's my good boy."

She sounded like I did. "Can Quiet come in, too?" I asked my mother.

"Well, I don't know if—"

"Captan won't hurt him," Cate said. "I can promise you that."

So my mother sent Samuel, who handed Quiet to me and then went out with her again, protesting loudly.

Through the door, I could hear him asking, "How is the hag going to use two dogs to make Daddy well?"

Cate smiled a real smile. "That's some boy you have there."

"Samuel?" I said. "Or Quiet?"

"Both. But especially Samuel." She looked at me gently. "Yes, of course you were in the way, too, Ellie. You did what you were supposed to do. Trying to save your little brother. And your father did what he was supposed to do. Trying to save you both."

I cleared my throat, which was still too tight. "Not just trying."

I held Quiet out so he could look his father in the eye. "This is Captan," I said into his little ear. "This is maybe your daddy."

"Oh, I'm not fond of maybes," Cate said. She watched Captan sniff Quiet's little head. "What is, is."

"Whether it's true or not?"

Cate huffed. "Tell me what true is."

I thought about that. "I know a million true things."

"As do I. And a million I can't explain, though they're real. And quite a few I can't believe, though they happened. Whether they should have or not."

She looked at my father in the bed next to where she sat. "Here's a true thing, and a good one."

I was surprised by that. "Good?"

She gave me a long look. "He might have died."

Which was also true.

I considered his face. How deeply he slept. "How will we wake him? I thought maybe we could try skunk stink or—"

"Skunk stink?" She looked amazed.

"The doctor who was here tried smelling salts, but they didn't do any good. I thought maybe skunk, though, would make him curious enough to wake up." I looked at my father's slack face. "And horseradish might do some good, too. I don't know anybody who could sleep through a dose of horseradish."

Cate took my free hand and held it to her cheek. "It's a terrible thing," she said, and I thought she was talking about my father. "That I have only just met you."

I smiled at her. "All this time you were up there, not far at all. But you're not so old, and that leg will heal, and we'll have plenty of time." But I heard the doubt in my voice.

"Perhaps," she said. "If I am to get well, it will be for Larkin and you both."

Which was when the flame decided to flare in my chest, as it had on the morning when Quiet was born. And the voice decided to speak to me again, so sure and strong that I didn't doubt it for a moment.

And I listened to that voice, which was as clear as my mother's as she opened the door and said, "Will you have some balsam tea, Mrs. Cleary?"

And I said, "We will."

And then to Cate, I said, "You will." Though I wasn't talking about tea.

Cate looked at me curiously. And began to smile. "You know what to do, don't you." It wasn't really a question.

I nodded. "I do," I said.

And I did.

Chapter Sixty-Five

I took Quiet to Samuel. "Will you give him back to Maisie?"

"Okay." He looked Quiet over carefully. "Did the hag do something to him?"

"Yes, she turned him into a goat, can't you tell?"

He made a face. "Don't be foolish, Ellie."

I looked around. "Where's Esther?"

My mother said, "She went with Larkin, partway back up-mountain." She sounded sorry about it. "He was upset. She thought he might want the company."

I tried not to care. Which wasn't too difficult, since I had other things to care about. But it wasn't easy, regardless.

When I turned to go back to my father, my mother gave me a worried look. "Are you all right, Ellie?"

"I'm fine," I said, the flame in my chest roaring.

I went into the bedroom and shut the door gently.

I went to Cate.

When I put out my arm, she took it without question and let

me help her around the bed to lie down next to my father so I could check her leg.

She didn't say a word when I pulled off her leggings and carefully unwrapped the bandages.

The wound was still as swollen and angry as it had been, despite the honey. Maybe even worse than before.

"I think we should send Mr. Peterson for the doctor now," I said, wrapping the wound again. "So he'll get here in time if the honey doesn't work."

We both knew what I meant by "in time."

"And if the honey works? And he comes here for no good reason?"

"He'll want to be paid either way." I thought about what I had to give in trade. I looked at my mother's mandolin.

"No," Cate said. "Not that. Not for me."

And I remembered another of the hundred questions I had not yet asked her. "Larkin said he used to help his father make mandolins. Doesn't he want to be a luthier, too?"

At which Cate closed her eyes. "I asked him that very thing. But all he said was 'Maybe someday.'"

I thought of what else we could use to pay the doctor. "Have you no wedding ring?"

"Gone," she said. "In trade. Long since."

I thought about the years since Larkin's father had died. The crash that had made those years even harder.

"The doctor won't know that we have no way to pay him," I said. "Until he's already here."

"And if you fool him like that, he'll never come back here again." She reached out to scratch Captan between the ears. "Cry wolf and you won't have him next time."

"Then we'll do what we can without him. But right now, no wait-and-see this time." I remembered the other things she'd tried. "Can I pour in some hot vinegar?"

She considered that. "I don't know what it will be like to pour it into an open wound. And we don't want to melt the honey away."

"Then I'll keep the cut mostly closed for now, to hold the honey in. And I'll build a . . . a dam around the cut and fill it with vinegar so it seeps in slowly and doesn't spill away."

She watched me without saying a word.

I thought about the possibilities.

There was a candle next to the bed. But I'd been burned by candle wax before, and I was not eager to give Cate a new hurt trying to heal an old one.

So I closed my eyes and listened to myself for a while, letting my mind tick through the possibilities, until I came to one I liked, for more reasons than one, all of them good.

I found my mother in the kitchen, tucking balsam chips into pouches.

"I need an old pot you might never be able to use again," I said.

She frowned at me. "Pots don't grow on trees," she said. "Are you making something for your father?"

"Not right now. This is for Cate."

"For Mrs. Cleary?"

I was amazed that she saw a distinction.

"Yes," I said.

My mother gave me a long look.

Just days before, she had sent me to the shed to sleep with the dogs, my belly as empty as a hat on a hook, for trying to wake my father. Now, with only a little pause, she fetched an old, blackened pot and handed it to me without another word.

I wondered if she was so willing because I had earned some trust . . . or because I was now trying to heal Cate instead of my daddy.

I decided it didn't matter.

I carried the pot back to where Cate lay waiting.

She watched me carefully as I took out my knife and sliced away a broad strip of deer hide from her leggings.

She said nothing out loud, though her face made a comment or two, especially her eyebrows, before it settled into a smile.

"Larkin told you some things about his father's luthing, didn't he?"

"He did," I said, wiping my knife on my sleeve and folding it away.

I draped the deer hide over my arm and picked up the old pot.

"This will take a while," I said.

"Not so long if you boil it hard," she replied. "An hour over a fire is all you'll need, though be ready to stir it right along." She smiled sadly. "It would be different if I were a mandolin. For that, all night long, slowly, in an oven, works best."

I didn't say, *We don't have all night long.* Nor did I say, *You're not a mandolin.* I said, "Close your eyes and rest while I do this. Captan's here, and I don't imagine he'll leave you."

Esther was in the kitchen with my mother when I came back through on my way to the yard.

"How's Larkin?" I said, though I didn't like to be the one asking . . . or her the one answering.

"He's sad and angry and ashamed of himself," she said. "For you being the one who's helping her."

So I was not the only one feeling out of sorts about such things.

I wanted to go find him, right then, to tell him that I understood . . . and to be the one he understood in return.

Later, I would do that. Find him.

After I'd helped Cate. After I'd helped my father. After all that. If he hadn't come to find me first.

"What's that?" my mother said, nodding at the deer hide that hung from my arm.

"Deer hide," I said.

"What for?" she said as I gathered up my pack.

"You'll see. It's hard to explain."

She followed me to the cabin door and stood watching as I laid the deer hide on the ground and scraped the hair away with my knife until nothing but leather remained.

But she went back to her work when I knelt to build a fire where we had made soap. Before the fire got too big, I laid stones in a small circle around its edge so the pot would sit above the ground and the flames would stay where I wanted them.

While the fire was growing, I cut the leather into strips and tucked them all into the old pot, added a little water from the well, and set the pot on the fire.

"What are you doing?" Samuel said as he crept out of nowhere and my shadow merged with his.

"Playing the piano," I said.

He made a sound that was mostly snort. "You are not, Ellie. You're cooking something."

"Then why did you ask?"

He peered into the pot. "But what is it? Is it something to eat?"

"Maybe if you're a wolf," I said. "A very hungry wolf."

"Well, I'm not a wolf," he said, though he sounded a little doubtful, as if he reserved the right to eat what I was cooking, should it prove to be something sweet.

"I'm making glue," I said, stirring the strips of hide with a bare stick as the water began to simmer.

"What did you break?" he said happily. For once, he was not the one who had done the breaking.

"Nothing," I said. "But I'm going to fix it anyway."

Samuel poked at the fire with a stick of his own. "How do you know how to make glue? Did Daddy teach you that, too?"

I shook my head. "I taught me how. I just hope I taught me well."

He made a face at that. "You're silly." He poked at the fire some more. "Do you need help?"

"Always," I said, though it wasn't true. Though it was.

Chapter Sixty-Six

Samuel and I spent the next hour tending the fire and the pot as the deer hide slowly melted down toward glue and the day trod on toward evening.

"I think it's done," I finally said, letting some drizzle from the end of the stir-stick.

"That's a lot of glue." He looked around the yard. "What's so big and broken that you need all that glue to fix it?"

"Cate," I said, using a rag to move the pot off the fire. I set it aside to cool.

"You mean the hag?" he said, astonished.

I nodded. "I do." But I knew he was astonished by the idea that I could glue her back together, not that it was a hag I meant to heal.

"What are you brewing out there?" my mother asked when we came into the cabin to check on Cate.

I liked that we were *brewing* something. I liked that word.

"Glue," Samuel said.

I could see that my mother wanted to ask more, but she didn't. She simply turned back to her work, which was a supper of corn bread and beans and one of the trout . . . and a pie. Something as uncommon as hen's teeth these days.

"Is that a pie?" Samuel said, his eyes amazed.

"Of a sort," my mother said with a sigh. "Dried blueberries and apples with walnuts and a little maple syrup. Which is hardly what I'd choose to bake. But bake it I will."

"For Miss Cate?" I said.

She nodded. "How often do we have a guest in this house?"

I wouldn't have called Cate a guest, but I was glad that my mother saw her that way.

At the bedroom door, we found both Cate and my father sleeping, though differently. I could see that just by looking at them. Even asleep, Cate looked as if she were . . . aware.

Esther was there, too, sitting alongside the bed in the rocking chair, reading aloud to both of them—and to Captan, too—as they slept. A very good book about a bear named Winnie and a pig named Piglet and a host of others that I had loved and still loved and would always love.

I was jealous at the thought that Cate might be meeting Pooh and Piglet for the very first time—like tasting a first strawberry or hearing a first loon—since the book was only a little older than Samuel and meant for children at a time when her son was already grown. But perhaps she had read it to Larkin when he was little, as my mother had to me.

As Esther had to me, too, I realized, when she had only just learned to read, the story coming out word by word, slowly and carefully, like a cat when a dog's nearby. But that hadn't mattered at all.

What I remembered best was lying next to my sister at bedtime, tucked in together, while she read that story to me.

When Esther looked up from the book to find me and Samuel standing in the doorway, watching, she stopped.

I expected annoyance. Impatience. But she simply paused, as if we were a couple of songbirds on the windowsill—not so much a distraction as something worth noticing—and I felt my heart swell, the way a bud will when the days grow warm.

And that's when Cate said, without opening her eyes, "Why did you stop, girl?" and I heard in her voice that she was in more pain than she should be. More pain than I'd thought.

And I knew it was time for me to do something about that.

"Is the hag going to live here with us now?" Samuel whispered after we'd crept out of the room.

"If *now* means right now, then yes," I said. "But beyond that I can't say."

Which seemed to satisfy Samuel, a here-and-now sort of boy if ever there was one.

"Can I have some vinegar?" I asked my mother

She looked at me curiously. "For your father this time?" she said as she pulled a jug of vinegar from the cupboard.

"Maybe later. Right now, for Miss Cate."

"Right now, supper," she said. "You can take her a plate and then eat your own. And then you can do whatever it is you plan to do."

"I'm not hungry," I said, though I was. "And I need to tend to her leg now. I'll feed her, and myself, after I get that sorted out."

My mother turned to Samuel. "Go fetch Esther," she said and then, when he had gone, turned to me with a hard look on her face. "Ellie, I can't make up my mind about all this. Mrs. Cleary seems to think it's all right that she's come here to . . . get better, I suppose, and help your father, though I don't see how when she's the one who needs a doctor. She needs a doctor, Ellie! Not some barbaric kind of glue . . . and vinegar . . . and Heaven knows what else you've got in mind." She sighed. "Yes, I'll admit it, you've done some . . . interesting things for your father, and he's no worse for them, maybe even better. But you're not a doctor, Ellie. You're twelve! You're just a girl, whatever else you might be. Whatever else Mrs. Cleary thinks you are."

More *elses.*

I waited.

This was my mother, sorting herself out.

Which was her job more than mine.

"I must be mad as a hatter to stand here baking a terrible little pie while Mrs. Cleary rots away in that bed alongside your bee-stung father." She wiped her hands on her apron and heaved another sigh. "But in the morning we will all come to our senses and send Mr. Peterson to fetch the doctor." At the look on my face she held up a hand. "And that is that."

She handed me the vinegar.

I poured some into a pot, careful to hold back the cloudy "mother" that we'd need to start the next batch, and put the pot on the back of the stove where the heat from the oven would warm it.

"Yuck," Samuel said, coming back into the kitchen, Esther with him. "Another bad smell."

"Just vinegar," I said.

"For what?"

"For you," I said. "You're too sweet. You need a little tart."

Samuel took a step back. "What does she mean, Mother?"

"Nothing," she said. "Now wash up and sit down and eat."

Instead, he sidled up next to me.

"But what's the vinegar *for*?" he asked again.

"For Cate."

"Glue *and* vinegar?"

"Glue and vinegar."

"Samuel," my mother said. "Get washed up. I won't tell you again."

But when I went out to the yard to fetch the glue, he followed me, as a puppy would, and I realized that when Mr. Anderson took Quiet I would need Samuel more than ever.

The thought brought me to a stop.

Samuel looked up at me as I stood there with dusk coming on.

"What's wrong, Ellie?"

I didn't want to think about losing Quiet. Losing anything. "Nothing. Go on in to supper now or you'll get no pie."

But I almost called him back as he scampered off toward the cabin.

Chapter Sixty-Seven

"This first part shouldn't hurt a bit," I told Cate as I settled a lantern and the glue pot next to the bed, "but I brought some willow tea down from your cabin and never used it. Would you like some now . . . for what's coming?"

"No," she said, after a moment. "It will lower my fever, and I need that fever right now, to fight the germ." She nodded at the glue pot. "It's cool enough?"

I nodded. "I think so."

It felt odd to be sitting with Cate, intent on her instead of my father, who lay just there, on the other side of her, without a sound or any suggestion of life except the slow bellows of his lungs, the heart that I could hear somewhere inside my own chest.

I turned all my attention back to Cate.

I untied the bandages again and gently unwrapped her leg.

"We should thank those bees," I said, leaning close to study the wound. It didn't smell as bad as it had before, but it was still foul enough.

"No *should* about it," Cate said. "*Do.* Every day. Them and the trees and the flowers and every other kind of doctor to be had."

Which was all true. And more besides.

"Now don't move. I want the glue to stay put."

Cate huffed. "Isn't that the whole point of glue? And why go to so much trouble? Why not clean things out and wrap me up again?"

She looked like she already knew the answer to that, but I sat back, the pot poised in my hand, and gave her one anyway. "I thought of just pouring the vinegar again and again, over the bandages so they'd keep the cut good and wet for a day or two. But I think the cut needs to be drenched. I think the vinegar needs to seep all the way in to keep the honey soft and sink down deep to the bottom of the wound. I think we need to clean it out from the bottom up, else we might not get at all the corruption." I leaned again toward the wound. "I don't want it to spread any more than it already has."

Cate smiled tiredly. "That's a lot of thinking."

I remembered what she'd said to me on the mountaintop. About whether a hag was the kind of person who would read books.

"A lot of thinking for a twelve-year-old girl?"

Which earned me her customary snort. "A lot of thinking for anyone."

Slowly, bit by bit, I spooned the glue in a ring around Cate's wound, then stirred what was in the pot while I waited for the stuff on her leg to firm up a bit.

In the lull, I wondered where Larkin was and hoped he would come back soon . . . and with no rancor.

It was more important that Cate got well than who got her there.

Captan, who had stayed as close to Cate as he could, climbed to his feet and stretched his front legs out before him, his tail in the air, threw his head back, and yawned a mighty yawn. Then he shook himself all over and looked at me expectantly.

"Do you need to go out, boy?"

"He'll go to the door if he does," Cate muttered without opening her eyes. "And he'll ask for some supper after you've had yours."

I spooned another ring of glue above the first, using the smooth side of the stick to nudge it back to neat, though I can't say it was a pretty business.

"None of this should feel good," Cate said. "But it does."

I smiled. "When I'm sick, I love how my mother takes care of me. The sound of her moving around my bed while I lie with my eyes closed. How it feels when she lays a cloth on my forehead." I began another ring of glue atop the last. "Almost worth being sick."

Cate sighed. "I'd like to think I made someone feel that way when I was a nurse."

Which astonished me. "Ask Esther," I said.

She smiled. "I can smell the hot vinegar."

I could smell it, too, sharp as broken glass.

She opened her eyes. "Won't it melt the glue away?"

"It might, a bit. But maybe not too much. And if it does, it does."

I didn't care what kind of mess it made.

Cate lifted her head up again to watch me working.

For a time we were silent while I added more glue, blowing on it until it had a skin, soft but firm.

My mother, at the door, said, "I've brought you some more tea."

The smell of balsam twined with the smell of the vinegar, and I felt as if I were in a fresh winter garden, though the stink of the glue failed to give much ground.

She brought two mugs of tea into the room and set them on the windowsill. She made sure not to look at what I was doing to Cate's leg. "Is everything all right?"

"It is," I said. "Will you bring that vinegar now?"

She waited for a long moment.

Then she went to do as I'd asked.

After a moment, she came back into the room, carrying the pot of steaming vinegar. "I don't know what you—"

But as she neared the bed, she saw Cate's wound, and she almost dropped the pot.

"Mercy," she whispered. *"What are you doing, Ellie?"*

"Here. Just put it on the floor by the bed. I'll need a ladle, too, please. And a clean rag or two."

She looked at us, a little wild-eyed, but then she stopped and took a closer look at what I'd made, at the glue dam and the swollen wound in the middle of it, and said, "You mean to pour hot vinegar in there?"

"I do. But not hot enough to burn her. And just a little at a time. So it can seep in with the honey and clean the wound."

She looked at Cate. "Is this another thing you've taught her?"

"Heavens, no," Cate said. "This is her idea. If anything, I've bungled the whole deal since the beginning. If I'd let her run the show, I'd be right as rain by now."

"Though I did plan to burn you with a hot chisel," I said.

Which made my mother flinch. She put the pot on the floor. "If it's bad enough to do this, should we not send for the doctor right now?"

I looked at Cate and could see that she didn't want to get into that again: the business of paying or not paying a man who might arrive in a day or two or three when she would either be better or beyond whatever help he could give.

"I believe we have a doctor right here," she said, nodding at me. "And I'm a nurse, don't forget. So all we lack is some medicine that people have been doing without for thousands of years."

Nobody said "and dying for lack of it," though I'll bet we all thought it.

My mother said, "If you're sure."

Cate nodded.

We waited while my mother went for what we needed.

When she came back, she paused.

She looked like she had something to say.

I knew my mother. I knew she was still struggling. But the hag was Mrs. Cleary. The same nurse who had helped Esther through a course of earaches so bad they'd made her scream. And I was the same girl who had made my daddy's hand twitch, and his eyes roll. Made him groan. Was maybe the reason he had opened his eyes, even if for just a little while.

I smiled at her, the flame in my chest so bright I was surprised she couldn't see it shining from my eyes.

But perhaps she could, since she finally said, "This is all so strange, and I don't much understand any of it, but I'm sorry for how hard I've been."

I thought of Larkin's mother. Esther. Cate. And me myself.

"Daddy's been asleep for months," I said. "How were you supposed to be? And you're right. I am a twelve-year-old girl. I'm not a doctor. So it's all right, Mother."

Which earned me a look I'd keep for a long, long time.

After she'd gone out again, I shut the door and turned back to the bed.

Cate said, "Would you really have burned me with that chisel?"

It was the same question Larkin had asked days before, though the answer was no longer true.

I shrugged. "I didn't know what else to do."

"I'm ever so glad you didn't have to do that."

"Me too. It would have made things worse."

"Yes, but something like that—" She stopped to choose her words. "It's something you should never have to do."

"Because I'm twelve?"

At which Cate looked disappointed. Hurt, even. "Because *no one* should have to do such a thing if there's another way."

If there's an *else*.

"Even this," she said. "The hot vinegar. What you're about to do will stay with you for your whole life."

I nodded. "I hope so."

Which earned me another look I'd hold on to forever.

"And then I'll know how," I said. "One more thing I can do."

Cate smiled. "Just hours ago we were talking about your father and skunk stink and horseradish."

"We were."

"And now this." She gestured at her leg.

Which reminded me of the balsam sap I'd given for Scotch's hoof instead of using it on my father's scar. The egg I'd fed to Maisie instead of using it to lure a skunk. The honey I'd left for the bees instead of adding it to my medicine brew. And the time I'd spent up-mountain instead of here, by my father's side.

"My mother thinks he will wake or he won't, regardless of what I try," I said.

"You think that's true?"

I remembered what Cate had said to me not long before. "Tell me what true is."

She smiled. Said nothing.

I tried to find the words to say something I'd never said before. "It seems to me that what I do for one thing is what I do for everything." Which wasn't exactly right. "I can do this," I said, looking at her wound. "So I will. And I have an idea that it will be . . . more than what it is."

Cate didn't say anything about that, and I didn't know if she understood me, but I thought maybe she did.

Chapter Sixty-Eight

Captan didn't like the sounds that Cate made as I ladled the warm vinegar onto her wound, bit by bit, letting it seep into the cut and then collect in a reservoir on her skin, inside the glue dam I'd made.

The dam slipped a little and shifted in the heat, but as it softened, it still kept a grip on her skin and held the vinegar pretty much where I wanted it to be.

What seeped out I wicked away with the rag.

"It's working well," Cate said through her teeth, her hands in fists.

"Are you all right?"

"I am," she said. "I will be."

After a while, my mother came to have a look.

"You've had no supper. Either of you."

I looked up at her.

"Ellie, you go on and have something. I'll stay with Mrs. Cleary until you're back."

"A name I'd nearly forgotten," Cate said. "Though I'll not forget my good husband, stuffy as he was." She tried to smile, but it was a struggle. "Doctor Cleary was Doctor Cleary, through and through, though he was Reggie to me when the world wasn't listening."

My mother looked at me. "We're all more than one thing." She went around the bed to lean over my father, kiss him on the forehead, smooth his cheeks with her hands. "Go on now, Ellie," she said. "Go get your supper. And when you come back, bring your father some broth. And bring Mrs. Cleary a plate."

"Oh, don't bother with me," she said. "I haven't much in the way of an appetite."

"Perhaps not, but you need your strength if you're to get better. You'll at least try some of the broth I've made for him."

So I went for my supper and found that Samuel had been right: The trout was the best I'd ever had, though being hungry had a lot to do with that.

I looked in on him before I went back to Cate. Found him sleeping so deeply that even when I kissed his warm cheek he didn't stir.

To Esther, who was reading by lamplight in her bed, I said, "You're kind to read to Daddy like you do."

She looked up, startled. "I suppose I am, but I do it mostly for myself, Ellie." She laid her book down in her lap. "It's terrible to feel useless."

Which I knew to be true, though I hadn't imagined how she must have felt as our father lay shrinking and fading to gray through the long, cold months.

We looked at each other in the golden darkness.

"Good night," I said.

Esther picked up her book again. "Mrs. Cleary is lucky that I wasn't the one who found her."

"Well, but you did," I said. "I just found her first."

It was an odd supper I took to Cate: a mug of venison broth and a slice of dried-blueberry-apple-walnut-maple pie. For Captan, the last of the trout topped with the soft, brown skin from the bottom of the corn-bread pan.

For my father, broth alone.

While my mother fed him in hummingbird sips, I fed Cate likewise, though she managed the pie in bites.

"At my age, making friends with a new kind of pie is an unexpected blessing," she said. "I would never have thought of putting those things together, though they make for a fine family. And such a buttery crust."

My mother smiled. "You're a terrible liar, but thank you." She collected the empty mugs, the plate, the vinegar pot. "Shall I heat this up again?"

"Just one more go of it, please," I said. "And then we wait for the morning."

She must have seen the question on my face—*And, in the morning, will you still send for the doctor?*—because she said, "That's fine, then, Ellie. We'll see how everything goes."

When she had gone, Cate said, "You're exactly like her and entirely different, aren't you." Another question that wasn't a question.

But since she'd asked, I gave her an answer. "Entirely different, yes, though I don't know what she was like when she was a girl, and

I don't know what I'll be like when I'm grown up. So I don't really know much of anything."

Cate gazed at me sleepily for a long moment. "You know a fair bit, Ellie."

"I wish I'd known her before she had Esther. And me. And Samuel. I wonder what she was like back then."

"Well, different, of course. And different, still, before she married your father. And different, again, before she picked up that mandolin over there for the first time. And, again, after she laid it down." She closed her eyes. "The sun never rises the way it did the day before. Not exactly. And it won't rise the same way tomorrow. But it's still the sun," she said. "And we'd all be just as cold without it."

When my mother came back with the vinegar, she said good night to all four of us.

"You can have my bed," I told her. "I'm happy to sleep with the dogs."

She looked a little sad at that, until I said, "It's a lovely thing, to sleep with puppies."

So we decided on that and she went off to bed, leaving us in a pool of lantern light beyond which the entire world disappeared again.

I let the vinegar cool a little and then slowly ladled in another small dose.

We waited quietly while it seeped into the wound, a puddle of it remaining on Cate's skin. "I think that will do for now," I said.

Cate was tired out but no worse than before. Perhaps a bit better.

I left the gash open and laid a fresh cloth across her leg before pulling the blanket over her.

Then I went around the bed to my father.

"I wish I could do something for you, too," I whispered.

"I believe you just did," Cate said. "Isn't that what you meant?"

I had to think back before I knew what she was asking. "About one thing and everything?"

"Yes."

"Or maybe if I do one thing, for you, someone else will do one thing, for him."

"I will," she said. "If I can. When I'm able."

But, in the end, it wasn't Cate who helped him.

Chapter Sixty-Nine

Later that night, from my nest among the puppies, I heard my mother call my name, and I was up and out of the woodshed like a cricket. But it was nothing to do with my father or Cate. At least I didn't think so at the time.

"It's Captan," she said. "He came and woke me up, but he won't go outside. I don't know what he wants. When I went back to bed, he came with me and won't leave. He keeps . . . singing in my ear."

I rubbed my eyes. "Singing?"

"Whining, like a big mosquito. Right in my ear." She pulled me inside and shut the door. Captan stood there in the darkness, his eyes like full moons.

"Is it Cate?" I asked my mother. "Did you check on her?"

"Of course I did, Ellie. A dog like that comes to me in the night, of course I went in to have a look, but she's sleeping soundly. Some fever still, but no worse than before." She bent down to look into Captan's face. "He followed me in to see her but then out again when I left. I don't know what he wants."

Which is when I felt what he felt, knew what he knew, and realized that he, in that moment, was a lot like me. Filled with both lullaby and shout. A dog split in two. A dog doubled.

He didn't budge when I went to him and rubbed his ears. "What's that song?" I said. "What is it, boy?" But he kept looking at my mother. Not at me. "This has something to do with you, Mother." I stepped aside.

When she held out her hand, he put his nose in her palm. Licked it. And sang some more of the song he'd apparently been saving for her.

Since I'd met him, he'd made no sound except a pair of howls, a little whining and, from time to time, a growl or two.

And this was no growl. Far from it.

When he turned toward the bedroom where Cate and my father lay sleeping, I waited for my mother to follow. And then I did, too.

The lantern burned so low in the room that it lifted the darkness only a little, like the very first moment of dawn.

I turned up the wick and held the lantern high.

Nothing seemed amiss, but Captan kept singing. And he went not to Cate but to my mother again, singing all the while.

"What's the matter with him?" my mother whispered. She bent to look him in the eye again. *"I don't know what you want."*

No more lullabies, I had said.

Captan seemed to disagree.

And he clearly meant this one for my mother.

But then he left her and went to my father's side of the bed, his nose close to my father's face.

We looked at him.

He looked at my mother.

Looked at her some more, still singing.

And then he turned back to my father.

And he barked.

One loud, shattering bark that nearly stopped my heart.

The first bark I'd ever heard from him.

"What!" Cate cried, startling like a grouse. "What is it, Cap?"

And then he barked again.

"Captan!" I cried.

And he barked again, even more loudly than before.

My mother covered her ears.

"What's wrong?" Samuel said as he tumbled through the doorway. "Why is that dog barking?"

For a fourth time, Captan barked.

And my father turned his head away.

"Oh, good dog," I said, rushing to the bed. "Good boy."

"What's happening?" Esther cried as she, too, raced into the room, her face wild.

And Cate said, her voice full of wonder, "I don't believe Captan has barked since my boy died."

And the fire in my chest flared even more.

I stepped out of the way and pulled my mother close to my father, Samuel pushing up, too, Esther with him.

And Captan barked again.

And my father flinched again.

"Oh, good dog," I said.

At which Captan began to sing some more of his dog-song, louder than before, looking up at my mother, though I was the one who understood him.

"Oh, you very good boy," I said. "You are a great and wonderful dog, aren't you, Captan."

And he sang some more, his eyes on my mother's face.

"What does he want?" she said, clearly baffled, her cheeks pink, her hands at her throat.

I went to the corner and picked up the mandolin my mother hadn't played since my father had gone to sleep.

"Oh, my beautiful, beautiful boy," Cate said softly.

But I didn't think she was talking to Captan, though it was clear that she understood him, too.

I held the mandolin out to my mother.

She took it from me.

Cate watched as if she might be watching a rose about to bloom. We all did.

And my mother looked at my father, listened to the song that Captan was singing, and began to pluck the strings softly, one by one, turning the knobs on the neck of her mandolin, of her Keavy, until the notes rang true. Whatever true is. And Esther went still. Even Samuel went still. And Cate began to smile.

And Captan looked at my father and barked again, a ringing bark that echoed as it rang. And turned to my mother and sang to her some more.

And I watched, and I watched, and I watched as my mother began to play. Something I couldn't name and hadn't heard in a long, long time. Something sweet, and sad, and wonderful that made Captan croon and tremble. Made us all smile like children, which some of us were. Which all of us were in that moment.

Even my father, who opened his eyes as if it were Christmas morning, he himself the gift.

He didn't say anything. He didn't say a word. But this time, when he looked at me, he was there. He was right there, in those eyes, looking out at me as he once had.

And I was right there where he could see me.

Chapter Seventy

None of us got another minute of sleep for the rest of that night.

We stayed in the bedroom and watched as my father slowly surfaced, blinking and sighing, all of us caught between hope that he was finally awake for good and fear that he would slip away from us once more.

Captan returned to Cate's side, quiet again. Samuel lay down at the foot of the bed and made up songs about brindled dogs and black snakes. Esther and my mother paced and murmured. And I checked on Cate's leg, fed her some tea, and said to my father, again and again, "It's all right, Daddy. It's all right now."

Just before dawn, he finally turned his head toward my mother and said, his voice full of rust, "What happened?"

It took a while for anyone to answer, what with my mother crying and Samuel asking Cate how she had managed to fix him; but after things calmed down, Esther said, as I'd known she would, "You were cutting down a tree and Ellie got in the way and you got hurt saving her."

"Esther, hush now," my mother said.

"Oh, I don't blame her," Esther said. "She's just a kid."

Which was how I felt about Samuel chasing that rabbit.

And Esther was only saying what she thought was true. And what *was* true. At least true *enough*.

But a part of me soared and sang when my father looked directly at me and said, "Not Ellie."

"But I was," I said, meeting his eyes but completely aware of Samuel, who had laid his little head on my father's chest and could hear every word we said. "Esther's right."

My father frowned. He held my gaze for another long moment, and I thought he might say something more, but then he put his hand on Samuel's head, and nodded slowly, and gave me the smallest of smiles.

I smiled back at him.

And then watched as he turned to find Cate lying in the bed next to him.

His eyes grew wide, and he leaned away from her and whispered, *"You're—"*

"Cathrine Cleary. I was a nurse in Bethel." She nodded at my sister. "Esther, there, used to come to us with earaches."

"But you're—"

"The hag. Yes, I know." She nodded at me this time. "Your daughter Ellie found me sick in my cabin. She's been taking care of me."

My mother stroked my father's hand. "And she's been taking care of you, as well."

_____

In the days that followed, we all helped my father and Cate mend, and ourselves along with them.

On the morning after he woke up, my mother sat by my father, who was now propped up in bed, and fed him a little porridge with maple syrup on it.

"If I'd known we had maple syrup, I'd have woken up sooner," he said, his voice still raspy from disuse, his head bowed a bit with the hard work of waking.

Cate liked that. "You remind me of my son." She stroked Captan's ears. "He made me laugh."

I'd spent more time on her leg, scraping away the hide glue and pulling open the wound to wipe the honey out, pouring vinegar into the breach and letting it scour her clean.

She had moaned with the pain of the acid on her raw flesh, Captan joining in, and Samuel had stood outside the room and said, "Will you stop hurting the hag please, Ellie?" until she called out to him, "It's all right, boy. She's fixing me up good as new."

But it wasn't easy for either of us. Or Captan, who had found his voice again in a big way and would bark and mutter if she cried out.

Bit by bit, her wound began to improve. Her fever to abate. And before long I was able to leave her leg alone, with nothing but a single ribbon of cloth to cinch it closed.

Still, I checked it again and again for any sign of trouble.

And every time I did, I found my father's eyes on me.

"Where did you learn to do that?" he finally asked me.

"Do what?"

"Heal."

Which I liked. "The things we need to learn to do, we learn to do by doing."

He looked at me thoughtfully. "Who said that?"

At which I smiled and said, "You did."

I turned to Cate. "And so did you."

Esther made herself useful and with good grace, helping both my father and Cate as they made their way slowly back toward well.

But it was Larkin who surprised us, on the morning of the third day after Cate had come to stay.

We had wondered at his absence. Cate, especially, had watched for him, sighing and fretting when he didn't come to see how she was doing.

"That mother of his," she said. "She must be keeping him away. Why else would he not come?"

And I had asked myself the same question. Felt a similar hurt.

But then he did come, and with him the doctor from town. The same one who had said *coma* when my father got hurt. The same one who had taken my mother's locket in payment for doing nearly nothing, though he *had* made the trip from town, the climb to our cabin, which was worth something.

"What's this?" Cate said when they came through the door, Larkin and the portly doctor in his just-so coat and his dinner-plate face. "Larkin, where have you been?" But she looked happy enough when she said it.

"To town," he said. "To fetch the doctor." Who had been away, delivering a baby in Rumford. "Right after I left here. Esther thought so, too, that I should go get help. So I told my mother," who had not been pleased, "and walked down the mountain and out to the road and caught a ride in a rubbish truck," which explained why he smelled like he did, "and had to sleep under a bridge," which also explained why he smelled like he did, "until the doctor got back the next day. And then it took us a while to get here."

"Just in time to tell me all's well," Cate said, her voice equal parts relief and apology.

And that's pretty much what the doctor told her, though he cleaned the wound with carbolic acid (which was one last and awful thing), stitched it up tight, and bandaged it in dressing so white it made my eyes hurt.

And I was sorry I'd been so hard on the man.

He'd managed to do, in short order, what I would never have been able to do half as well.

But he said some kind things about what I *had* done.

"And you just twelve," he said. "You'll make a fine nurse someday."

Which did not bother me a bit, that he didn't say *doctor*.

Perhaps I *would* be a nurse, as Cate had been. As she still was.

Or a doctor.

Or something else.

The *else*s, I had found, were everywhere.

Chapter Seventy-One

While he was there, the doctor examined my father as well, listening to his heart, his lungs. Looking into his eyes and ears. Testing his reflexes, which were understandably sluggish. Had him roll his tongue. Close his eyes and stretch his arms out, one at a time, and bring his index finger to the tip of his nose. He was spot-on with his left arm, a little off with his right.

"You may have some problems along the way," the doctor said. "But you won't know until you have them."

"Like what?" my father said.

The doctor shrugged. "Could be some dizziness. Some permanent weakness in your muscles." He looked at my mother. "No seizures?"

She shook her head.

"But maybe some confusion. Time will tell."

We'd already had my father on his feet once, helping him slowly into the washroom for the first proper bath he'd had in months, and that had been an ordeal.

His legs didn't want to work very well.

The doctor, when he saw for himself, told us another word we hadn't known. "Atrophy," he said. "He needs to build up his muscles again." Which wasn't so frightening after all.

"But you must watch those sores of his and get them closed up quick as you can," he said, looking at my mother. "You've done a good job keeping him clean. And you must not stop doing that until he's well."

For that, he gave her a salve, though she'd already brewed a fresh batch of vinegar with the "mother" from the last batch.

"Any trouble with your words?" the doctor said.

My father looked bemused.

"What's this?" The doctor held up the stethoscope that hung around his neck.

"A stethoscope," my father said.

"And this?" the doctor said, pointing at Captan.

"A loud dog."

Which made Captan smile.

"Do you have a book handy?" the doctor said, looking about.

My mother stood up and left the room. She came back with the book that Esther had been reading to my father while I was up-mountain with Cate.

She handed it to the doctor, who handed it to my father, who let it fall open where it wanted him to begin.

He read the words aloud, slowly, but not as if he didn't know them. " ' "It doesn't happen all at once," said the Skin Horse. "You become. It takes a long time. That's why it doesn't happen often to people who break easily, or have sharp edges, or who have to be carefully kept." ' "

He looked up at me. "So that's another thing that seems to be all right."

"How's your memory?" the doctor said.

My father tipped his head. "How can I know what I might have forgotten?"

"Well, it's clear you know everyone you ought to know. Do you remember your childhood?"

My father nodded.

"Coming here to live?"

"Yes, all of that."

"What about how you got hurt?"

But that drew a frown. He looked at my mother. Then he looked at me, for just a moment, and I saw something in his eyes. Something that wasn't confusion. Something *else*. "No, that's a day I can't recall. They've told me about it, but I can't bring it back."

"Anything about that day?"

He glanced at me again. "Not really."

"Which is probably a blessing," the doctor said, snapping his bag shut. "No sense in remembering something like that."

When it came time to pay him, the doctor waved us off. "The boy has already paid my bill."

We all looked at Larkin.

"Not with your father's last mandolin!" I gasped, remembering what his mother had said.

"Not that," Cate said in a small voice. "Not for me."

Larkin shook his head. "With my first one. Though I have yet to make it."

The doctor cleared his throat and rubbed the bridge of his nose. "He doesn't know how to make one yet. And I don't know how to play one yet. So we both have some work to do."

Yet. Another word I'd hold on to.

And I promised myself, right then and there, in that moment that will always be, for me, an *else* worth trying, that I would never again make up my mind about anything too quickly. Not ever again.

Including doctors.

Chapter Seventy-Two

I didn't blame Esther for sending Larkin in search of better help than I could give. Or better than she had *thought* I could give.

Cate had scared us all with her sad goodbye on the day she'd come to stay with us.

But, had I not been so scared, maybe I would not have been what she needed me to be.

No more lullabies, I had said.

Not for my father.

And not for me.

Until they were what we needed most.

Nor did I blame Larkin, for leaving as he had.

He'd done a brave thing, to face his sad and angry mother. To go to town despite her wrath. To make the long trip, ride in a rubbish truck, sleep under a bridge. All the while thinking that Cate might be leaving him, as his father had, though more slowly.

And I didn't blame myself, either, for being in the way when that tree fell. As Cate had said, I'd been trying to help, which was never a bad thing.

I'd been in the way quite a lot since then.

Saving Quiet.

Helping Larkin treat his black eye, which the doctor had said was healing nicely, though he had his doubts about a medicine made from potato.

Trying to wake my father, bit by bit.

Looking after Cate.

Picking up that lonely mandolin and handing it to my lonely mother.

I knew a thing or two about loneliness.

And so did Larkin, who climbed the mountain with me on the fourth day after my father woke up, to get Cate's cabin ready for her again.

"Does she have a broom?" I asked when we got there and found the floor littered with dead flies.

"Of course. In the shed behind the cabin."

He led me around there, opened the door.

I'd expected a washtub. And, of course, a broom.

But I hadn't expected a great pile of wood in chunks too big for a hearth. Or walls and rafters hung with wood cut rough and raw but clearly meant to be mandolins someday. Necks and bodies. Coiled strings hung from nails. A bowl of turning keys.

"Your father left all this," I said.

Larkin sighed a sigh too big for a boy, even one like Larkin. "He did."

Some of the cut wood had warped from years of cold and hot and the steam from Cate's bath, but I knew that wood was both forgiving and eager to please.

"You'll make the doctor's mandolin here," I said.

Larkin nodded. "And another for you, too, if you want."

Which I did, of course.

"Will you teach me how to carve things?" I said.

He ducked his head. "Anyone could do that."

"No, anyone could not. And I'm pretty sure I won't be any good at it. But I'd like to try."

Which was something I *could* do. So I would.

Larkin's mother had been so happy and relieved to have him back and likely to stay, at least for a while, that she'd made some promises and vowed to keep them.

"When I told her I was going to try to make mandolins like my daddy did, she started to cry," he said as we made up Cate's bed in clean sheets.

I didn't blame her one bit for that. "Maybe now she won't mind you learning to read or how to make a poultice."

"I just hope I remember enough from watching my father," he said as he scooped cold ashes from the hearth. "Otherwise, there's no one to teach me how to make a mandolin."

"You'll remember," I said. "And you'll learn as you go."

"You sound like Cate," he said.

"And my father."

"And mine, too," Larkin said, while his father's tools watched us, their heavy, black hearts beating a little more quickly at the idea that they would soon be put to use again.

Chapter Seventy-Three

As I helped my mother grind corn the next day, she said, "I've changed my mind, Ellie."

I thought she was talking about making corn bread instead of corn cakes, or when it would be best to help Cate move back up-mountain, or almost anything except what she said next.

She gave me a small, sad smile. "Quiet can stay."

I let out a breath I'd been holding for a long time. Since even before Quiet had been born. "And the others?"

She turned back to her work. "We'll see."

And I knew what she meant. If my father got well enough, fast enough, to manage a passel of dogs. To do without Mr. Anderson's milk cow.

We couldn't know any of those things. Not yet.

But there were some things I *did* know.

That Quiet was mine. And I was his. And there, right there grinding cornmeal, close enough so I could touch her, was the mother I had missed. Who'd been coming back to me, bit by bit, over these past few difficult, wonderful days. And was all that much closer, now, because I'd met her halfway.

When we finished with the corn and cleaned up the mess, my mother said, "Cate's not ready to go home yet, but I think we can move her now." She gave me an apologetic smile. "To your bed, perhaps?" I'd continued to sleep in the shed with Maisie and the puppies while my mother gave her own place to Cate, and I hadn't minded one bit. So I nodded, smiling at the thought of Cate and Samuel and Esther all sharing a room, telling stories by lantern light.

It was easy to move Cate from one room to another, carefully, slowly, with Captan dancing alongside and Samuel in the lead, chattering about a dog army in which Captan was a captain and Quiet was a general and Maisie was a lieutenant, until we all told him to hush and get out of the way.

I was the one to go back for Cate's pillow. So I was alone with my father for the first time since he'd woken up.

"Ellie," he said, as I turned toward the door with the pillow in my arms.

When I looked back, ready to fetch him something, to give him some water . . . whatever it was he wanted . . . he gave me something that *I* wanted, instead.

"Ellie," he said, softly. "I do remember."

I went to stand close to him. "What do you remember?"

He took my hand. "That day. The day the tree fell."

At first, I thought he meant that the memory had finally surfaced. And I said so.

"No," he replied. "I always remembered. As soon as I woke up all the way, I remembered all of it."

And *I* remembered how Esther had told him about the accident and how he had looked at me—straight at me—and said, "Not Ellie." How I had heard, in those two words, everything I needed to hear.

"I wish you could have been with me these past weeks," I whispered. *"To watch what happened."* Though much of it would have been different, had he been well.

My father smiled at me, his eyes full of sun in the shadowy room. "I see it all very clearly," he said. "I see it in every bit of the girl you've become."

Quiet was waiting for me when I went out into the sunshine later that day.

He had managed to find his way into the yard while Maisie was busy with the other pups, their eyes open now, too.

I found him watching an ant make its way up a blade of grass.

When he felt my shadow, he turned toward me, his little tail wagging, his tongue like the tip of a pink ribbon.

"Oh, what a fine present you are," I said, scooping him up and rubbing his nose with mine. "What a boy. What a good little Quiet you are."

And I realized, then, that Quiet wasn't the first person I had saved.

Or the last.

Captan, coming up the path from below, stopped at the sight of us and then came on again, more quickly.

He had taken to spending most of his time near the cabin door, no longer welcome inside, but patient about that.

No more howling. Still, though, the occasional bark and a certain amount of singing, as if he had something to say. To which I always listened.

And I did now, as he came to me and crooned for Quiet.

Some father dogs could be unkind to their pups, but not Captan.

When I put Quiet on the ground, Captan licked him with his big, rough tongue. To clean him, yes, but to kiss him, too.

And I knew again that doing one thing was doing everything.

I knew the same thing, all over again, later that day, when we led my father and Cate out to sit in the afternoon sun and take another step toward well.

They had become friends as they'd healed, side by side, and even better friends when they both grew strong enough to do small chores together at the kitchen table, and to help us with our lessons, all the while talking about their lives on Echo Mountain.

"You're lucky to have a girl like Ellie," Cate said as I settled them in the chairs we'd brought out to the yard, one facing down-mountain, one facing up, so they faced each other.

"We are," he said, smiling at me.

And I was lucky, too, when I left them to their conversation and went into the woodshed to lay fresh straw for the puppies, only to find the stool not where I had left it but just there, by the high shelf where I kept my small treasures.

And I was lucky when I stepped up on the stool and found not ten carvings waiting where I'd left them, but eleven now.

A new one, right next to the one that looked like me.

This one was of a boy. Tall. Lean. With hair like a bear's fur, and a face with so much music in it that I laughed out loud.

And climbed down from the stool.

And went out into the trees to find him.

And did.

ACKNOWLEDGMENTS

I am grateful to many people who helped with *Echo Mountain*.

First, those who have suffered my amateur ministrations over the years, especially my husband Richard (whose broken tooth I once sanded down with my Dremel), and our sons, Cameron and Ryland. I sometimes think I should have gone to medical school and become a diagnostician. As it is, I like to investigate sickness and do what I can to cure it. My friends and family have been very patient patients over the years, and I thank them for that.

My grandmother, Ann McConnell, who made everything better when I got banged up playing on the family farm. She used things like balsam of Peru, baking soda, vinegar, poultices, and mud for everything from bee sting to bruises. And she relied on scoldings and sweets for almost everything else.

My mother, Mimi McConnell, who bought some land in Maine and built a little camp there so we could retreat from the chaos of our lives and let the mountains remind us of what's important. That land inspired *Echo Mountain*. So did she. I thank her for that and for her thoughts about Ellie's story.

My sister, Suzanne Wolk, and my father, Ronald Wolk, who were among my first and best readers and helped me see how to make this a better book. My uncle, Calvin Richard McConnell, who built his own cabin in a place called Wolf Hollow and helped to inspire *Echo Mountain*.

As always, the members of my writing group, the Bass River Revisionists, especially Deirdre Callanan, another early reader who never fails to push me into better, stronger work. And Jack Harrison, whose voice I sometimes hear when the work is most difficult.

Beatrice and Frieda Bilezikian and Zoë Reese Gameros, young readers whose insights helped me see *Echo Mountain* in a new light.

So many colleagues and friends—including Bob Nash, Amy Neill, Meg McNamara, Laura Kelley, and Patty Creighton—who make me feel stronger than I really am. (Amy is also a lovely hag skilled at making potions and tinctures and brews of all kinds. She helped to inspire Cate.)

Lila, Tanner, Rascal, Spike, and all the other dogs who helped me create Captan and Maisie and their pups . . . especially Quiet.

Wendy Newmeyer, co-owner of Maine Balsam Fir Products in West Paris, Maine, whose little shop I visit whenever I go to the Oxford hills to camp. When I asked Wendy about the healing properties of balsam, she took me to a tree at the edge of the woods behind the shop and told me about the many ways to use its wood and sap.

Elaine Wilson Young, who lent me a mountain of very old books on healing, which I shared with Ellie and Cate, and which helped me understand what people in those days knew about illness and medicine. And what they didn't know.

Julie Strauss-Gabel, who has an incredibly sharp mind paired with a tender heart: a rare combination that makes her the perfect editor for someone like me and books like mine.

And the rest of my family at Penguin Young Readers, all of whom bridge the gap between my books and those who read them, especially the extraordinary Jen Loja; Anna Booth, Melissa Faulner, Rob Farren, and Natalie Vielkind at Dutton; marketing wizards Venessa Carson, Christina Colangelo, Andrea Cruise, Carmela Iaria, Trevor Ingerson, Bri Lockhart, Summer Ogata, Matt Phipps, and Rachel Wease; my publicist Lindsay Boggs; US jacket designer Maggie Edkins; and a boatload of amazing sales reps.

Jodi Reamer. There is no finer agent anywhere. And her cohorts at Writers House who make my literary life easier, including Alec Shane, Cecilia de la Campa, and Alessandra Birch.

And of course all my other family and friends—especially Cally, Denise, and Ashley Wolk—whose love and encouragement make all the difference in the world.

If you enjoyed *Echo Mountain*, you might also love Lauren Wolk's other award-winning books!

WOLF HOLLOW

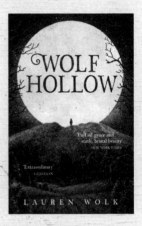

Annabelle has lived in Wolf Hollow all her life: a quiet place, still scarred by two world wars.
But when cruel, manipulative Betty arrives in town, Annabelle's calm world is shattered, along with everything she has ever known about right and wrong.

When Betty disappears, suspicion falls on strange, gentle loner Toby. As Wolf Hollow turns against him, and tensions quickly mount, Annabelle must do everything in her power to protect Toby – and to find Betty, before it is too late.

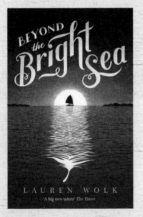

BEYOND THE BRIGHT SEA

Crow has lived her whole life on a tiny, starkly beautiful island. Her only companions are Osh, the man who rescued her from a washed-up skiff as a baby and raised her, and Miss Maggie, their neighbour across the sandbar. But it is only when a mysterious fire appears across the water that an unspoken question of her own history forms in Crow's heart, and an unstoppable chain of events is triggered.

Crow sets out to find her lost identity – and, ultimately, to learn what it means to be a family.